INTRUDERS

E. C. SCULLION

INTRUDERS

Red Door

Published by RedDoor
www.reddoorpress.co.uk

ISBN 978-1-913062-29-3

A CIP catalogue record for this book is available from the British Library

Cover design: Dissect Designs

Typesetting: Jen Parker, Fuzzy Flamingo

Printed and bound in Denmark by Nørhaven

To Paul, Isabel and Thomas, with love

Prologue

Elnur Huseynov.

Along London's City Road the rain had been torrential, a slick sheen on the concrete now visible under gleaming street lights. On the number forty-three northbound, steam rose up the inside of the double-decker windows, outside splattered with wet streaks, the wool moquette fabric of the seats giving off a stale, mildewed scent. The upper deck of the bus was crowded, yet no one had chosen to sit next to him. He knew that the sight of his face meant most passengers would keep their distance.

He sat seven rows behind her, watching her, catching his reflection; the sight of his profile always reminding him of Elnur Huseynov.

At fifteen, Elnur had thumped him in the face, in a shirts-off, bare-knuckle brawl in the courtyard at the back of his uncle's boxing academy. It was a place where rats would linger in the shadows for scraps of food. The year was 1988. There were other boys involved, yet he remembered only Elnur. He could still recall with some clarity the sound the cartilage in his nose had made as it was crushed against the older boy's bony fingers.

When it was over, his uncle had handed him an ice pack

and strip of plaster. Elnur's father was a paying client. His uncle had no money for surgery. There had been no mother to fuss over what he looked like. The cartilage unrepaired, his nose had remained squashed over to one side ever since. As he grew into a man, it became a blot on his face, unequivocally deformed. For this, he had that over-privileged motherfucker Elnur Huseynov to thank.

Arriving in England four years later, he stepped off a ferry to shake hands with his contact. The wiry looking individual, by the name of Benedict, had appeared shocked, raising questions over the possibility of plastic surgery.

Yet it was Capricorn who insisted the nose stayed as it was.

On the upper deck of the bus he watched her pull the phone from her handbag, and start typing a message. She wasn't glamorous, but he had always thought her pretty. Tonight she didn't seem herself, and not just because once or twice she had caught him staring at her in the reflection.

He knew why. He had been informed of her letter of resignation, sent via email two hours earlier from her work computer. Whilst she hadn't yet gone to the police with what she knew, it was expected that she would, and imminently.

She had left them with no choice.

He was thankful she had selected to wear such a bright shade of green. When the bus lurched to a halt opposite Angel Underground station, she got to her feet, three stops earlier than he had anticipated. As she took the stairs to the lower deck, head down, he reached into his pocket for the cheap Nokia phone he had purchased that morning. He typed out the words before hitting the 'send' key:

Angel. Heading north on right side. Green coat. Phone in the handbag.

He glanced down out of the window, following the flash of lime coat-tails, and caught sight of his nose again, considering that perhaps now was time to get it fixed. He determined to get out at the next stop, allowing enough time for her to catch up with the route of the bus on foot.

Perhaps she was already running.

He waited for the bus to move again before reaching up and pressing the red 'stop' button.

She could try and run all she liked. When it came to Capricorn's enemies, he caught them all eventually.

One day, if time allowed, he would catch up with Elnur Huseynov too.

Chapter 1

Monday 4 July, 2016. 10 a.m.

'My client would expect you to commit a crime,' the lawyer with unruly eyebrows, who called himself Albert Denham, said, 'and under no circumstances get caught doing it.'

There was a silence. Tom Holt swallowed the brittle lump in his throat.

'I don't expect an answer right away,' the lawyer continued, leaning forward and placing his now empty coffee cup on the surface of the table. 'But I have a team waiting in Buenos Aires who require some direction.'

Denham got to his feet. Tom followed, rising from his sofa, shaking Denham's hulking hand when it was offered.

'Perhaps you could show me out,' the lawyer said.

Tom followed him on the stairs to street level. In the hallway, he opened the door. The driver of the BMW Denham had arrived in had returned and now parked kerb-side.

'I just have one question,' Tom managed. 'Why me?'

Denham pushed his hands further into his pockets. He'd worn an overcoat even in the July heat. 'Because on paper it seems that no one would miss you,' he said. 'And it is my opinion that you care little for anyone but yourself. My number is on my card.'

The lawyer left without giving him a backward glance.

Tom closed the door, retreating to his flat, allowing the events of the previous thirty minutes to wash over him.

Albert Denham had arrived without fanfare at 09.35. Before the shriek of the doorbell had echoed through his North London flat, Tom had been standing beside the Venetian blinds, wearing the previous day's underwear and three-day-old stubble. The foul, meaty stench drifting past his nostrils had been that of his own body odour. From his vantage point, he had watched the silver BMW estate pull up. For forty minutes, no one got in or out.

He had felt it in his gut. He was being watched.

In the living room, dim light emanated from his laptop. On the screen was Roxy Palace Online Casino; one of three online gambling sites he'd frequented since his dismissal. The sofa cushions, like memory foam, had still been in the shape of his vegetative self, definition enhanced by a line of toast crumbs.

He had let go of the slats, showered and shaved. Within fifteen minutes he was back in his living room wearing only a towel, peering outside.

The BMW was still parked.

When the lawyer finally emerged, glancing up at the window, Tom let go of the blind a fraction of a second too late.

He'd had time to pull on jeans and a shirt from the wardrobe, his frame slender for six foot two, and check that his sand-blonde hair wasn't doing anything wacky.

Denham was tall, barrel-chested, with dark, slicked-back hair. From the looks of it he was fifty or thereabouts. He had deep frown lines, chasms in his forehead that spoke of untold

2

years of stress, or that he'd seen a thing or two. No one with a happy life had lines like that.

'Can I help you?' Tom had asked, voice still hoarse from the two-thirds' bottle of Rioja he had polished off the previous evening.

The lawyer introduced himself, handing over a business card containing a name, job title and a contact phone number.

'What is it you want to talk to me about?'

'I have a job offer to discuss.'

'How did you find me?'

'My client came to me with your name. I was given your address.'

'Who's your client?'

'I'm afraid I'm not at liberty to disclose that information. My client is a powerful man. He would like to keep this discreet.'

Curiosity got the better of him.

'Well you'd better come in then,' he had said.

The lawyer Denham had a prior knowledge of things. He had known Tom was ex-military, completing two tours in Helmand in '06 and '07. Knew his date of birth: 6th of February 1976. Knew he wasn't married, nor currently in a relationship. He had even known about his parents' divorce when Tom was eleven, Oliver Holt walking out on his mother, taking with him only a backpack and a bottle of rum. He'd known about South Africa, though Tom acknowledged that that part of his history wouldn't have been so hard to unearth. The story had featured in the Cape Town local press five months earlier, concerning his dismissal from Vlok

Petersen and Associates after having been caught gambling company funds at the Grand West Casino, something he had managed to do for weeks without detection.

The lawyer knew about Eden: eight months prior still calling herself his fiancée, the oldest daughter of Hendrick, his immediate boss. Eden Van de Vlok, whose pleas to her father had been the sole reason he hadn't pressed criminal charges.

He paced, kept the blinds closed, wiped the sweat from his upper lip, going over in his mind what he could recall from the conversation.

'I know that you and Mr Van de Vlok have come up with a system of repayment for his lost assets,' Denham had said, 'one that will probably cripple you financially for the next twenty years.'

He hadn't denied it. The arrangement he and Van de Vlok had made was substantial on his part, a form of punishment for the upset he had caused both to Hendrick's family and business.

'I understand you can speak Spanish,' Denham had said.

'I studied Spanish at university. Completed a placement in South America.'

'Where in South America?'

'Mendoza, Argentina. Six months with a homestay family.'

'Have you ever been to Uruguay?'

'Uruguay? No.'

'Do you know anything about Uruguay?'

He had given a shrug. 'The Argies like to spend their summers there on account of the better beaches.'

4

'So you know what a *Barrio Privado* is?'

'It's a private neighbourhood. A gated community.'

Denham had gulped the coffee Tom had made him. 'The job you did for Hendrick Van de Vlok, tell me about it.'

'I was a consultant, Hendrick's deputy. Our business was badged as secure living. We devised housing communities based around high security, secure compounds, implementing security measures to protect domestic properties, that sort of thing. One in ten South Africans will still choose a house in a gated community given the choice.'

'So you know all about the systems people put in place; locks, fences, CCTV, that sort of thing. The things that are supposed to keep other people... out.'

Tom gave a nod.

'Why did Van de Vlok give you the job in the first place?'

'He thought I had the right background. Thought he could train me up. He liked army men. He liked Brits.'

'He just didn't know you were a gambler. In more ways than one.'

The coffee Tom had been drinking tasted bitter at the back of his throat. The story of his dismissal wasn't a topic he had been fond of sharing with the world outside his flat.

'Why didn't you stay in the army?'

He had sat back into the cushions, brain flooded with so many different memories. 'My commanding officer believed I could lead, and that I'd make a sound colonel one day. If only I hadn't enjoyed spending time playing cards with the soldiers. We came to the mutual decision that it was better if I moved on.'

'My client came to me with your name,' Denham said. 'He

5

likes to keep a close-knit circle of trusted individuals who work for him. He needs someone he can trust to lead a small team.'

Tom had waited for more. It had not been forthcoming. 'To do what exactly?'

'We would expect you to sign a non-disclosure agreement to cover the duration of the project,' Denham continued unabated. 'You would be handsomely rewarded, if successful.'

'And if unsuccessful?'

'You would still be adequately compensated for your time and effort.'

He had searched Denham's features for any sign he might be lying, quelling the momentary rush of exhilaration in his chest. 'This job, is it legal?'

'Technically, no.'

'And you would expect me to travel to where... to Uruguay?'

'The team is currently based in Buenos Aires, but yes. To Montevideo, the capital of Uruguay.'

'This team... who are they? Are they British?'

'Yes, all of them.'

There was another silence before he had asked the question, a hot lump already forming in his throat, unsure of his precise reaction if Denham were to confirm his suspicions.

'And we are to commit a crime?'

★★★★★

He sat facing Denham on the other side of a chintzy-looking desk in Butler's Wharf on the south side of the Thames, brick walls painted off-white. It was an office of sorts, above a flower shop with partial views of Tower Bridge, a room with a vaulted ceiling and iron rod supports. He'd worn a suit, no tie. Two chairs, upholstered in a dirty shade of brown tweed, both equally moth-eaten, had been placed opposite one another. A large metal filing cabinet dated back to the seventies, the entire place thrown together as if Denham had looted his childhood family home.

He had said no to Denham. Had avoided one jail sentence in South Africa and wasn't of a mind to set himself up for another. He had sat on his sofa, staring at his iPhone with its abandoned WhatsApp chat groups – *so-and-so has left* – wondering if he had made the most colossal mistake.

At 7 p.m., the same phone started to ring.

'I spoke to my client,' Denham had said. 'If you accept the terms of our employment, he has offered to clear your debt to Hendrick Van de Vlok… in its entirety.'

He had capitulated, perhaps more quickly than he should have. Three hefty lump sums would be paid into the account of Hendrick Van de Vlok of Cape Town, South Africa, from a London-based lawyer over the following three months. He would be free. The South American angle had heavily influenced his decision. The allure of the place was strong, given everything he had left behind. His Spanish was rusty but still buried in the recesses of his mind. *Only a criminal if you get caught*, he had told himself. Life could go on as it was, with no purpose, his family fragmented. Eden, now his ex-fiancée, had changed her phone number, so had some of his friends. Now he didn't have any.

7

He could start again. Forget about another decent job in the private sector, he'd reasoned with himself. The moment anyone carried out a background check, *Christ*, even a Google search on his name, it was all over.

Nothing like uncertainty to get the adrenaline pumping, a commanding officer in the army had once said.

He had googled Denham's name, come up with a rough history: a former corporate lawyer now with his own small firm in Canary Wharf. The man seemed genuine enough. Tom had signed the contract, together with the gag order. He would only be able to discuss the job with those directly involved in it.

In Albert Denham's private office, he sat back in the moth-eaten chair and waited for the lawyer to begin.

Denham turned a laptop around on the surface of the desk so that Tom could see the full image on screen.

'This woman is Sabina Cordero,' Denham said. 'The photograph is about two years old. She's from Argentina, thirty-eight, with two children: Beatriz, eleven, and three-year-old Mateo. She is married to Feliciano Ledesma. He's a surgeon at the British Hospital in Montevideo.'

Tom leaned forward. Sabina Cordero wore sunglasses, white shorts, a shirt tied at the navel, feet splashing in the ocean on some idyllic beach somewhere. She had a hint of Hispanic colouring, an expensive smile.

He nodded once. Denham turned the laptop back around, tapped at the keyboard. Tom was looking at the screen again. 'And this,' Denham said, 'is where they live.'

The front page of a website displayed the aerial view of

a golf course, seemingly built around an expansive series of interlinking roads and houses. It all looked highly familiar, only on a different continent. 'Aves de Las Colinas' swirled across the screen in a sophisticated typeface. *Birds of the Hills.* It was the mirror image of the kind of compound Vlok Petersen had recently designed in Wynberg, a suburban area of Cape Town, though the pictures expertly omitted any evidence of garrison-style fencing.

'Uruguayans, Argentinians, if you have any kind of money along the banks of the River Plate, this is where you build your house, or one of your many houses,' Denham continued. 'Purchase your plot, design your dream home, finish it with a pool and garden and you're living six months of the year in a sun-drenched paradise with no one but a few keen golfers to bother you.'

'Golfers and friendly neighbours all basking under the warm rays of mutual exclusivity,' Tom added. 'So this is the *Barrio Privado* you were talking about.'

'Correct,' Denham nodded. 'Fifteen kilometres east of Montevideo, outside the city limits because inside the city gated communities are unlawful.'

'But this is Latin America,' Tom said. 'You move there for your own personal safety. Or to launder your money.'

'Precisely.'

'But if you do live there, you have guaranteed security. That compound will be surrounded by a towering electric fence, CCTV and controlled vehicle access, more than likely with a fingerprint-recognition entry system.'

'It has a security checkpoint, manned twenty-four seven, only one way in, one way out.'

'Music to Hendrick Van de Vlok's ears,' Tom added with a half-smile.

Denham walked around to Tom's side of the desk, where a coat was hanging up. Tom watched as he rifled around in one of the pockets, pulling out an old-fashioned key. He returned to the other side of the desk, bending to open one of the drawers hidden from Tom's view. Straightening, Denham tossed an envelope on the surface. Tom reached forward, tore it open. He pulled out a credit card and a smart phone.

'I take it your passport is valid and in date?'

He nodded.

'Good. You leave tomorrow night on a flight to Buenos Aires,' Denham said, handing him a printed e-ticket. 'Everything is booked. The phone is for direct contact with me and me only. My number is already plugged in. Use the WhatsApp account – it's encrypted. The credit card can be used for day to day living expenses, supplies, whatever you need. There is no credit limit, it will be paid for each month and I will be scrutinising the bill. Each member of the team has one. Whatever you need to get the job done. The pin is sixty sixty. Six zero six zero, don't forget it, because in five minutes from now I will have forgotten it.'

'Sixty sixty,' Tom repeated, eyes levelled on Denham's. 'So once we are inside the compound, what is it exactly you want us to do?'

There was a moment before Denham replied. 'There is a safe, inside Sabina Cordero's house, house number 8024 inside Las Colinas. Your job… the job of your team, is to bring me the contents of that safe.'

Chapter 2

Buenos Aires, Argentina

He had been roaming inside the ancient walled cemetery at Recoleta for fifteen minutes, clutching a small black holdall, staying visible, avoiding the spider web of shadowy passages leading off in every direction, age-old crumbling mausoleums crammed in left and right, a sea of ornate gothic marble. He kept well within the view of the cemetery's only entrance, a gated marble portico supported by Doric columns, waiting for a stranger to make himself known. The words over the entrance to the cemetery read *Expectamus Dominum. We expect the Lord.*

Tourists were milling about the place, cameras about their necks, searching for the gravesite of Evita herself: Eva Perón.

Denham had given Tom a name – Ray Caulder – and provided him with the location of where to meet: not a hotel, Tom noted, but inside a city full of dead people. He wore a jacket and crisp white shirt, purchased twenty minutes earlier at Etiqueta Negra, a men's clothing boutique a short walk from the cemetery. *Take only what you really need*, Denham had instructed. *Buy everything there.*

He sidestepped some more American tourists, the whirr of traffic not so far away. He could still recall the taste of the

Malbec at the back of his throat… the steak… the women… the jazz… the unchecked passion of it all. Buenos Aires: a city that knew how to leave even the most prudish personality all hot under the collar.

The wind rustled the trees overhead. There was a chill in the air, Argentinian autumn coming to a close. He hadn't slept. Wished he'd bought lunch as plane food only went so far to fill a man's stomach. As he continued to meander through the maze of granite vaults, allowing himself a surreptitious glance over his shoulder, he mused on the various aptitudes of this so-called team, who they were, where they came from, how many. Above him were corpseless heads, stone angels scattering stone flowers. Only in Buenos Aires could death feel so in vogue.

Only a criminal if you get caught. It was the antithesis of a security manager. He had been asked to take everything he knew about security and turn it on its head in order to break in… In order to beat the system.

Ten past twelve. He yawned. Ten past four in London. He was considering retiring to a nearby café when a man entering the cemetery caught his attention. Seasonably overdressed in a suit, beige trench coat and dark glasses, he shuffled rather than walked. He looked like a presidential bodyguard, or worse still, some kind of covert operative on the verge of retirement, pushing sixty, weary with his job, white hair, moustache, leathery skin.

Tom stood still outside the imposing tomb of someone called Manuel Dorrego, watching. The man was trundling towards him.

'You Tom?' the man grunted in a thick northern English accent as he reached him, clearly out of breath.

'Yes. Ray?'

'Good to meet you,' was the reply as they shook hands. Ray had pudgy fingers. 'Mr Denham said to expect you.'

'How long have you been here?' Tom asked.

'Couple of weeks. He told us to sit tight whilst we waited for you.'

A rudderless ship: that's how Denham had described them. 'Funny, he only offered me the job three days ago.'

Ray forced a smile, teeth stained from too many cigarettes. 'Seems they found their man then. Come on, I'll take you to the flat. You been to Buenos Aires before?'

'A long time ago.'

'Speak any Spanish?'

'Some. I'm rusty.'

They were heading for the exit. 'Good,' Ray said, ''Cause the rest of us don't speak a bloody word.'

The apartment was a ten-minute walk away from the cemetery down Riobamba, north of Avenida Santa Fe. The buildings rose up from the ground in the most elaborate fashion – a preserved Paris of old, smudged with soot from car exhausts – the architecture all European. Most buildings in Buenos Aires had a name: theirs was Edificio Tijuana. Inside the narrow marbled lobby sat a dozy-looking Argentinian concierge with a sizeable belly. The lift was old-school with a sliding caged door that didn't quite close all the way. Ray followed him inside and pressed the button for the tenth floor without a word, keeping his gaze facing upward. Tom had asked after the nature of Ray's job. Ray had responded that he'd once worked for Manchester Police, and that Tom should consider him the logistics man in the team.

At the tenth floor Ray collapsed back the metal grate. The corridor was straight and narrow with speckled marble flooring, a small barred window at one end. Tom counted five separate apartments. Ray turned left and walked to the end of the corridor.

'Oh, I, *uh*, should mention,' he said, without making eye contact. 'This is only a three-bedroom apartment.'

'How many people in the team?'

Ray put a key in the lock. 'You're the fourth,' he said, and opened the door.

Ray shrugged out of his coat as soon as he entered. Tom stood in the doorway, still clutching the holdall, looking at the vast red velvet three-seater sofa in front of him. A striking redhead wearing a thin sleeveless vest and skinny jeans was sat cross-legged, talking and smiling at someone out of his eyeline. She must have been around thirty, with poker straight, shoulder length auburn hair, pointy nose, cheeks dappled with freckles. She stopped talking when she saw him, staring him in the face, her expression collapsing into a frown.

'Come in,' said Ray, holding open the door.

The apartment had gone silent. Tom took three steps forward, enough so that Ray could close the door behind him. A second man came into view, a little older than the woman but less hostile, of Asian, possibly Indian origin, wearing slim jeans and a leather jacket, hairline slightly receding and greying at the sides, slick with too much product.

'Tom Holt,' Ray said, 'meet Rebecca Wylde and Anil Choudhury.'

14

'It's Becca,' the woman corrected Ray.

'Alright, mate,' Anil said in a cockney-sounding accent, leaning forward and shaking Tom by the hand, 'When did you get in?'

'Couple of hours ago,' Tom said, setting the holdall down on the wood floor. There was an armchair that matched the sofa and a small television set. Through an archway to his right was a small kitchen. The walls were a reptilian shade of green, much of the paint chipped, with a clapped-out looking air-conditioning unit attached at ceiling height. To his left was a dark corridor with what he presumed to be bedrooms. Behind the sofa, a set of balcony doors, the audible hum of traffic below; in the corner a circular rustic wooden table and chairs.

'So is this everybody?' he asked.

'This is us,' Becca responded. 'This is your team, oh *Wise One*, oh *Dear Leader*. You say "jump", we say, "how high?"'

His lips twisted into a sardonic smile. 'Albert Denham hired me three days ago,' he stated.

'I'm aware of that,' she said, uncrossing her legs. 'Ray just about manages to keep us informed.'

Ray screwed up his face in mock offence.

'Look, I'm just here to do what I'm being paid to do,' Tom said. 'I'm not here to put noses out of joint.'

She raised her chin an inch. 'Does my nose look out of joint to you?'

Anil was back in the kitchen, making tea.

'So what are you doing here?' he asked her, changing the subject.

She rolled her eyes in annoyance, getting to her feet,

15

walking around to the back of the sofa, swiping up a brown leather backpack and military style coat with a hood. 'I'm going out,' she announced in Anil's direction, brushing past Tom and stopping only to pull on a pair of scuffed boots. She opened the door and was gone, slamming it loudly behind her.

'D'you bring any pesos?' Anil asked, emerging from the kitchen. 'I forgot the pin on my credit card and now it's effing blocked. Cupboards are a bit bare like.'

Tom reached for his wallet, handed Anil over a large pile of pesos he exchanged at the airport.

'I'll go get us some food in a bit,' Anil said. 'Make yourself at home, put your feet up.'

'It's Anil, right?' Tom said.

'That's it, yeah.'

'What are you doing in Argentina?'

Anil puffed out his cheeks. 'That's a good question, mate, I've been asking myself that a lot lately.'

'Did Denham get you here?'

'Yeah. Turned up at my door in the middle of my kid's third birthday party. My wife was spitting blood when I went off to speak to him.'

'Where are you from?'

'Hackney.'

'And what is it that you do?'

Anil offered him a grin, brown eyes sparkling. 'I'm here for the safe, man. Ain't no one else in this room will get you into that safe but me.'

Anil finished his tea and left. Ray excused himself, went to his room. Tom stood alone, unsure of what to do next. So this was his team. He peeled off his jacket, unbuttoned his cuffs, rolled up his sleeves. He opened the balcony doors, air rushing in and a cacophony of horns, sirens, engine revs and pneumatic drills rising up from the space below.

Buenos Aires.

He breathed her in, almost tasting the exhaust fumes.

He had missed her. Like a long-lost girlfriend, he'd often thought about her over the years, fleeting memories charged with so many emotions. Those days in Argentina had been a thrill ride. 1997. Twenty-one years old on his year abroad learning Spanish; a wide-eyed, sexually naive university student, he'd been introduced to Gabriela Autino in a Palermo nightclub on a glacial September night. Through his inexperienced eyes she'd been a Latina princess. Forget Mendoza... he had lied to Denham about that much at least. Faced with a choice of travelling north-west to live with a local family on a six-month homestay, or staying in Gabriela's bed, he had swiftly abandoned the idea of the former, drafting a handwritten letter of apology to the homestay family with a promise to wire them cash in exchange for a glowing report on his language progress. They hadn't bothered to report his absence. His Spanish he picked up on the street, from Gabriela, in illegal backroom casinos run by her father, over long nights at the blackjack table, sleeping in with Gabi all day, going out after dark to a city coming to life. He made good his promise of a hefty reward to his Mendoza hosts, won on the roulette wheel. He had paid them a visit in the end, clutching an envelope stuffed full of US *dólares*. Reluctant at first, it hadn't been hard to persuade them – in fluent Spanish no less – to write to his university back in the United Kingdom a report that was gleaming. They made good on their word in exchange for the contents of that envelope. And then there was Gabi, eight years his senior, a hustler's daughter, a woman he had positively worshipped... He wondered what had become of her since their last fateful meeting.

He closed the balcony doors again and lay down on the sofa – apparently now his bed – resigning himself to spending the night there and addressing the issue of moving to a bigger apartment the following day. Jetlag washed over him, kicking up a notch. He glanced at his watch. It was one of the only things he'd chosen to bring with him: a Bulova Accu, an expensive birthday gift from his brothers some years ago, the word 'Papercut' engraved into the titanium back, a reference to a game they'd played as adolescents: who could administer the worst paper cut to the flap of skin between the thumb and forefinger. In London he had called his younger brother Christian minutes before the taxi came, left a voicemail saying he was going away for a while but not to worry. That Christian could even tell their mother if she still cared.

In his room, Ray was now talking to someone on his phone, muffled sounds emerging from underneath the bedroom door. Eyelids drooping, Tom crossed his arms over his chest and attempted to listen to what was being said.

He woke with a start to the sound of Anil crashing through the door, laden with bright blue plastic shopping bags. He sat up, back of his neck clammy, looked at his watch again. He'd been asleep for three and a half hours.

At 9 p.m., in front of him lay open a copy of *501 Spanish Verbs (Sixth Edition)*. *Futuro perfecto*. *Perfecto de subjuntivo*. All flooding back. The remnants of cold pizza sat in the kitchen. Ray was back in his room, Anil snoring a few feet away in an armchair in front of an old dubbed episode of *Friends*. Jennifer Aniston squawking in *español* didn't quite possess the same allure.

She entered like a whirlwind, slamming the door behind her, heading straight to the table, sound of her boots clomping on the floor. Yanked open her bag and emptied it onto the wood surface in front of him, the contents crashing down. Anil stirred. Tom counted four wallets, two ladies' purses, two passports and a delicate gold necklace with a heart-shaped pendant. She'd been gone almost nine hours.

'What is this?' he asked.

'That's what *I'm* doing here,' Becca said, leaving her haul on the table and stalking off in the direction of her bedroom, slamming the door shut behind her.

He stared at the table contents. Picked up the passports first: two Canadians, in the name of Hannigan, seemingly man and wife, in their late fifties. Both now paying a visit to the local police station and then to their Embassy first thing in the morning. He felt a pang of guilt in the pit of his stomach. The wallets and purses all belonged to Argentinians. He removed a few wads of pesos before stuffing everything, including the necklace, into one of the blue plastic shopping bags Anil had brought back, and tied the handles.

Anil was shuffling off to bed, eyelids drooping. 'Sleep well, mate,' he muttered.

'So she's a thief?'

'Slip of a thing, ain't she?' Anil yawned. 'You'd never believe it looking at her.'

He was pretty sure it worked to her advantage. He sat in

silence, no desire to sleep, particularly not on a sofa. Swiping up his jacket, he pulled it on, and locating a key for the apartment, slammed the door behind him.

Outside, the air was cool on his cheeks. He meandered north back towards Recoleta, the area where his memories of the city were still most vivid, traffic still humming despite the late hour. The architecture was dripping with Parisian style, all wrought iron balconies and heavy ornate windows. His eyes darted over the buildings on Ayacucho, a short stroll north of Riobamba, searching for Gabriela's apartment, until he located her fifth-floor balcony. He stood at the bottom of the building on the street underneath it, craning his neck in the darkness. There was childproof netting on it now, no red roses entwined between the railings. Gabriela would leave them there even after they had died, adding new flowers to the mix every now and then. She had probably sold the place years ago.

He thought about telling Denham he'd changed his mind, that he didn't come halfway across the world to lead a rag tag bunch of petty criminals on a wild goose chase across South America. The redhead, Becca, in particular was a liability, and he wasn't sure he could entirely trust Ray – of whom he knew virtually nothing other than that he liked to make secret phone calls in his room.

There were some rules to be made.

On the corner, he entered a Chinese supermarket with the aim of buying a bottle of wine or some beers. All paid for by Denham of course. He entered, meandered past the checkout and a sour-faced Chinese woman barking orders at an employee in Spanish. He walked down the narrow aisles, shelves piled chaotically with canned goods and provisions, looking for the fridges, his movements almost swan-like, a feeling of exhilaration washing over him. Despite the urge to quit the job, it still felt good to be back in South America.

He headed for the fridges at the rear of the store, surveying the choice of lager and settling on a six-pack of Italian-imported Moretti.

From the corner of his eye he noticed two men standing in leather jackets, behind him where the surplus supplies were kept, talking in hushed voices, exchanging wads of money. Tom closed the fridge, turned slightly to find both men, both thick-set Argentines, staring at him with impassive faces. One, the taller, broader of the two seemed to squint at him, tilt his head slightly to the right, as though some distant memory was dawning on him.

A distant memory dawned on Tom too, as if in slow motion. Suddenly not so distant anymore. His blood ran cold. The man on the right he had seen years before, in a barn in Rosario, coming at him with a blade in his hand.

A small explosion detonated in the pit of Tom's stomach. The six-pack dropped to the floor.

Run.

Chapter 3

Thirty-three years old. An *estância* north-west of Rosario. Gabriela, in her wedding dress, hair pinned back off her face. A pungent stench of manure in the air. Brown leather saddles and stirrups suspended from the stables' ceiling, sweat drenching Tom's shirt. Open-mouthed kisses reminiscent of the nights spent in her Buenos Aires apartment. Her second marriage to an architect with a shady family tree.

Three burly Argentines, ties removed in the heat, standing in the doorway. Armed.

'Federico,' her terrified whisper. *'Puedo explicarlo.' I can explain.*

★★★★★

He opened his eyes.

His cheek was hot, pressed up against a red velvet cushion. There was a crick in his neck, a kink in his spine.

That said… he was alive.

Tom sat up on the sofa, dawn sun peeking through the curtains. He leaned his elbows on his knees, memory raw with the events of the night before, high-tailing it back between the supermarket aisles, causing an avalanche of tinned tuna. The Chinese cashier had cried out in crude Spanish as he passed her in a blur.

He'd kept running, thighs pumping, crossing intersections in the dark, skimming over the bonnets of cars. When he glanced back, the two Argentines were more than fifty metres behind, but he could tell from their movements they were slower than he was. He took a sharp right, ducked into a wine shop where a dark-haired assistant with a high bun stood behind the counter. She must have been fifty. Her eyes widened as he pulled out two one hundred-dollar bills, the only money left in his wallet since giving all his pesos to Anil, and held it out for her to see.

'*Por favor, necesito esconderme,*' he whispered, out of breath. *Please, I need to hide.*

The woman stared at him, looked at the notes in his fingers. She must have seen the desperation in his eyes. Coming out from behind the counter, she went to the door and locked it, switching off the light. '*Detrás del mostrator,*' she said. *Behind the counter.*

Tom sank behind the glass stand. Over the whirr of traffic he heard the sound of footsteps running on concrete. The two men were outside, shouts going up between them. They had lost him.

He waited, heart pummelling his ribs. When he peered out from the counter the woman had pressed her figure against a shelf, obscured by shadow.

'*Hay otra puerta,*' she whispered, minutes later. *There is another door.*

He thanked her in Spanish. When he tried to give her the dollars, she refused. '*Esta ciudad,*' she mumbled, clicking her tongue.

He guessed it was around five-thirty or six, still no sound from the bedrooms. He swung his legs over to the floor, arched his back. Sooner they moved apartments the better.

He watched the sunrise in his underwear from the balcony, an hour later dressed in his running gear, one of the few things he had bothered to pack inside the holdall. Took the key to the apartment and the stairs to the ground floor. The same sleepy guard was still on duty. He jogged north, at a noticeably easier pace than his sprint the previous night, back past the cemetery gate, down the small hill to Avenida del Libertador.

It had taken him some time to remember. The man in the Chinese supermarket's name was Mazzanti. He didn't recall a first name. Mazzanti was one of Fede's men. He had been at the stables that day.

Which meant that by now, Federico Hernandez would know Tom Holt was back in Buenos Aires.

And if Fede knew he was back, Fede would want his blood.

Federico Hernandez. In Buenos Aires, they called him 'The Bullet'. There was a rumour years ago that he had murdered his own mob boss for the sole purpose of taking his throne. In Rosario, Gabriela had married Fede's brother.

Tom slowed to a halt, within view of the *Floralis Genérica*, a steel flower structure that opened and closed with the rising and setting of the sun. If Denham's job was going to go ahead successfully, he needed to make peace with Federico Hernandez.

His mind made up, he circled back around, descending some steep steps back down past the cemetery wall, dodging

24

a dog walker leading seven tethered canines along the pavement.

The apartment was still quiet. He showered, headed out again.

The Bullet was only half his problem. He had a team of three to manage who at that moment had a boat-load of potential to get them all thrown into a South American lockup.

Twenty minutes later, Tom purchased a new laptop using Denham's credit card. In the daytime he was safe. The night-time hours were when Fede's men would emerge from whatever rock it was they had been lurking under. Ducking inside *El Ateneo Grande Splendid*, a grand theatre-turned-bookstore, he located the language section on the upper galleries.

When he returned to the apartment, Anil was in the bathroom, Becca on the balcony with the doors wide open clutching a coffee, Ray in the kitchen boiling eggs.

'Morning,' Tom said, putting his bags on the table.

'How did you sleep?' Ray asked.

'Like I spent the night on a sofa. Maybe we could look for a new apartment today.'

'No can do,' Ray said, 'We paid cash up front for this one for three months. Still two months left on the lease.'

Tom gritted his teeth, felt a muscle tick in his jaw. Through the glass doors, Becca was staring off into the distance, hair blowing in the breeze. She was prettier than he'd first thought, or else when she wasn't scowling.

'Hurry up and finish eating,' Tom said, walking to the balcony doors as Ray looked up in surprise. 'We've got work to do.'

He poked his head out to the balcony, catching Becca off guard. 'Meeting in ten minutes.' Didn't give her the opportunity to respond, instead stalking off towards the bathroom.

He banged on the door.

'What?' Anil moaned on the inside.

'Meeting, ten minutes.'

'Eh?' came the reply.

'It means get your shit together.'

Five minutes later – the apartment filled with the slightly unpleasant odour of Ray's boiled eggs – they had assembled at the table. Becca studied her fingernails. Ray sat with his arms crossed over his chest, a ketchup stain down his white polo shirt. Only Anil was paying any sort of attention.

'First rule,' Tom began. 'You are my team. That means my decision is final.'

He paused: no reaction.

'Second rule,' he continued. 'If we are going to be here, we are going to blend in. That means' – he reached into the shopping bag, pulled out the language textbooks, dumping them with a loud bang on the table surface – 'that we are all going to learn some Spanish.'

He handed them out to a stunned silence. Anil swiped up a book, already interested.

Becca rolled her eyes. 'Enough of this, I'm going out,' she sighed, moving to Tom's side of the table.

'You,' Tom interjected. 'Third rule. No one does *anything* that gets us any undue attention here. That means no stealing from anyone, no thieving, no doing anything that gets captured on CCTV and us arrested. Not unless I instruct you to do so. You keep your heads down. Understood?'

She'd raised her chin in defiance. He stood his ground, her face like thunder.

Anil sniggered. 'He's got you there, Bec.'

'I know more Spanish than you think,' she stated, walking back to her chair and dragging it across the floor, planting herself on it.

'She's lying,' Anil laughed. 'She knows less than I do.'

'And they both know less than I do,' Ray said.

'It's agreed then,' Tom said. 'For the next five days we study. Then we head to Uruguay.'

'What, we just pile onto a plane?'

'No, we visit as tourists. We travel separately, two by plane, the other two on the ferry down the River Plate. Becca and I travel together as a couple, as fiancés, Anil and Ray as golfing buddies.'

'I'm sorry, what did you say?' Becca asked.

'We can work out the detail later.'

'I'll be Anil's fiancée if I'm going to have to pretend.'

'I have a question,' Anil piped up, saving them another awkward silence. 'Anybody know what's in the safe?'

He had wondered who would be first to broach the subject, Anil being the obvious candidate. 'Denham didn't mention it, no.'

Anil looked to Ray. 'Care to enlighten us, Ray Charles?'

'Do I look like a black fuckin' blind singer to you?' Ray snapped, frowning at Anil.

'Chill, man,' Anil shot back. 'I'm a curious mo-fo. I mean, it's gotta be diamonds, right? What else is worth going to this much trouble for?'

★★★★★

There were two places he knew he could count on someone getting a message to The Bullet, or at least one of Federico's goons. One of those places, he didn't want to go. Not if he wanted to come back alive. The second place…

His father had taught him how to play blackjack on his tenth birthday. He'd always suspected his father's habit had been the main reason for his parents' divorce. His older brother Jacob had gone to work on the London Stock Exchange, a gambler in his own way, but someone who was wholly disapproving of trying their luck at casinos, perhaps because gambling had been the ruin of Oliver Holt. His father had never taken him to a casino, not a real one, his mother vetoing that idea from the start. A poker game in a smoke-filled room at the back of a pub in Bromley a couple of times when he was seventeen, when his dad had still been part of his life, but that had been the closest he had come. His mother had warned that gambling was in his genes, and to steer clear of it. Until his first trip to Argentina, he had not thought about gambling much at all.

In the apartment he stared at the ceiling, lying on the red velvet sofa: his bed, everyone else's seat. Ray was back in his room. Outside it was dark. Anil was chewing gum, the TV on low, distracting him from learning any Spanish. Becca was reciting something, her Spanish book open on the table. He was intrigued by her. How did someone like that become a pickpocket? He thought about asking, sensed her venomous response before he'd even opened his mouth.

He swallowed the nervous lump of anticipation in his

28

throat, showered and changed, emerging from the bathroom looking a little slicker.

'I'm going out,' he announced to a bored audience.

'Don't do anything to get us any attention now, will you?' Becca hummed, lips twisting into a taut smile.

'You raised the bar on that one, don't you think?' he said, closing the door behind him.

Four hundred *dólares* worth of chips at an improvised blackjack table. The room was fuggy with cigarette smoke, a low-slung haze in a makeshift basement with black walls. No conforming to fire regulations here.

The moment he'd sat down at the table, he'd made eyes at the dealer.

'*Necesito hablar con El Almendra,*' he said in hushed tones. *El Almendra* was the Spanish for almond, also slang for The Bullet. Asking to speak to one of the most powerful gangsters in Buenos Aires was not without its risks, but this was Gabi's father's casino. He had been the one to show up that day at the stables, to diffuse the situation and send Fede and his thugs packing, and him away from Rosario, back to Buenos Aires.

The dealer stopped what he was doing, raised his chin to one of the security guards in the shadows. The guard came over, the dealer whispering something in his ear. Tom swallowed. There was no going back now.

He waited. Played a few hands. Bet simple. Wasn't here for money. All he had to do was bide his time and someone would show.

An hour passed. He bowed out of the game, wished an old Argentinian couple *buena suerte*. Picked up his drink, leaving a tip and cashing in his chips at a dimly-lit booth manned by a leathery old fellow reading the *fútbol* pages of *Clarin* under the light of a cheap anglepoise, glass protected by thick wire mesh. Tom glanced up at the mirror to see two would-be security guards whispering to one another before exchanging positions. He locked eyes with the taller of the two: black, receding hair but longer at the back, the style of choice for Argentinian males. He had unusually high cheekbones, a long nose, badly grown beard. He was the third man from the stables. His name was Arturo Baresi.

'Buy me a drink?'

His head snapped round. There she was, completely unexpected, smiling pleasantly for once, taller than usual, auburn hair glimmering under the spotlights on the ceiling.

'What are you doing here?' he breathed, eyes flitting to Baresi.

'Denham installed a tracking app on all our phones,' Becca said, taking in her surroundings. 'He thinks we don't know that but Anil worked it out quickly enough. You were easy to pinpoint, although I don't think the taxi driver appreciated my shouting at him in broken Spanish. Couldn't work out where you'd disappeared to until I spied the concealed door. What is that you're drinking?'

Tom looked down, glancing at a pair of seemingly uncharacteristic gold strappy sandals at the end of her tight black jeans. When he looked up again over her shoulder, Baresi was fast approaching.

'It's called a Gancia Limone.' He grabbed her by the elbow. 'Why don't we move to the bar?'

Mazzanti had appeared behind Baresi. Becca frowned, yanked her arm away from Tom. He silently cursed her bad timing.

'I need you to stay here,' he breathed. 'There's something I need to do.'

'Other than drink and place bets? I wouldn't have pegged you for a gambler.'

'And I wouldn't have pegged you for a thief. I need you to order yourself a drink, stay here at the bar. Don't talk to anyone.'

It was too late. Baresi had stopped within inches of Becca's back. Tom watched as she felt his presence, turning, glancing up at his face. Baresi looked down at her, gave her a lustful once over. Becca frowned in disgust, moving away from him.

'*Te lo dije... él ésta de vuelta,*' Mazzanti said from behind Baresi, gaze positively murderous. *I told you... He's back.*

Baresi stroked Becca's arm with his fingers. She recoiled in disgust, thrusting him off. 'I thought you only had eyes for Fede's sister-in-law,' Baresi said in Spanish in Tom's direction. 'Who is this we have here?'

'I've come to make peace with Fede. That's all in the past.'

Baresi was admiring Becca's hair. Redheads were quite the novelty in Buenos Aires, packed full of Latina women with olive skin and mounds of coarse dark hair.

'We need to leave,' Becca spat.

'You wanna come back with us, *mi coloradita*?' Baresi crooned, switching to English, fingers reaching out and stroking the skin on her bare shoulder.

'Touch me again and I'll put a knife in your throat,' she spat back.

'Leave her, let me talk to Fede,' Tom said, also in English, trying to reel Baresi back in.

Baresi was mesmerised. Keeping one eye on Becca, Tom barged past him, grabbing hold of Mazzanti. 'Forget about the girl,' he snapped in Spanish, for there was no way a thug like Mazzanti could understand any level of English being spoken. 'Where is The Bullet?'

Mazzanti grinned, revealing a set of grills covering his teeth. *'Fede no puede esperar para verte,'* he said. *Fede cannot wait to see you.*

No sooner had he said it, Tom witnessed Becca's elbow plough upwards into Baresi's front teeth. As Baresi doubled over, blood shooting from his nose, Becca had whipped out a knife. In one swift movement, Tom saw the glint of the blade under the casino lights as she buried it into Baresi's upper thigh, below his hip, before wrenching it out again. Baresi went from being bent forward to throwing himself backward as the pain in his nose paled in comparison to the agony in his leg.

He gave Mazzanti no time to open his mouth before throwing his first punch. His knuckles made contact with Mazzanti's chin, sending the Argentine sprawling backwards and a judder shooting up Tom's right arm.

He watched as several things happened in quick succession. Mazzanti was thick set but would be back on his feet in an instant. The security guards' attention had been piqued by Baresi's howling. Tom knew they had seconds to get to the stairs and out of the door. He grabbed Becca's hand, bolting towards the exit.

He pushed her up the stairs in front of him. 'Go! Now!' he shouted as the guards were on them, approaching seemingly in slow motion. Becca tripped on her heels. As she reached the door, light flooded in from the bar at ground level. Tom followed, exiting the casino and grabbing her hand again, pulling her out into the cold air to the streets of Palermo Soho, under the nose of a door guard who hadn't yet cottoned on to what was happening.

'This way,' he shouted, mind swirling as they bolted, weaving in and out of late-night Palermo drinkers lolling out of the clubs, Becca now surprisingly agile in her heels. There were men on their tails, he could hear the cries going up, didn't dare look back for fear of losing precious seconds of escape time.

Becca flung out her arm to a yellow and black cab going the right way. The vehicle rolled to a halt as they launched themselves into the back.

'Drive, drive, go, go!' Tom hollered at the cabbie in Spanish, who did as he was told, behaving like the driver of a getaway car before the passenger door was even closed, tyres screeching along the tarmac. Tom looked back to see two casino security guards disappearing on the horizon.

'Jesus Christ! What the hell was that?'

'I could ask you the same question!' she yelled back. She was folding away her switchblade.

'You knifed him in the fucking leg!'

'He's lucky I didn't put it in his throat!'

'Do you have any idea what you've done?'

'Why were you even there? Who is Fede? And what's he to you?'

He leaned back into the seats, caught his breath. 'Something happened a long time ago.'

She made eye contact. For a split second he pictured himself kissing her.

'You've been here before,' she hissed, incredulous. 'Haven't you?'

He tried to steady his breathing. 'It's not my first time in Argentina, no.'

'Does Denham know?'

'He doesn't know about Fede, no.'

'Jesus!'

The taxi driver demanded to know where they were going. Tom shouted the address, unable to tear his eyes from her, street lights flickering across her features. She was wiping bloody fingers on the seat. If she was distressed, she was doing a good job of concealing it.

'Do you always carry a knife?' he breathed.

'Comes in handy when you need to cut the straps on a handbag,' she responded matter-of-factly, lifting her hips and sliding the whole thing back into her pocket. 'Do you owe them money?'

'Things might be easier if I did.'

Any further conversation was put on hold as from behind, back down the street, there came a roar of engines as two motorbikes came into view, beaming headlights, one on each side of the back end of the cab.

'Get down!' Tom shouted, barking at the cabbie to accelerate. The driver began to rant in Spanish, Tom couldn't hear it all, but their car did not speed up. As the motorbike caught up on Becca's side, it was clear one had two riders, faces shielded by helmets. On the back, the smaller of two males was reaching for what looked like a baton. The first bike lurched and the second rider took a swing, smashing Becca's window, sending glass into her lap.

Tom yelled at the cab driver to get off the street and before he knew it the car was swerving to the right, sending Becca tumbling into his lap.

'I'll take you as far as Santa Fe then you're on your own,' the driver barked, visibly shaken, as Becca pulled herself back into a sitting position. 'No *policias* but I want cash for the window.'

At Edificio Tijuana, they rode the lift in silence, Becca yanking open the metal grate at the top, Tom leaning out into the corridor to check the coast was clear. His movement caused the motion sensor lights to switch on. All was quiet.

Inside, Tom immediately locked the door to the apartment behind him. Becca located a small table lamp and switched it on.

'When do we leave?' she breathed.

Standing opposite her in the shadows, eyes locked together, he felt a second bizarre urge to take her in his arms. It was gone the moment Anil appeared in his baggy white underwear, face groggy from a few hours of sleep.

'What's going on?' he croaked. 'Where you guys been?'

'Pack your things,' Tom told him. 'We leave for Uruguay tonight.'

Chapter 4

London. Five months earlier

Court Three, the Old Bailey: a sentence hearing on a dull, grey February afternoon. Sat in the viewing gallery looking down at the back of Richie's head. Becca kept her coat on, the only individual in her particular designated seating area, waiting for the judge. Most times Richie seemed to be looking at the floor. She would lie awake at night, desperate to exchange places with him, wishing that the events of that night could have been different. Wished he would turn around, but he had never once acknowledged her presence in court.

The courtroom was packed. Journalists, mostly. Those guys would be chasing something with juice, and a young lad hauled up on a murder charge, the murder of a prodigious Justice of the High Court, was juicier than most. Public interest was high, or so the lawyers said. Some of the journalists she had begun to recognise, the ones who had spent a week taking notes on both sides of the argument. The key line of the defence team had been intent, or lack of in Richie's case, backed up by her brother's personal history, the absence of any role models or previous convictions. He had intended to rob a judge of his belongings, that much was true; he had not intended for the judge, Lord Justice

Whitinger, an esteemed individual in his mid-sixties, to hit his head on the concrete kerb and later die in hospital of his injuries. The case of the defence rested on the charge being reduced to manslaughter by an unlawful or dangerous act. The prosecution had petitioned for a second-degree murder charge, therefore a longer sentence if found guilty. Impact statements had been read out by both the judge's daughters. She had watched Richie's shoulders trembling with sobs that day.

The lawyers had warned her to expect a nine to fifteen year sentence following a manslaughter verdict. Her brother would likely serve ten before being eligible for release.

The call went up. All rise.

A café on Carter Lane. Far enough away from the Old Bailey that she wouldn't risk running into the victim's relatives or members of the press. She sat in front of a coffee and a Danish pastry, the former going cold, reliving the moment the judge had read out his sentence: thirteen years, given the malicious nature of the intent.

Her eyes drifted shut. Richie would be out in eight if he was lucky. He would be thirty-five. As he was removed from the courtroom bound for Wandsworth Prison, sobbing, he'd looked up, for the first time straight at her, as if he'd known her exact position all along. She'd raised her fingers to her lips, kissed them, waved goodbye.

She opened her eyes. There was a rustling beside her table as a man took his seat. Broad shoulders, unruly eyebrows, black woollen overcoat with deep pockets. He squeezed into his seat, shook his newspaper open. A waitress brought him coffee. He thanked her gruffly, looking up to meet Becca's stare.

Albert Denham.

'What are you doing here?' she asked.

'I was in court just now.'

'I didn't see you.'

'Well I was there, sat at the back. I'm sorry, Becca, I really am.'

Denham moved himself to her table, removing his overcoat, slinging it over the back of the chair.

'He hasn't been here. Not once,' she said.

Denham was good at making excuses for his would-be employer. 'It would bring unnecessary attention, you know that.'

'No, it would bring *him* unwanted attention. People would start to question why he was at the trial of a lowlife thief, there's a difference.' A silence passed between them. 'I'm sorry,' she said at length. 'I appreciate you coming.'

'He's talked to me about a job,' he said. 'Wants me to try and convince you to come aboard.'

'Anton already spoke to me. He thinks it's a fool's errand, that the chances of getting caught are fifty-fifty. That Capricorn should hire professionals.'

Denham glanced over his shoulder. 'He's worried that if he contracts it out, Sabina Cordero and her family will end up dead.'

'Would that be such a bad thing?'

'You know how he feels about that woman.'

'And yet she's the one threatening him.' Becca folded her arms over her chest, sank her teeth into the inside of her cheeks. 'I can't go. I don't even own a passport.'

Denham shrugged. 'Sign some forms, have the pictures ready, I can do the rest.'

Somehow it felt like there was no squirming out of this one, despite Anton's reservations and her own doubts about breaking into a safe in a country she couldn't even pinpoint on a map. She leaned forward. It had been playing on her mind ever since her conversation with Anton.

'I'll do it,' she hissed. 'On one condition. Get my brother's sentence reduced. No, get him out. If Capricorn can do that, I'll crack open that safe myself. I swear to God.'

Denham seemed to contemplate what she had put to him. 'That could be… complicated. The justice system is a maze, I'm not sure he has that kind of reach.'

'Come on, Al. You must know somebody. Isn't it your job to do as Capricorn tells you? Can't go back and tell him I'm still saying no, can we?'

'Becca—'

There was a warning in his tone. She didn't care. She wouldn't do it for anything less. She was gathering her things, getting ready to leave.

'Nice seeing you again, Al,' she said. 'I'll let you get the bill. You know where to find me.'

*****

Becca stared from the window of the *Francisco*, huddled in the corner on a mint green-coloured faux-leather seat, bag and coat at her feet. The ferry skated across the River Plate's murky brown waters, Uruguay's coastline visible through a layer of mist on the horizon, Buenos Aires a distant memory.

She'd been on one ferry ride before, from Liverpool to Belfast as a child, not long before her parents' death. Coming to Argentina was the first time she had left the British Isles, and the first time she had even been on a plane.

Across from her, stretched out over three seats, Tom Holt's head rested awkwardly on his holdall, mouth open, chest rising and falling as he snored. He looked like the kind of man whose education had been paid for, not a career criminal.

Back at the apartment, heart still pumping from the evening's events, she hadn't had the energy to argue with him about who should travel with whom. At 5 a.m. they had bundled into two separate taxis, Ray and Anil bound for Aeroparque, Buenos Aires' airport-in-the-city; she and Tom for Puerto Madero, with an agreement to meet at a bookshop in Montevideo, the Librería Puro Verso, in the city's old town.

On the ferry, Tom stirred, sitting up to rub his eyes. 'How long was I asleep?' he asked.

'An hour,' she responded.

He yawned, rubbed his stubble. She watched him stand up and stretch up to the ceiling, revealing a light sprinkling of hair around his belly button, a belt holding up his jeans. He then picked up the holdall, tossed it on the floor next to her bag and took a seat by her side. She bristled.

'I'll get us some coffee,' he said.

'I'll have a Coke.'

'Want something to eat?'

She shook her head. 'You still haven't told me who those men were,' she said.

Tom took a deep breath, leaned his head back against

the seat. 'They work for a man called Federico Hernandez. About seven years ago, I got a little too close to Federico's brother's new wife for his liking. And it appears Fede hasn't forgotten my minor error of judgment.'

He was looking over to the main passenger area, to the *Francisco's* coffee counter and Duty Free shop.

'Why did you go to the casino?'

'Because they knew I was in town. I went to try and make peace with Fede.'

It dawned on her then. What he'd meant in the taxi, when he asked if she knew what she'd done. 'Oh.'

'It doesn't matter. He probably would have tried to kill me anyway. Or Baresi would have done it.'

'Who's Baresi?'

'The one who took a shine to you.'

He got to his feet, bending to pull his wallet from the holdall. She suddenly felt satisfied that she'd put a knife in the man. She looked up at Tom, wondering how it was a man would go to so much trouble for a woman. 'Was she worth it?'

He grinned. 'I used to think so.'

He backed away. 'Don't forget you owe me a ring,' she called out.

He frowned at her, apparently not understanding her meaning.

'If I have to pretend to be marrying you, you can at least buy me a ring.'

He was away for some time, out of her line of vision. She reached for the mobile phone she kept buried at the bottom of her bag, the one that Denham had given her to use along with the credit card, and punched in the security code. As if by coincidence, a text message appeared from the man himself:

Why have you left Buenos Aires?

Becca looked up, eyes searching for Tom. He came into view, meandering around, clutching something in his hand. She wondered whether he had been the one to tell Denham, whether it had been Ray from the airport or whether the lawyer had been paying attention to his phone tracker. It didn't make a shred of difference: Al Denham was one step ahead. She could tell him the truth, risk freaking him out, but she didn't want to do or say anything that could jeopardise Richie's early release. Ignoring his question, she typed her reply slowly:

Did you go and visit Richie?

Denham responded immediately.

Not yet. Tomorrow.

She winced, hating the idea of her brother having no visitors, wondering why she hadn't been to see him. She would give Denham one more day.

Back over in the Duty Free, Tom was paying for something. She returned the phone to her bag. When he came back over, he was clutching a mug of coffee and a bottle of Coke. He handed her the drink before reaching into his pocket, pulling out a small, black velvet box.

'I hope you're not expecting me to get down on one knee,' Tom muttered as she took it.

'You really shouldn't have,' she said, opening the box and staring at its contents. 'Oh no, wait, you *really* shouldn't have.'

'What can I say? You're not marrying me for my money.'

'Clearly.'

Becca unsecured the cheap narrow gold band and pushed it onto her left ring finger. It slid on easily. She held out her hand, frowning at the minuscule, cut-rate stone nestled on top. Picked up her Coke and held it out to Tom.

'To false pretences,' she toasted.

He chinked her bottle with his paper cup. 'To false pretences.'

★★★★★

Montevideo. The capital of Uruguay. A city by water. Departing the city's port they walked side by side through a maze of streets to Sarandi, a slightly decrepit yet oddly charming pedestrianised street in the drizzling rain, wind coming in strong from the coast, following a set of notes Tom had scribbled for himself. They barely spoke, too shattered even to make small talk.

Outside the Librería Puro Verso, Tom stopped, Becca noting that he appeared vaguely pleased with himself. He was looking up, squinting in the rain at the large window and what appeared to be a café inside.

'You look like a boy scout who just worked out how to read a map,' she said, walking ahead of him inside, eager for a hot drink and to escape the worsening rain.

Inside, walls upon walls of books climbed all the way to a vaulted ceiling. Becca headed for the grand curved staircase at the rear, turning back on herself to get to the second floor balcony and the café at the end. Books had never really been her thing.

'You made it,' Anil grinned from a table in the corner, Ray in the seat next to him.

She slung her bag down, yanked off her coat. Two other customers were both immersed in newspapers.

'So where's your fiancé?' Anil added.

'Funny,' she shot back, taking a seat opposite Ray who acknowledged her presence with a slow nodding of his head.

Becca forced a smile as Tom appeared, removing his jacket and wiping the rain from his hair. She watched him take note of their surroundings, sinking down into the chair before swiping up the menu.

'Well look who it is everybody,' Anil announced. 'The leader of this shit show. You want to tell us what we're doing here?'

Ray leaned forward towards Tom, eyes narrowed. 'Why did we have to leave Buenos Aires?'

For a split second, he exchanged glances with her. He had brown eyes with a hint of green. Her stomach did a little flip. It wasn't a sensation she had experienced before. She didn't like it.

'We had to go,' Tom said. 'It doesn't matter. Montevideo is where we need to be.'

'You're a liar, mate,' Anil cut in. 'You're gonna lead us, I want a little honesty, yeah?'

'We were doing fuckin' fine until you came along,' Ray mumbled.

'Forget Buenos Aires,' Tom snapped. 'I am asking you to trust me. We're going to need an apartment and a car. Ray?'

'What kind of car?'

'Buy something outright if you can. Nothing that stands out. Get us an apartment for at least a month. Pay cash if you can. Avoid giving out names. Somewhere around here will do. Four bedrooms this time.'

'Right,' said Ray, slapping his knees, getting to his feet. 'Apartment first.'

'Get going,' Tom said. 'Anil, find somewhere that sells golf equipment. Get us each a full set, clubs, couple of golf bags, gloves, the works. I'm going to buy us some mobile phones. Meet back here in four hours.'

She had been waiting for her instructions. 'What am I supposed to do?' she blurted.

Tom got to his feet. 'You can look after the bags.'

'You want me to sit here for four hours and babysit your shit?'

'Somebody has to.'

Within seconds, she hated him again.

Two hours later she was still simmering with anger, unused to being made to feel redundant. She liked to be up, light on her feet, darting in between the shadows, one eye on her next target. Below her at street level, tourists passed by clutching handbags, cameras and purses, all ripe for the taking. All missed targets whilst she was a lame duck.

The phone at the bottom of her bag began to buzz.

'Are you alone?' Denham said at the other end of the line.

'I am,' she replied.

'Where are you?'

'In a café in central Montevideo.'

'You didn't answer my question.'

He sounded irritated. 'You haven't been to see Richie,' she stated.

'And I will. Tomorrow. Why did you leave Buenos Aires? What changed?'

A woman walked past, a white pleather bag hanging wide open. Becca resisted her magpie urge to get up and follow.

'It's been five months, Al. You told me my brother would be free by now.'

'Answer the question.'

She dug her nails into her palm. 'There are people in Buenos Aires who seem to want Tom Holt dead.'

Denham went silent for a moment, the line crackling. 'Will it compromise anything?'

'It could if we have to go back there.'

'I need you to get close to him.'

Becca sat up. 'To who? To Holt? No. That wasn't part of the bargain.'

'Things change. Get on with it. Capricorn wants to know everything.'

She was halfway across the world, helpless to argue.

'He always does,' she murmured before hanging up.

Chapter 5

London

The train pulled into Streatham Hill Station not long after 7 p.m. Albert Denham stepped onto the platform clutching his briefcase and a week-old copy of *The Economist*. He appreciated the lighter evenings. He followed his fellow commuters, thumping footsteps causing the entire bridge over the platform to quake. Outside the station he took his usual route up the hill, turning right into Culverhouse Gardens. At the sight of a shiny black Mercedes-Benz parked imposingly on the kerb across the street from his front door, he ground to a halt.

'You *hev* visitor,' Tatiana snapped in her glutinous Polish accent the moment he entered his kitchen.

Without looking up from the kitchen sink, his wife – his third, more than twenty years his junior – lifted a hand sheathed in a bright yellow Marigold rubber glove that matched the shade of her hair dye, and pointed out of the window. Denham put down his briefcase without a word, leaning his head a little to the left.

A familiar figure towered in the back garden, his back to Denham, surrounded by high hedges, wearing an expensive suit, twirling a glass of red wine whilst contemplating the vast open sky above his head.

'How long has he been here?' Denham asked.

Tatiana gave a shrug. 'Thirty minutes.'

'What did he say?'

Her lips twisted in irritation. 'Go ask him.'

A knot formed in the pit of his stomach as he stepped outside onto the patio. On the table was an open wine bottle, an empty glass and a brown manila envelope.

'How's it going, Al?' Solomon Capricorn said without turning around. 'Go ahead, have a drink. It's from my collection. From Argentina.'

Denham cleared his throat, poured himself a glass. 'How appropriate.'

Capricorn wore a pink shirt, mahogany hair slicked back, curling a little below the ears. He was about five years his junior, a fact which Denham had always accepted with a twinge of resentment. It was the first time Capricorn had ever come to his South London home.

'I need answers, Al,' Capricorn continued with a degree less than his usual composure. Capricorn didn't turn around. 'I had another email today. The seventh in the last eight weeks. She is trying to intimidate me.'

'With respect, sir,' Denham continued. 'You could ask Belosi to back off a little. Maintain a sensible distance. Or flat out leave her alone.'

It was a moment before Capricorn answered. 'But you're missing the point, Denham. *She* is trying to threaten *me*.' He turned around. For a moment, Al considered whether he might have taken something. Capricorn's eyes were wild, bloodshot. He hadn't shaved. Denham was unused to dealing with the man face to face. 'I need what's in that safe.'

'I spoke to Becca earlier. They're in Uruguay. It's going to take time.'

He watched Capricorn down his wine.

'You know the reason I didn't give this job to Anton?' Capricorn asked.

'Because if you had, Anton would have sent Sancho Belosi in a long time ago. Or he would have gone himself.'

'That's correct, Al. Sabina Cordero's blood would be smeared up a wall. You know I don't want that, but I'm not prepared to back away. If Holt can't get me what I need—'

'Holt will succeed.'

He had learned a long time ago not to relay any concerns. Capricorn was a classic narcissist. He didn't dare tell him either that Holt seemed to have enemies in Buenos Aires.

Capricorn took a step closer. His right arm shot up. Denham barely had time to think, the pressure on his neck instantaneous, Capricorn's nails biting into his flesh, the shock causing Denham to drop his glass. It shattered on the patio, sending Pinot Noir splattering across concrete slabs. Tatiana appeared at the back door, still wearing the Marigolds.

'If he doesn't, I am holding you personally responsible.'

Capricorn let go. Denham stumbled back across the patio, into the grass, clutching at his windpipe, gasping for breath.

'Tatiana looking well, I see,' Capricorn added. Denham glimpsed her look of contempt, disappearing back inside.

'It's good to see you, Al. Enjoy the rest of the bottle. I'll expect an update soon.'

After dark, Denham sat in his study, top two buttons of his shirt open, forehead dappled with moisture. After Capricorn had gone, he had smoked two of Tatiana's cigarettes in the garden, pacing the hedgerow, shoes in the mud. His wife had picked up all the fragments of glass from the patio. He picked up his wine glass from his desk, polished off the last of the Pinot Noir and tore open the manila envelope Capricorn had left for him. He teased out the three slim pages it contained. Capricorn had printed out three separate emails he had received from Sabina Cordero, each one showing the exact time and date that it was sent, nothing but vitriol. Denham sat back in his chair, sucked his teeth. He thought about what Belinda, his first wife, had said to him soon after their divorce. That working for Capricorn would ruin him: that it would burn a hole in his chest until there was nothing left but a charred heap of flesh where his heart was supposed to be. Sometimes he suffered shortness of breath and he would think about those words. He missed her, the first love of his life.

He considered his future for the briefest of moments. After Holt and his team had completed the job – *if* they completed the job – he would cut ties.

This would be his last job for Capricorn.

He walked out into the garden carrying the copies of Cordero's emails, a can of lighter fluid and one of Tatiana's lighters he had used earlier. Lifting the lid on the kettle-style barbeque, he tossed the sheets of paper onto it, sprayed them with fluid, lit them up and watched them burn.

★★★★★

Tom paced through the streets of Ciudad Vieja, Montevideo's old town, on edge, no way of assessing how far Federico's network of spies spread. Montevideo was a small city in comparison to Buenos Aires, like an irritating little brother to an older, cooler, adolescent one. There wasn't the same bustle: a smattering of tourists, the odd market, some shabby looking shops, an artisan deli. He was yet to shake the image of Becca thrusting her knife into Baresi's thigh, fingers bloodied as she yanked the blade out again. Now they both had targets on their backs. So much for making peace.

It was still raining. He tried to relax, let his shoulders drop, put his head down and kept moving. He'd sent Denham a message on the boat. Kept it brief, telling him that the team was making a move to Uruguay. No need for Denham getting panicky before they had even started the job.

The job. He stopped for a moment, glancing over his shoulder, reeling his mind back in. Saw an ATM and crossed the road to withdraw a wad of local Uruguayan pesos. Hailed a cab and asked the driver to take him to a shopping district.

'Which one?' the driver spat in Spanish.

'Any,' Tom replied. 'Whichever is closest.'

In Punta Carretas, as the driver reliably informed him it was called, he purchased two mobile phones from a kiosk, one from a shady looking record store and one from an electronics shop that also sold a line of police accessories, crime scene tape, body armour and the like. Finally, he bought SIM cards and phone top-up cards from two separate tobacconists on opposite sides of the street.

He was back at the Libreria within two hours. Still waiting in her chair, Becca looked bored out of her skull. It didn't evade his attention that she avoided eye contact as he reclaimed his seat. Anil had already come back with six hefty bags containing new golf kit.

'You should see me in this outfit,' he enthused as Tom was sitting down, 'I tried the whole thing on. I look like the Indian Tiger Woods.'

'Try Jeev Milkha Singh,' Tom corrected him. 'What do you know about golf?'

'Only what I seen on the telly,' Anil came back, rubbing his hands together.

Tom signalled over to the waiter. The sandwich he'd wolfed down on the ferry seemed like a distant memory.

'Have you eaten?' he asked Becca.

'Several times,' was her terse reply.

It was another hour before Ray returned to the group.

'Got us a four-bedroom apartment,' he said, pulling his chair up to the table. 'We can move in this afternoon.'

'Good work,' Tom nodded, inwardly relieved.

'Paid cash up front,' Ray continued, 'No ID required. Owner is South African. I paid her a healthy deposit. Only bad news is that the fourth bedroom is out of action.'

Anil sniggered.

'Fuck's wrong with it?' Tom asked.

'No floorboards. And a gaping hole in the ceiling from a burst pipe last month. I say we draw lots for the three bedrooms.'

'How 'bout we shotgun?' Anil offered. 'Shotgun.'

'Shotgun,' Becca seconded.

'Shotgun,' Ray piped up simultaneously.

Tom stared at them around the table, teeth clenched. Becca got to her feet, unfazed.

Anil offered him a shrug. 'Looks like you're on the sofa again, chief.'

The apartment was a fifteen-minute walk away, back towards the Port of Montevideo. On the top floor of a decrepit three-storey building – façade painted butter yellow over a web of age old cracked stonework – it featured high ceilings and two balconies overlooking the cobbled street below, both with wrought iron railings in a Spanish colonial style. A portable heater sat in the middle of a central living area, which also contained an open kitchen.

Tom could taste the damp, signs of mould already mottling the powder blue walls from top to bottom. He threw open the door to the fourth bedroom, slammed it shut again immediately. Uninhabitable didn't even come close.

Tossing his holdall on the floor, he tested the purple sofa cushions with his hands, confirming his suspicion that he wouldn't be the first body to use it as a bed.

After dark, following a meal of over-cooked pasta, Tom said, 'We need to talk strategy.'

Anil fiddled with the back of the portable heater in an attempt to get it functioning. 'Here's my strategy, we never let Ray cook dinner ever again,' he offered up.

'Fuck you,' Ray said with a frown. Tom's eyes travelled from Ray to Anil and back again. He didn't know either well enough to figure out their beef, but something was there, smouldering. Almost reading his mind and diffusing the situation, Becca picked up an open bottle of wine, nudging Ray and filling his glass. Tom wanted to tell Anil to watch himself but steered the conversation back to more pressing matters.

'Las Colinas,' Tom continued. 'We start by locating Sabina Cordero's house, work on getting in and out of the compound without being detected. Those are our start points. First decent day's weather we get; Anil and Ray you go and play an initial round of eighteen holes. Try and locate house number 8024. Anil, is there any way we can video your visit?'

There was a clicking sound and the portable heater came on. 'I'm on it, guv. I'll have a GoPro attached to the cap that woman sold me today. People like to video their golf swings these days, yeah.'

Ray started laughing, a too-many-fags laugh. 'All the gear, no idea,' he wheezed.

Anil got to his feet, taking umbrage. 'Oh, I'm sorry, mate, I forgot I was supposed to be here working on my golf game. You're a former bent copper, isn't that what all bent coppers do all day, be on a golf course being shit at golf?'

Tom barely absorbed the words before Ray shot out of his seat, tossed his wine and lunged at Anil. Cheap red Uruguayan Tannat spilled all over the floorboards, the glass shattering as Ray gripped Anil by the throat in between pudgy fingers, Anil practically lifted off the ground as Ray pinned him to the wall. With his free hand, Ray reached behind his own back, lifting his shirt and in one seamless move yanked a handgun from his waistline, pressing the barrel flush to Anil's temple.

'*Woah! Woah!*' Tom shouted; he and Becca on their feet, Anil's eyes squeezed tightly shut in panic, hands grappling to loosen Ray's ironclad grip.

'Who are you calling a bent copper you little prick?' Ray seethed, forcing the barrel harder against Anil's temple, causing the latter to let out a whimpering sound.

'Jesus Christ, Ray, put the gun down,' Tom hissed, jumping over a chair to get to them. 'We're all on the same side.'

'This motherfucker definitely isn't on my side,' Ray snapped. 'Are you, you little cockshit lowlife scumbag? You think I spent my time as a copper on a sodding golf course, you're wrong. I was putting pricks like you behind bars. Only in your case somebody beat me to it.'

Unable to inhale enough breath, Anil's legs had started to twitch, Ray's grip on his throat unrelenting.

'Ray!' Tom snapped again, the anger raw in his tone now, 'Put it the fuck down, now!'

Ray let go of Anil, the latter dropping like a lead weight. He gasped for air, fingers grasping his throat. Becca rushed to him, leaving Tom to square off with Ray.

'You bought a gun?'

'This is Uruguay, it was easy enough,' Ray shrugged, holstering the weapon in his waistband.

'What the hell made you think we'd need a gun?'

'This is South America; everybody needs a gun.'

'I sent you out to find us an apartment. That was all. Next time, do as I ask. Tomorrow, get rid of the fucking weapon.'

'You scared of it?'

'I did twelve years in the British Army; I think I can handle a damn weapon.'

Ray made a grunting sound, as though the news had come as some surprise, or possibly in defiance, it occurred to Tom, before he was turning and walking towards his bedroom, slamming the door behind him.

'Are you alright?' Tom asked Anil, now lying on his back on the floor, hands covering his eyes, face screwed up in anguish.

'I need sleep,' Becca murmured softly.

He woke in darkness to the sound of bottles chinking together. He'd been wrong about the Buenos Aires' sofa. It had been a bundle of warmth and comfort in comparison. He shifted, pain shooting thorough his hip, eyes squinting towards the kitchen. The light from the fridge hit her hair, making it glow. She was bent over, in only her underwear, her bra a camouflage green, or possibly a dark purple, hard to tell in the light. She had a flat stomach and no hips, small, flat breasts, her figure virtually androgynous. The red hair made up for it. Eventually Becca reached inside the fridge, pulled out a can of drink, tapping the lid with the tip of her fingernail before the ring pull let off a loud hissing sound. She took a distinctly unladylike slug.

'Stop watching me,' she said, wiping her mouth with the back of her hand.

'I can't help it, you're in my bedroom.'

She closed the fridge and the room went dark, except for a small light emanating from her room. He could hear the padding of her bare feet against the wood floor, the air a degree cooler as she went past.

'I suppose since I'm your fake fiancée I could offer you a place in my bed.'

Tom lifted his head, neck twisting in her direction. 'Yes?'

56

She disappeared into the bedroom. He scrambled up, rearranging himself, wincing at the pain in his back. Headed for the light.

The bedroom was sparsely decorated; a wispy pair of curtains covering a single-glazed window, in turn blacked out by a rolldown shutter on the outside. Becca stood on the opposite side of the king-sized bed, feet apart, eyeballing him.

'There are *quid pro quos*,' she said. 'No touching, no watching me, no wandering hands, definitely no hogging the blankets and most important of all, no snoring. Understood?'

He resisted a smile. 'Anything else?'

'Yes,' she said, indicating with her arms at her portion of the mattress. *'This is my dance space; this is your dance space.'*

Tom leapt into the bed, fluffing the pillow. The mattress wasn't half bad. 'Alright, Patrick Swayze, let's see how we go.'

'A thank you wouldn't go amiss.'

'Thank you, Becca. My darling fiancée.'

'Don't call me that.'

She climbed into the bed, back facing him, switched off the light. For a moment, in the darkness, neither moved.

'Becca?'

'I should have added no talking.'

'Did Denham ever tell you the name of the client?'

There was a beat before she gave her answer. 'No. Go back to sleep.'

Chapter 6

Tom let Anil do the driving; Anil still gnashing his teeth over the incident with Ray, mouthing off about the latter's lack of professionalism. *Can't work with dat, man, can't work with dat.* Tom stared from the window then back at Anil, driving on the right-hand side of the road for the first time in his life with a GoPro video camera strapped over a Titleist golf cap. Seven months earlier Tom had had a respectable job, an attractive fiancée, better-than-average salary, company 4x4. Now he was sat in the passenger seat of a 2002 white Suzuki Vitara convertible – a car Ray had bought for peanuts from a second-hand dealership in central Montevideo – next to a Hackney thief, about to plan an all-out robbery. There was some irony in there, that a security consultant sacked for gambling company money was now staking his very existence on the unknown contents of a domestically-held safe.

The drive took them east along Montevideo's La Rambla, a long winding coastal road bordered by white sand beaches and the murky brown, polluted waters of the River Plate. Outside it was eleven degrees with sunshine. He had put himself in Ray's shoes as Anil's golfing partner, unwilling to risk the pair of them coming to blows in the middle of Las Colinas, ordering Ray to go and drop the gun somewhere no one would see him. He knew full well that was not what Ray would do.

He liked Anil, appreciated his frankness. He'd known the moment they'd left Buenos Aires that he'd have to build some bridges to get the team back on side. Things had improved with Becca. Ray was a whole different story.

'Tell me, Anil,' he said. 'How did you learn how to rob a safe?'

Anil offered him a grin. 'Still in school, wasn't I? Two kids I used to hang with, parents ran a locksmith. They sold safes too, for domestic properties, you know, like the ones you put in the back of your wardrobe. We did it for fun to start with, to see if we could. Then we got pretty good at it. So later we started robbing properties, all around North London. Me, I went along for the ride, but it kind of got addictive, yeah? Seeing what we could get our hands on. Few years down the line the Old Bill caught up with us, and I ended up in the slammer.'

'How much time did you do?'

'Six years, Pentonville. Then later, another five. Second stint I did for a mate.'

'You went to jail for somebody else?'

'First time they sent me down I had a wife and daughter, I was twenty-six. She left me when I was inside, took my girl back to India, divorced me and re-married. Not seen my girl since. Second time, my mate, the one who was guilty yeah, he was the same. Had a wife and a little boy. We didn't look too different. So with the CCTV footage, I told the pigs it was me that did it. Didn't want to see what happened to me happen to my mate too.'

'That's decent of you, Anil. Can't be many men who would do that.'

Anil gave a shrug. 'Didn't have anywhere else to be, did I?'

'But you re-married. You said you had a daughter.'

'Meena. That's my little girl. She's three. She's my life; I miss 'em both so much. I stopped messing about when I met my wife, the second one. That's why this job, it's my last, yeah? Took me two weeks to say yes to Denham. Haven't done this shit in a while, and never on this scale. Then again, nobody ever offered to pay me for it neither.'

'How old are you, Anil?'

'Forty-six.'

'Jesus. I would have guessed thirty-five.'

He laughed. 'Always was a bit baby-faced.'

The drive took them out of the city, past the airport, into the district of Canelones, where, following Google Maps, they turned down a long straight road littered with potholes and patched-up tarmac. They passed cars held together with various strips of duct tape. On one side rose tall eucalyptus trees, distinctive narrow trunks of white bark crowding the landscape. On the other, two other *Barrio Privados*: gated compounds, new houses in various states of construction behind high security barbed wire.

Tom caught his reflection in the wing mirror. For the first time in a while, a sensation of guilt washed over him. Less than a year earlier, he had got away with gambling almost five million in South African Rand, afterwards walking away a free man, losing his job and fiancée but without even so much as a police interview. Anil had rotted away in prison for a crime he didn't even commit.

'What's the deal with Ray?' Tom asked.

'Former copper, innee? Looks at me like I'm the shit off his shoe. Because I done time, I'm a proper crim.'

'So is Becca.'

'Ah, but Becca's different. She got talent. Never once got caught, never had a record. That makes her different in Ray's eyes, makes her special.'

It wasn't long before Aves de Las Colinas came into view: rolling fairways, pristine houses, well-manicured lawns, all packaged up inside a three-metre-high electric fence.

'There she is,' Tom said, straightening in his seat. 'Are you recording?'

'Way ahead of you, boss.'

'Then let's play some golf.'

At the security gatehouse, Anil brought the car to a juddering halt. Their vehicle third in line to enter the compound, Tom allowed his gaze to sweep the area. The gatehouse separated two roads, one in, one out. On each side, there were two channels to take, one for visitors, and one for residents marked *'solo si está registrado'* or 'only if registered'. As he had expected, Tom observed the owners of cars in the residents channel using a fingerprint reader to gain entrance through a red and white barrier, which moved automatically. Inside the gatehouse he glimpsed a guardroom. It was impossible to see inside. Only the top part of the perimeter chain link fence appeared to have an electric charge.

'Can you hear dat?' Anil asked in the driver's seat.

Tom lowered the passenger side window. 'Alsatians,' he said at the sound of dogs barking, breathing in and out. It was South Africa all over again.

Anil nudged the car forward. Inside the compound was a small car park backing into a driving range, and a golf shop. To the left in the distance appeared to be some kind of clubhouse. The sound of a helicopter whirred overhead.

'We're up,' Anil said.

A burly guard approached clutching a clipboard, wearing a sky-blue polo shirt and a six o'clock shadow, trousers slung low under his protruding belly.

'*Hola, buen dia,*' he said, eyeing them.

Tom did the talking. From the passenger seat he produced his most charming smile, ensuring his Spanish was pitch perfect. 'We're here for a round of golf. I called ahead.'

'You're members?'

'No, just visiting.' Purposely avoided saying where from.

'I'll need both your identifications. Open the trunk of the car please.'

Anil reached down and pulled a lever as Tom handed over both their passports. The guard checked their names against his list, staring at Anil's camera, or possibly his Asian appearance for a little longer than was necessary, before meandering to the back of the car, opening up the boot to peer inside.

Satisfied, he returned both passports. 'Park over there please. You are not permitted to drive around the complex, unless you are in a buggy. And, sir, no filming allowed.'

'Understood,' Tom grinned. 'Thank you very much.'

The guard wished them a good day and raised the red and white barrier. Anil raised the window, removing the GoPro from his cap.

'Hold onto it; keep it running,' Tom said under his breath.

A short while later he emerged from the shop clutching the receipt for their round of golf.

'You mean we're not getting a buggy?' Anil asked, sounding disappointed, unloading the clubs from the back of the car.

'This way we get to take our time,' Tom said. 'Get a good look at our surroundings. Besides, they just gave me a map of the complex. Every single house is marked and numbered. So now we know exactly where Sabina Cordero lives.'

Anil took the piece of paper, eyes widening as though he'd been handed a route to buried treasure.

By the time they reached the eighth, a combination of exasperation and anxiety had reached his chest. They were yet to get a glimpse of Sabina Cordero's property, and whilst he considered that there was a satisfactory lack of CCTV around the entire Las Colinas complex, there seemed to be no point of weakness, nothing other than scaling the electrified fence in order to get inside, without going through security. Floodlights lined the perimeter fence from the inside; each one positioned two metres from the fence and five or six metres apart. Outside the fence, there was precious little bush or shrub. Getting in and out of Las Colinas undetected appeared to be nigh on impossible.

Anil dragged his feet. He was still holding onto the GoPro, letting it record as they went.

'We're almost there,' Tom said as Anil teed up, practicing

his swing. 'We should be able to walk past the house halfway down the ninth. Don't thwack it. It's only a par three.'

Anil took the shot. Tom winced. The ball swung off wildly to the right, way behind the hole and into some tall trees. Anil had mastered distance in his golf game, but possessed little or no finesse.

'I hate this fucking game, man!' Anil yelled into the air and Tom rubbed the bridge of his nose.

'I'll get it,' Tom said, tucking his leather glove into his pocket. 'Give me the GoPro so I can get a look by those trees. I'll see you on the green.'

Anil passed him the camera as Tom turned and walked down the fairway towards the trees carrying his bag of clubs, leaving Anil mumbling under his breath. He peered off right towards the horizon, beyond the chain link fence at the rear of the Las Colinas complex, forcing any feelings of edginess from his mind. He kept the camera pointing forwards, arm relaxed. In the very far distance there looked to be some kind of copse, possibly more eucalyptus trees, but little else for cover. In the near distance was some kind of quarry. It was a disconcerting sight.

Beyond the eighth hole was a row of hedges, separating a dirt road leading to a small building from the fairway. He continued towards the fence. At the perimeter was a muddy path not meant for use by golfers, lined with the dried tracks that came from the boots of the security boys making patrols. He followed the path along the line of the fence, making gestures as though searching for a lost ball, should someone see him. Anil's ball was nowhere to be seen. Behind him was some kind of water supply plant, two large silos at the back between two open stretches of putrid-looking water. It was impossible to tell the depth. He crouched down, ran his eyes along the line where the fence met the ground. A little further on, he froze.

Anil's ball was in the rough beyond the green. Tom swiped it up, went back to where Anil was waiting.

'Find it?' Anil asked lazily.

'Better than that,' Tom replied. 'I just found us a way in.'

★★★★★

'Show me again.'

In the apartment, huddled around a table, Tom watched Ray rock back on his chair legs, chuckling privately to himself and shaking his head, arms crossed over his chest. Becca, in contrast, was leaning forward on her elbows, squinting at the laptop screen, trying to mentally unpick what she was looking at as Anil rewound the video footage from Las Colinas for a second time. Granted, it was largely fuzzy images of grass.

'This is the eighth hole,' Tom said, talking them through it. 'The fairway stops here. And here's the line of trees right near the edge of the green. Behind the trees, bit further, here's the path that goes down by the perimeter. Here's the water supply plant, or some kind of overspill, that borders the perimeter path. Here's the fence again, *and...* ' He hit the pause button. 'Here's the pipe.'

Tom watched as Becca squinted again, lips twisting in dissatisfaction. She sat back.

'That's not a pipe. It's some kind of run off. There's only three sides look, and you'll not get a human being through there.'

'Yes you will,' Anil piped up. 'OK, if we was doing this tomorrow, then *you* might be the only one to get through, but if we boys lose a bit of weight—'

He was watching her. She looked disenchanted. 'Don't take this the wrong way, Ray, but that's a hell of a lot of weight you're going to have to lose.'

Tom gritted his teeth. Ray grinned at Becca, gave her a wink, got up from the table.

It was Becca's turn to look at Tom, eyes pleading. 'You're not seriously considering this option, are you?'

'I don't think we should ignore it.'

'As opposed to going through the fence with a pair of wire cutters or smuggling in the boot of a car?'

'They search cars on entry.'

'Not the residents' cars.'

'You're suggesting we bribe a resident to get us in?'

'It's a better idea than squeezing through some kind of concrete drainpipe.'

'Did you not hear me about the canines?' Anil butted in nervously.

Tom leaned forward, meeting her gaze. 'The less people who know about this, the less chance we have of getting caught in the long term. And that's the condition, isn't it? That we don't get caught? We take a pair of wire cutters to the fence we might as well leave a sign saying "sorry about the break in".'

'You think Miss Cordero's not going to notice somebody broke into her house, took her stuff and ran? It doesn't matter if we leave a footprint, so long as we get the job done.'

'Hey, hey, *chill*,' Anil interjected, Tom realising the levels to which their voices had risen. 'This is only the initial. We got a lot more work to do. Becca, just give us the benefit of the doubt, yeah?'

'Fine,' she said. 'What else?'

'We got another lead,' Anil smiled.

'Show her the footage,' Tom said.

Anil leaned forward, nudged the cursor along the timeline with the mouse, pressed play, pushing the tip of his index finger against the side of his head. 'Ignore the visual, yeah, it's just grass, you gotta use your ears.'

Both Tom and Becca leaned in. Anil tapped the volume up. 'This is on the fairway on the way up to hole nine. Can you hear?'

Becca closed her eyes. Tom felt eager to have her back on side, to believe in what he and Anil had discovered.

'I can hear voices,' she said. 'A child laughing, and a woman talking.'

'But you hear what language they're speaking in?' Tom asked her.

'Sounds German. Or Dutch or something.'

'It's German,' Tom confirmed. 'Anil, move it forward. We got some footage of the car outside the house. See this? The number plate. It's an SCD plate. And see the flags stuck on the back? German.'

Becca looked blank. 'SCD?'

Ray had wandered back to the table, his interest piqued again.

'I looked it up. In Uruguay, SCD is *Cuerpo Diplomatico,* it indicates a diplomatic car. So chances are, the people who live in the house bordering hole nine work for an Embassy in Montevideo. Very possibly the German Embassy.'

'So… ?'

'So I checked the website for the Ministry of Foreign Affairs in Uruguay. Four individuals listed for the German Embassy: the German Ambassador, Hermann Möller, the Deputy Head, someone named Jan Schaus, Liesel Kurtzmann and a secretary, Meike Grassl.'

'You're assuming that one of them lives in this house on the ninth hole?'

'Could be. The woman we heard on tape could be the wife of either the Ambassador or Jan Schaus.'

'And how do we find that out? How do we know if either of them is even married? Did you get a look at her?'

'A glimpse,' Anil volunteered. 'Reddish hair. Big hips, like.'

'Helpful,' Becca said, getting up out of her chair, puffing out her cheeks. 'Sounds like me without the hips.'

Tom watched her walk away, perturbed by his quickening heartbeat, and as to why it was her opinion that suddenly seemed to matter to him quite so much.

Ray tapped him on the shoulder, held out his hand. 'I'm actually impressed,' he announced as Tom shook it. 'I had my doubts about you. But that's not bad for a morning's work.'

'Anil was there too, Ray.'

'*Mmm*,' Ray muttered. Tom got to his feet, gave Anil an encouraging smack on the back. He hadn't yet voiced his concerns to the group over the level of security at Las Colinas. He had been paying attention, taking in every detail between each golf swing, every floodlight, every uniformed guard. He swallowed the lump in his throat. Getting through the fence alone would be enough to get them all killed.

Chapter 7

Five minutes after she had viewed the footage taken from Las Colinas, it had started to rain.

Five days later, it was still raining: perpetual and unrelenting, rain that hammered against the shutters all night, causing damp patches to emerge on the walls and ceiling. Ray argued that raising the issue with the landlady would only alert her to their existence as a foursome. Tom agreed; they needed to lay low. So Becca listened to the hollow sound of *drip-drip-dripping* all day, water splashing into a copper saucepan which would require emptying into the kitchen sink, before the *tap-tap-tapping* of drips would resume. She felt cold. Something about the place reminded her of the crumbling house she grew up in.

She was used to being busy. No work: *create your own*. No money: *go steal some*. Take the tube to Covent Garden tailing unsuspecting passengers through the ticket barriers. Walk a route towards Oxford or Carnaby Street, where she could find wallets to snatch in abundance, handbags under chairs, ripe for the taking, whatever caught her glimmering eye. Pedestrian crossings and traffic lights tended to be profitable, women standing blathering on their phones, so concentrated on their conversation or the latest free magazine to notice anything amiss. Open season.

She sat huddled on the sofa, near the portable heater, watching Anil rehearse breaking a loose pin-tumbler lock with a variety of different tools: a small lever, a hairpin and what looked like a set of bump keys, all items she was familiar with.

'How long does it take you to get in?' she asked.

'Depends on how much money somebody spent on their lock,' he replied. 'Most cheap locks I need a couple of minutes. You mean you don't break locks?'

Becca half-smiled, gave him a shrug. 'Usually I just go through the window.'

Anil chuckled. The sense of uselessness gnawed away at her stomach. Her thoughts turned to Richie languishing in his cell. Denham had put off his visit twice more.

She got out of the chair, stretched, puffed out her cheeks. Walked to her bedroom and changed clothes to skinny jeans, her military-style jacket, a pair of dog-eared lace-up boots, and a lick of black eyeliner.

'I'm going out,' she announced.

Outside it was already dark. 'Still raining,' Anil commented.

'Where are you going?' Tom asked.

'I'm not going to steal anything from anyone if that's what you think.'

Montevideo wasn't the city she had expected. At night, the old town was dark and foreboding, too many shadows for muggers and thieves like herself to lurk in. She had grown used to walking the back streets of London, but even they were better lit after midnight, and with less chance of somebody pulling a knife. She glanced at her phone. 8.15. She quickened her pace, opening up her umbrella, pulling it down close until she could feel the metal prongs digging into her scalp.

There was no Metro system in Montevideo, nor were there any trains, leaving her with a choice of bus or taxi. The city was old school. A short time later, after some confusion over how many pesos she would have to pay the driver, Becca found herself sitting at the back of a dilapidated yellow cab, heading towards the German Embassy.

Darkness. Only street lights, not a soul around. Her socks wet through, the umbrella now half-broken, discarded, hair dripping water down her neck. She waited motionless under the protection of a tree on the opposite side of the road to the Embassy compound, rainwater lashing her cheek and face. Cold had seeped into her bones. Without something to focus her mind on, her thoughts always returned to Richie, and to Capricorn, one of the two people in the world she had come to fear.

She wiped her eyes, spat out the gum she'd been chewing onto the pavement, shifting her attention to the dull greyish building with a grand portico behind a security fence, lethal spikes protruding at the top. There were no lights on and careful examination of the guard hut appeared to demonstrate a lack of a human presence. Still, it would prove impossible to get inside.

She wasn't entirely sure why she'd come, to see an actual Embassy perhaps, or to escape the cabin fever. All she knew was that she had to help get this job off the ground so she could go back to England and visit Richie in jail. As teenagers, following the death of their parents, they had come to rely on one another, yet now, years on, she had no one, and the feelings of loneliness had come back to haunt her.

She remained there for a few moments more, water dripping from the tip of her nose, counting the number of CCTV cameras she could see.

It was then that it caught her eye. Stepping out from underneath the tree, she allowed the rain to soak her entire being before walking a few paces down the road, out of sight of the compound. Repositioning a boulder with her foot to allow herself some leverage, she shifted the grey-black lid backwards on its hinges. The rain somehow lessened the smell inside the iron dumpster, yet the stench was still vile. Rain hammered down on the inside, splattering against plastic. Placing one foot on the boulder, she leaned up and glanced inside, the contents about visible. It was half full. She smelled the distinct odour of human piss and wondered whether it was worth her trouble, coming to the conclusion that it probably wasn't, but that she was going to do it anyway.

Leaning back, she grabbed the edge of the dumpster. Gymnastics had been her favourite class at school. Her teacher had once told her she had the grace of an elite Soviet gymnast, though now Becca couldn't recall the woman's face as she used the boulder to neatly flip herself inside, landing on two feet on a pile of wet stinking refuse sacks.

She retched more than once, locating her flick knife in her back pocket and stabbing at bag after bag until she was surrounded by rotting food waste, plastic bottles and soggy cardboard. She dug deeper, cursing herself for not bringing a torch, flinging out some of the bags onto the street, hardly caring if they landed with a loud crash on the uneven concrete. She gagged again at the sight of excrement, finally laying her hands on some thicker black sacks, breaking them open to find mounds of shredded paper. The shreddings stuck to her wet fingers, turning her hands white. In the third bag was a pile of plastic cups, more paper: office waste, not domestic. Using the side of the bin to yank herself upwards, she held out some of the documents, trying to read the contents under inadequate street light, rain wetting the paper.

She was about to discard them, until she caught sight of four names she had heard before.

At the apartment, she kicked the door closed behind her with her boot, allowing the water to pour off her hair and clothes.

Her male counterparts were huddled round the table, a laptop open in front of them showing a map of Google Earth. Except none were looking at it, instead staring at her as she wrestled to extricate herself from her jacket, paper shreddings still coating her skin.

'Fuck is that stink?' Anil asked.

Only Tom stood up. 'What the hell happened to you? Where did you go?'

She caught a glimpse of herself in a mirror by the door: eye makeup streaked across her face, hair matted against her forehead. Tiny pieces of paper shredding stuck in every contour. And yes, the funky smell. She didn't want to talk, wanted only to shower. Discarding her jacket on the floor, she kicked off her boots and wriggled out of her skinny jeans, before reaching into the back pocket, landing the piece of paper hard against Tom's chest.

'Now I don't know any German, but this could be interesting.'

*****

'Becca.'

In darkness, her eyes wrenched open. Tom Holt's face hovered inches from hers.

She bolted upright, thrusting him off with unsteady breaths.

'You were having a nightmare.'

She felt cold. In her dream she'd been back in London, grappling invisible forces.

'Who is Anton?' Tom asked. 'You were saying that name.'

She swallowed, throat constricting. Lay back down, rolling away from Tom.

'He's no one,' she said. 'No one.'

Chapter 8

When the lawyer, Denham, had first arrived at his door in '96, Ray Caulder recalled being slumped on the sofa in his underwear, a bottle of Laphroaig in his hand, 'Champagne Supernova' playing on radio Key 103. He'd been one of three Manchester Police officers convicted over taking bribes from the criminal underworld running an illegal prostitution ring, still getting phone calls from *The Sun* newspaper, until he'd thrown his telephone – yellowy beige and still with a rotary dial – out of the fourth-floor window of his Salford block of flats. Twice divorced, he had been contemplating the rest of his sorry life pulling pints at the local boozer, serving out maintenance payments to two ex-wives.

The streets of Montevideo seemed somehow like a step down from the grubby streets of Manchester. Ray didn't enjoy being quite so far away from home. He missed his daughters. He tried to speak to at least one of them most nights, on mobile phones he had given to each of them, the bills paid for out of his own pocket. Working for Albert Denham for the last twenty years had turned out to be immensely profitable.

It had finally stopped raining, the sky blue again. As Ray trudged back from the Plaza Hotel in the centre of Montevideo's Old Town, his phone started ringing in his pocket. He didn't have to guess who was calling.

'Holt's asking for money for a tux, a cocktail dress and a goddamn diamond ring, what the hell is going on?' Denham ranted.

Ray relished it when his boss's blood was up. It usually meant that he was working on something important, which in turn made Ray feel good about himself, knowing a bumper pay-packet was coming his way.

This job… This job was different.

'The girl went out two nights ago,' he informed Denham, 'Came back with summat. We think it was put out with the rubbish. It's a flyer for a casino event at the Plaza Hotel. Sponsored by the German Embassy. I've just come back from there with four tickets for the event.'

'What does that have to do with anything?'

'We think a German couple live out in Las Colinas. Within spitting distance of the Cordero house. Think we've got the wife on video. The diamond is for Becca posing as Holt's fiancée. He's not bad, your security fella. He's already made his way into her bed.'

'You mean they're—'

Ray let out a snort. 'Think he'd like there to be. The feeling's not mutual. Becca feels sorry for him sleeping ont' sofa.'

'Is this plan going to work?'

Ray stopped in his tracks. 'Who knows? Right now we'll try anything to be one step closer to that safe.'

*****

A sea of bodies: too many for Tom's liking. Men in tuxedos and bow ties, ladies in floor length gowns and their finest jewels, jostling for space at the individual tables. Sporadic laughter, squeals of delight. A lucky streak. Above his head, lilac-coloured fluorescent lighting, dipping to raspberry red. Behind him, Becca stood in a floor length gold sequined dress in the middle of three roulette tables, sipping on a cocktail; an upgraded diamond on her ring finger. Ray was at the bar, Anil skulking in a corner.

They had found the couple on Instagram; Jan Schaus's wife Katrin a prolific user of social media with no regard for her own privacy settings. Within a few minutes, Anil had discovered everything from her dress size to her favourite holiday destination. Pertinently, she had posted several pictures of her diplomat husband, together with their young daughter, several of the photographs tagged with a location of Aves de Las Colinas. And she was about seven months pregnant.

Therein lay the problem. The chances of a heavily pregnant woman turning up to a casino night were slim at best. Tom made the decision to focus on locating the husband. Yet if the pair showed up together, there was a good chance they would not stay, given the wife's condition, giving the team a very small window of opportunity to locate them.

Of all the tables, roulette required the least amount of concentration, allowing him to make small 'outside' bets – on the outside section of the betting layout – whilst scanning the crowd at the same time. It was a minimum ten US dollar table. Each bet he alternated between red and black, even and odd, winning some spins too. This was no time for 'inside' bets – lower odds, higher stakes on the central section of the betting layout – the kind that really got his adrenaline pumping.

Becca toured the room. Before long, she was back at his side, placing one hand on his back and leaning up to kiss his cheek.

'We screwed up,' she whispered.

As the dealer announced the next spin, Tom placed three of his blue chips on red.

'How so?'

'The German Ambassador was here, he came and went. There was a small opening ceremony, he cut a ribbon, made a speech then left after a glass of Moët.'

'*No más apuestas!*' the dealer shouted.

The bettors around the table leaned closer, watching the white ball as it hopped around the spinning wheel. Tom leaned closer into Becca. 'We keep looking. There's nothing to say they won't be here.'

The ball landed on black. Tom shook his head, shared conciliatory smiles. Becca took a step back, enveloped by the crowd.

By 11.30 p.m., sweat was pouring off his back. The crowd had increased in both size and volume. At the bar, Ray was half cut; Tom could tell by the way he was swaying in his chair. He stood with Becca in the centre of the chequered carpet, arm in arm, knocking back vodka tonics.

He heard her before he saw her. Barely ten metres away at another roulette table, shrieking with delight as she won another spin. Anil had heard it too, he and Tom sharing a look. The noise even got Ray's attention. The crowds parted for the briefest of moments, and he glimpsed Katrin Schaus, perched on a bar stool, heavily pregnant, with auburn hair and wearing an evening gown, surrounded by other faceless players, backed up by her husband who in contrast seemed wearied by the entire experience. Everything about Katrin seemed larger than life.

Tom felt Becca squeeze his arm, downing her drink, readying herself to close in.

'You know the thing about roulette, don't you?' he asked her.

'What's that?'

'There's no strategy. It's all about luck.'

Becca raised her eyes level with his. 'I don't believe in luck.'

Tom felt a smile tug at his lips. 'Get talking to the husband. I'll get close to the table.'

They heard another loud shriek. Katrin was rapidly gaining the attention of both the other gamblers and spectators alike. Tom elbowed his way forward towards the table, admiring the way Becca was able to glide unnoticed through the throng, smooth as a manta ray. Such was the interest in Katrin's winning streak, a crowd three bodies deep had congregated around her. Tom was quick to see why: this wasn't a woman betting on ordinary red or black. Katrin was making inside bets, with some knowledge of the table, perhaps prior experience or simply pure bluff. Either way, it appeared to be working. He watched her make a corner bet, placing her red chip on the intersection of four numbers: twenty-three, twenty-four, twenty-six and twenty-seven, causing some of the spectators around her to suck in their collective breath. The pay-out was eight to one. She'd bet twenty-five dollars. It wasn't high-risk as things went, but for a total stranger he took pleasure in her sheer bravado. The dealer spun the wheel. The crowd leaned in, all eyes on the white ball as it spun. The dealer announced no more bets. The ball kicked up, rattled from one number to the other, finally settling in the nook of number twenty-four.

Katrin raised her arms in disbelief; the crowd surrounding her going wild. Even Jan Schaus managed a grin as his wife grabbed his face enthusiastically and planted a kiss on his cheek. Then he was whispering something in her ear. She seemed to nod, holding up her index finger, pointing to the table, *one more bet*. Her husband rolled his eyes, reluctance written all over his features.

Tom couldn't see Becca. Ray was standing on the opposite side of the table, caught up with the stragglers. There was no opportunity to get close to either of them.

Katrin took all her chips, everything that she had won, and placed them on red, in Tom's eyes a wild, irrational strategy that spoke volumes about her inexperience of the game. She looked to her husband, who gave a nonchalant shrug. Go-big-or-go-home strategies were more about grandstanding. The crowd was whooping and Katrin Schaus was egging them on. Tom glanced towards Anil, now mingling with the crowd on the other side of the table, the excitement palpable.

The dealer spun the wheel. Without warning, Katrin changed her mind, moved her chips to black. There were gasps; some covered their mouths. The ball spun round, bouncing erratically, taking its time to settle. And when it did, it was on red.

There sounded out a downward, swooping cry of disbelief, not only from Katrin but from her new-found fans, disappointment written across their taut faces. Katrin's husband was laughing, one of the lucky few who would never get sucked in by the pageantry. He whispered in her ear.

Tom watched Jan Schaus help his wife off the stool as the dealer removed her chips from the table. She waved a fond goodbye to the gathered crowd, now dissipating having lost interest in the next spin. Tom stood his ground, teeth gritted, shoulders knocked from all sides, watching the pair as husband escorted wife across the floor, heading towards the exit and the cloakrooms, Katrin opening her bag and handing over two tickets. He followed at a distance, unsure of how he planned to strike up a conversation, perhaps in the coat queue, or waiting for a taxi in the lobby downstairs. He needed to stay close.

A moment later, he felt a tug on his arm.

'Let them go,' Becca said, under her breath.

'We need to make conversation. We're going to lose them.'

'And we will. Let them go. Trust me.'

He looked at her, her eyes sparkling under the casino lights. 'Why are we letting them go?'

They looked towards the couple, heading for the exit, coats on, Jan Schaus's arm draped protectively around his wife's shoulders.

'Because I have his wallet.'

A few minutes later, on a moving escalator near the hotel lobby, a hastily convened meeting.

Anil's eyes were wide, nervous. 'What about CCTV?'

'There's no way,' Becca shrugged. 'It was a crush. Easiest lift I ever made.'

Ray's elbows were resting on the moving handrail, the look he was giving Becca proof enough that he harboured some paternal soft spot for her.

Anil didn't back down. 'He's going to notice, yeah, and they'll be straight back here.'

'Not necessarily,' Tom interrupted. 'If they do, then we'll stage something, before they can talk to security.'

'Give it twenty minutes,' Becca said. 'If they haven't come back, call the number on his business card. Explain you have his wallet but don't hang around; make arrangements to meet him tomorrow.'

Tom and Anil exchanged looks as they swung round and took the escalator back down. Anil had calmed. It made sense.

'He may not even have noticed yet,' Becca added. 'They'll be halfway to Las Colinas by the time we call.'

Tom and Anil were nodding in agreement. 'Go back to the tables,' Ray said, finally speaking up. 'I'll watch the door'.

The crowd was thinning out. Tom stood behind Becca, maintaining a view of the main entrance. Her first time ever at a roulette table and Becca was already placing inside bets, perfectly focussed and winning the occasional spin too. Just her style.

After thirty minutes, Ray sauntered back into the room. He looked up at Tom, and with a shake of his head proceeded to the bar.

'How about we finish up here, darling?' Tom said to Becca, with a nod to Anil who was sat playing blackjack.

In the lobby of the hotel, Tom dialled the mobile phone

number on Schaus's business card, one of several tucked into the back of the latter's tatty brown leather wallet. The man answered after a couple of rings.

'Jan Schaus.'

'Herr Schaus. My name is Thomas Holt. I'm at the Plaza Casino. My fiancée found your wallet under a roulette table.'

There was a shuffling sound. '*Scheiss*,' the voice hissed, adding in English, 'I must have dropped it.'

'Are you close by?'

'No, I am close to my home. I live out near the airport. *Scheiss*. I'll have to come and fetch it. Can you leave it with security there?'

'I'd be far happier giving it to you in person. What about tomorrow? My fiancée and I were planning on going up the coast but I'm sure we could drop it round on our way back.'

'You sound British, are you British?'

'Yes, yes, we're travelling around, taking a sabbatical, that sort of thing.'

'Well, of course. Come round to our place in the afternoon for beers.'

'That would be lovely. Whereabouts do you live?'

'It's called Aves de Las Colinas, one of these gated communities. On a golf course. I can send you directions, but you can Google it. It's the least I can offer. You've saved me a journey.'

Tom laughed, continuing the charm offensive. 'Wonderful. How's five o'clock-ish?'

Chapter 9

Tom allowed Jan Schaus to fill his wine glass with a Uruguayan-produced Tannat for a second time. They had called ahead, confessed to running late, arriving at Aves de Las Colinas at 6 p.m. as planned, gaining access to the complex following a call to Jan's mobile phone. They had parked their new hire car – an unremarkable silver Peugeot legally requisitioned by Ray – outside the Schaus's Mediterranean-style villa in the centre of the Colinas complex just as the sun was beginning to dip below the horizon. It wasn't yet August, mid-winter in Uruguay, though recent temperatures had been favourable. They sat outside on the Schaus's terrace – having returned Jan's wallet as promised – under a bamboo-lined wooden canopy, looking out onto a large garden and swimming pool, and over the back fence to the ninth hole fairway on the golf course. The back of Sabina Cordero's house was visible in the near distance.

Next to him, wrapped in a chunky knit cardigan she'd purchased that afternoon, Becca looked every inch his adoring fiancée, gazing at him as he spoke, occasionally touching his arm or face, playing her part to a tee. She was almost as good an actress as she was a pickpocket. Real or not, he enjoyed having her undivided attention.

'I'm so sorry again we were later than planned,' Tom

said again, as Katrin Schaus waddled out onto the terrace wearing her coat, clutching a bottle of fizzy water and a bowl of nibbles.

'Not at all,' she replied before her husband had a chance to, in her Bavarian drawl, 'Elise is asleep now and we don't get many visitors out here.'

'It's so peaceful,' Becca commented as though admiring the view, or, Tom considered, perhaps trying to work out the best way to get to Sabina Cordero's house without being seen.

'Too quiet,' Katrin said with a chuckle, easing herself slowly into her chair. 'I can go a whole day without seeing a soul, nothing but golfers in those little buggies.'

'But you must feel secure though,' Tom added. 'I saw the fence.'

'Oh completely,' Jan said. 'Part of the reason we chose it. But it's a long way from anywhere.'

'I imagine you can probably leave your house open all day.'

'You probably could,' Jan mused, 'but this is still South America. Anyway, we're done now, getting ready to pack up and go.'

'Oh?' asked Becca. 'Go where?'

'It is back to Berlin for us,' Katrin said, rubbing her swollen belly. 'It is the end of our three years here. I have to go soon before I'm a flight risk.'

'When do you leave?'

'Two weeks left. The packers they come the day after tomorrow.'

Tom felt Becca's hand slide its way down his thigh before

giving his knee a hard squeeze. The plan was to keep them talking, as late into the evening as possible.

'So how did you two meet?' Katrin asked.

'We should get out of your hair,' Becca announced around 10 p.m., a couple of hours after moving to the couple's living room for yet more wine, having spoken at length about her role as a freelance photo journalist. She'd spun a yarn about their first meeting at a bar in Sydney.

'She's right,' Tom seconded, getting to his feet. 'We should get going.'

'I really appreciate you coming out here,' Jan said at the back door, shaking his hand. 'It's been a pleasure meeting you both. I envy you, taking a sabbatical like that to travel.'

They collected their things, Tom's heart going from a gentle *thud-thud-thudding* to smashing up against his ribcage.

'Darling, I can't seem to get this thing to work,' Becca said, standing outside on the gravel in the driveway and dangling the key fob to the car from her fingers.

Tom took it from her, pointed it at the Peugeot, pressing the button. Nothing happened. 'What's wrong with it?'

The failed attempts lasted several minutes.

'Looks like you're stuck here,' Jan laughed, taking the key fob and giving it a go.

'Is there a problem?' Katrin asked, emerging into the driveway.

'Can't get the key fob to work,' Tom grimaced. 'I think it's broken, or the battery's gone. We can't get into the car. Bloody hire car place is closed.'

He put in a fake call for effect.

Becca let out a weary sigh. 'I suppose we could call a taxi and get the hire car people to collect the car in the morning. Do taxis come all the way out here?'

'I tell you what,' Katrin sighed at length, 'Why don't I make you both up a bed and you can call the hire car place in the morning?'

Seven hours earlier, Tom and Becca had sat opposite Anil at the table, an array of tools spread out in front of the Hackney thief, his eyes bulbous due to excessive consumption of coffee and diet cola.

'A key fob works using a radio frequency, yeah?' he had addressed them. 'Take away the ability to emit that frequency, and it's a useless piece of plastic, *capiche*? So take two identical key fobs, disable one, keep the other functioning as it should. Classic switcheroo. Use the useless piece of plastic to try and unlock your car when you don't want to go anywhere.'

Tom gave a single nod. 'And in the morning it miraculously works again, providing that is, they let us stay over.'

In the bedroom on the ground floor of the Schaus's villa, Tom hovered by the set of glass patio doors, unwilling to lie down on the bed. He peered into the inky darkness, the sky strewn with more stars than he'd ever recalled seeing at any one time. It reminded him of being on army exercise, stranded out on a rocky outcrop on Salisbury Plain in the biting cold, laden down with kit, face smeared with army-issued face paint.

Becca lay on her back on the double bed, shoes kicked off, listening to the gentle sound of footprints from the upstairs floor as an average married couple got ready for bed. A single bedside light was on. Outside, music echoed into the night, the sounds of a house party nearby.

'Why Sydney?' Tom asked, keeping his voice low.

'What?'

'You told them we met in Sydney. Why Sydney? Why not London?'

'I looked at the pictures on their walls. It's a faraway place. They don't look like they've ever been. Wouldn't ask questions.'

'Have you ever been to Sydney?'

'Of course not,' she snorted. 'I've never been anywhere.'

'Where have you been? I barely know a thing about you.'

A pause. 'You don't need to know a thing about me.'

'Tell me something. Anything. Who are your parents?'

'My parents are dead.'

He fell silent, unsure if she was telling the truth or simply trying to shut him down.

'Do you have brothers or sisters?'

She moved to the edge of the bed, eyes to the floor. 'I have a younger brother,' she said finally. 'His name is Richie.'

'What does he do?'

'He does what I do. Except he's better at it than I am.'

They fell silent. Upstairs had gone quiet. Becca lay back down on the bed. 'Tell me something,' she said. 'Why does it say the word "Papercut" on the back of your watch?'

His fingers moved to his wrist. 'How did you know that was there?'

'It's your watch. I'm good at stealing watches.'

'It was a gift from my brothers, years ago. It's a reference to a game we used to play as kids. Who could withstand the worst papercut.'

'Who won?'

'Usually my brother Jacob. He had a high pain threshold.'

She turned on her side. 'One day I'll lift that watch from your wrist and you won't even notice.'

'I'd like to see you try.'

They waited. He battled drooping eyelids, the pulsating music outside willing him to sleep, the wine from earlier pervading his brain. The only thing that kept him awake was his memory of being on exercise, where falling asleep would have got you kicked out of the regiment.

He waited one hour, watched the hands on his watch crawl round. Becca had fallen asleep. When he felt ready, he poked her in the arm. She bolted upright.

'It's time,' he whispered.

The night felt cool, at ground level fireflies blinking in the dark. In contrast, the party, somewhere across the golf course, was still in full swing. They aimed for a line of steps, staying close to the shadows, criss-crossing the garden until they reached the side fence.

'We can cross over there,' Becca mouthed, indicating a direction towards the tee-off point at the ninth hole where the tall trees allowed for more shadow.

Tom's heart raced. Walking through the long grass in the darkness, only the moon to light their way, the idea that they could never get caught doing what they were doing suddenly seemed like an absurd notion. And trespassing was the easy part.

Crossing at the top of the hole, Tom led the way back down the hill towards Sabina Cordero's garden some fifty metres away, skirting the rear fences of the houses to their right, slithering through the long grass to the side of the fairway. The house party was nearer than he had thought, two doors away from their target property. Though the music had died down, partygoers had spilled out into the back garden, smoking cigarettes on wooden deckchairs, a disco light throwing out coloured shapes onto the grass. The light didn't extend to the end of the garden, meaning he and Becca could pass by unnoticed.

When they came to it, he was taken aback. Crouching low in the grass, down a gentle slope, both he and Becca witnessed the splendour of Sabina Cordero's residence stretching out over a double plot, fully lit inside and out, floor to ceiling windows spanning most of the ground floor, a smaller upstairs level. On the inside, a woman he recognised from Denham's photograph as Sabina Cordero, around forty years old, was in her open-plan kitchen, entertaining her guests in a living room space which stretched out in front of her, hair tied loosely off her face.

Tom took out a small pair of binoculars borrowed from Anil, attempting to take in every detail, knowing there would be plenty to recall later on. Next to him he could hear the sound of Becca's breathing. Something in particular caught his eye, something behind Sabina's head. The upstairs was smaller than the expansive ground floor, but there was a door that divided the two separate levels, a set of stairs visible on the inside, the door frame unusually thick. He knew straight away that he was looking at a steel-reinforced door, with hinge dog bolts and a three-point lock. Heavy-duty, common in South Africa, to allow residents a 'safe keep', should anyone ever attempt to break into the house. On the opposite side there was a back door, surrounded by glass and white plastic. There were bars on the upstairs windows.

It came out of the shadows. Stealthily at first, yellow eyes, a low hollow snarl reverberating in its throat: head low, lips curled, fangs bared.

'Easy,' Tom whispered, lowering the binoculars and meeting its gaze, feeling his way to Becca's arm. She was staring at the Bullmastiff, frozen to the spot.

'Gently move back,' he whispered.

No time. All hell broke loose as the snarl became a vicious bark, the Mastiff's muzzle lunging through the holes in the wire fence, baying for their blood, saliva trails hanging from its jaws. Tom dove backwards into the grass, arse over shoulders, yanking Becca with him, the pair tumbling down the slope into the safety of darkness. From the house there sounded a light whistle, followed by a call of *'Rico! Riiico!'* Rico the Mastiff quietened, standing rigid to attention, hackles up and glaring, confused by the dark space they had disappeared into. Shaking its entire body, the dog trotted back towards the house.

Tom allowed himself a breath, realising he was still holding onto Becca, partially atop her. She was lying on her back in the grass, his face almost touching hers. She frowned, wriggled out from underneath him. He got to his feet, glanced around. They needed one last look. A curt nod said she was alright.

Inside the property, the Bullmastiff was making a fuss of

its owner. Sabina Cordero had moved to the living room, sipping wine on a sofa. Tom's attention was drawn back towards the door to the upstairs. The door was open, but it was more than likely closed at night. And wherever the safe was located, it was more than likely to be behind that door.

Becca took the binoculars.

Tom checked around for signs of life. The music from the party ceased pounding, the air around them plunged into abrupt silence. A second exchange of looks said it was time to go. He followed Becca, shuffling down the hill, only getting to their feet again in the long grass.

The flash of a torch came from the direction of the party.

'Kiss me, do it now,' Becca hissed, and without warning placed her palms at the back of his neck, yanking his face forward to meet her own, capturing his lips and dragging him two steps sideways until she was backed up against the silvery bark of a eucalyptus tree. Caught off guard, it took a moment for him to empty his thoughts and focus on her mouth, pushing himself up against her shape, gliding one arm around her waist, kissing her deeply, sliding his other hand up towards her ribs. It took him another moment to understand her plan, the idea that the approaching guard and his Alsatian would assume two amorous lovers were party guests craving a little intimacy. Becca let out a gentle moan as Tom detected the guard, metres from them, dressed in a green polo shirt and coat *swish-swishing* through the grass, accompanied by a panting Alsatian.

'*Volver a la fiesta por favor*,' the guard chided them, barely giving them a moment's notice. *Go back to the party.*

Tom lifted his head, squinting into the light. '*Si, si,*

disculpe,' he mumbled, eyes back to Becca, panting breaths mixed together. For a split second it felt like she was his and he couldn't help but lower his mouth again, this time like he meant it.

'*Que pase bien, buenos noches,'* the guard threw back in farewell and was gone, evaporating into obscurity.

Chapter 10

Al Denham had indigestion. It was the result, he knew, of a late-night jar of ale combined with a deep-rooted anxiousness at meeting Solomon Capricorn face-to-face. It didn't happen very often: now it was twice in a matter of weeks.

There was – had always been – a definite order to things. There was rarely direct contact, only messages passed back and forth via an intermediary, otherwise known as Anton: the gatekeeper, the dark side to Capricorn. Nothing had changed in twenty years.

This time it was different. Capricorn had come to him direct with the job in Uruguay: desiring him, and not Anton, to take things forward. To talk Becca into leaving her brother and to find him someone who could easily crack into a safe. Ever since Sabina Cordero's emails had started arriving, he had noticed a change in Capricorn, in Capricorn's attitude towards Anton, as though he no longer quite trusted the latter's opinion. Left up to Anton, Denham considered, Sabina Cordero would be in the ground by now.

Denham had contacted Capricorn direct, something he had never done before, to request a meeting. He had received a one-line response, with an appointment time of midnight, at the usual rendezvous: Lauderdale Road Private Gardens in Maida Vale, north-west London.

It was mid-August, temperatures hovering around twenty-seven degrees. Everywhere, windows had been flung wide open, a sweltering city with no air-con as standard.

Denham had taken a late tube to Warwick Avenue around 10 p.m., sat in the Prince Alfred on Formosa Street until last orders before wandering the streets, killing time. If he wasn't there precisely on time, he knew Capricorn wouldn't wait.

At midnight he tiptoed through a small gate at the top end of Lauderdale Road, descending into a private garden with a patio. On the far side was a larger gate, leading to the private gardens behind the row of houses. Locating the same loose brick in the wall, in the middle, two up from ground level, he teased it out, releasing the key behind it and let himself through the gate. There he descended a second set of steps, the garden on his immediate right containing an elaborate rabbit run and some child-sized bicycles. He kept walking to the centre of the gardens, under cover of a gargantuan beech tree, where Capricorn was waiting for him on a bench.

'Evening, Al,' said a voice from the shadows. 'Have a seat.'

Denham did as he was told. It was difficult to see Capricorn in the gloom. He was wearing a suit, chewing gum.

'It's good to see you again so soon. How's Tatiana?'

'Tatiana is very well, thank you for asking,' Denham said.

'Relax, Al. You sound so formal. How does she like England?'

'She has found some Polish friends.'

'I'm grateful to you, you know. Her father was a good man. Would put his mind at rest, knowing his daughter was being looked after by someone like you.'

Denham joined his fingertips together. Tatiana had spent the previous evening on FaceTime with her mother, moaning that he had refused to buy her a Balenciaga handbag.

'Tell me, how are things going?' Capricorn continued.

'I spoke to Holt. They've managed to get near the house. He says there is a secure door that separates the downstairs of the house and the upstairs. He said it has a solid core, he thinks steel-reinforced with a three-point lock. I don't know exact specifications. And there are bars on the upstairs windows.'

Capricorn chuckled to himself. 'She really has gone to town.'

'Holt says Anil Choudhury can't get them past that door. It would take him too long to break through leaving no time for the safe. He believes it will be impossible to force entry through a door like that, provided that Sabina Cordero keeps it locked at night, or when she goes out.'

'Which she will, no question.'

'He says the windows on the other side of the security door face the street, not the golf course. That they won't be able to break in that way. He believes they will need the key, or someone on the inside who can get it.'

'What d'you tell him, Al?'

'I didn't. I thought perhaps we could ask Belosi to help us in some way.'

Denham had seen a thing or two, but the name gave him chills. He recalled a photograph he had once seen of a woman beaten to within an inch of her life, her wounds courtesy of Argentine Sancho Belosi, the image forever scarred on his memory.

Capricorn clicked his tongue. 'I'll send you his number. He speaks a reasonable level of English but the man is like a fucking yeti. Tell Sancho to speak to the maid. I forget the name of the latest one. If Sancho is the one to speak to her then she'll cooperate.'

Denham gave a nod, knowing what a request from Belosi amounted to. 'What about Becca?'

'I'll recall her in good time.'

'She's stubborn.'

'We have her brother. We have everything she wants. So long as we keep up the illusion of his impending freedom—'

'About that, sir—'

'Go on.'

'I went to see Richie Wylde in prison. The boy is not coping with incarceration well. He's struggling with depression. He's lost a significant amount of weight.'

'Is he skeletal? Are we going to lose him?'

'No, but we might want to think about pulling some strings before the situation worsens.'

Capricorn spat out his gum onto the grass. 'Leave him there for the time being. Keep visiting him.'

'And what do I tell Becca?'

'What you always tell her. That we are working on his release.'

*****

Tom went alone, as instructed, followed Denham's instructions to the letter. Took a cab to the Carrasco area of the city, where crime was as high as the security fences protecting

97

the affluent houses, early on the Saturday morning. He got out on Arocena, the main shopping strip, before walking the rest of the way on foot, past the Lawn Tennis Club, turning right, a graffiti-covered church to his left.

The children's playground in front of him was an apocalyptic sprinkling of run-down looking swings and slides made of nailed-together wooden slats, spread over an area of rough sandy terrain, half the size of a football pitch.

The maid was alone but for a young boy playing in front of her on his bike at the farthest most end of the playground, sitting on one of the metal swings, feet propelling her back and forth. Tom pushed his hands further into his pockets. In the seven days that Denham kept the team waiting, the mercury had dropped ten degrees.

As he approached she seemed to notice him, anticipating his visit. She had dark hair and coffee-coloured skin not typically seen in Uruguayans. She wore a grubby pair of workmen's jeans, checked shirt and jacket, both a couple of sizes too large. The boy, nine or ten, had shoulder length hair and wore a muddy pair of frayed tracksuit bottoms with a long-sleeved Barca FC shirt. He was cycling a sweeping figure of eight pattern. The screeching of her swing was like something out of a Stephen King film.

He took a seat on the swing next to hers. It had been painted red once upon a time but there was little by way of paint left, the chain links oddly old-fashioned. She kept her eyes down, shoulders hunched. Denham had told him that she only spoke Spanish.

'*Hola, buen dia,*' Tom said, his tone gentle.

'*Buen dia,*' she responded.

'My name is Tom,' he continued in Spanish. 'What's your name?'

'Manuela,' the woman replied. 'Manu.'

'It's nice to meet you, Manu. Is this your son?'

'He is my eldest grandson. Alejandro.'

Tom smiled at the boy, who continued to cycle in circles. 'Manu, did they tell you why I'm here?'

She nodded, Tom trying to catch a glimpse of her face. 'Where are you from?' he asked.

'Asunción,' she replied.

'You're Paraguayan?'

Again, a nod. Tom glanced over his shoulder. There was no one about, the playground abandoned, wind rustling in the trees.

'I need to ask you some questions about Sabina Cordero's house, Manu. You are the maid there, is that right?' He used the term *empleada domestica*, uncomfortable at the idea of calling her the maid to her face.

'*Si, Señor.*'

'I need to ask you something about the house at Las Colinas. There is a door inside. It separates the two parts of the house. Do you know the one I mean?'

'*Si, si*, it is for security.'

'That's right. Manu, do you know where your *señora* keeps the safe in her house? Is it behind that door?'

'Yes. Inside the cupboard in the study.'

'And does the *señora* lock the door at night, or sometimes in the day?'

'*Siempre*,' she said. *Always*.

'What does the safe look like, can you tell me?'

She gave a shrug. 'It's black. Small.'

'Do you know the code?'

She shook her head vehemently, as though outraged at the very suggestion. 'No,' she said. '*Noooo*.'

'And do you know where she keeps the key to the door?'

'She wears the key on a chain around her neck. She locks the door at night from the inside, this I know. In the day time, if she leaves the house, she will also lock the door, making sure I am on the outside. She has always done this, ever since I started working at the house at Las Colinas. She is very careful.'

'Does she ever leave the key in the lock?'

Manu shook her head.

Tom had an uneasy feeling in the pit of his stomach. Whatever was in the safe was worth a great deal to Denham's client, but if what Manu had to say was true then Sabina Cordero was going to quite some lengths to keep the contents of the safe secure at all costs. Tom looked up to find Alejandro had brought his bike to a halt, an inquisitive scowl on his face.

'Is there a spare key, Manu? Do you know where it is?'

Manu shook her head for a second time. 'I have never seen a spare key. But I think... I know... *Señor* Nico. He keeps a key to the door.'

'Nico?'

'Nicolás Cordero, *mi señora's* brother. He lives in Buenos Aires, in an apartment on Avenida Libertador. Sometimes he comes to Uruguay.'

'How do you know he has a key?'

'I have seen him use it. It is on a keyring with some other keys. He had it in his pocket.'

'What else can you tell me about *Señor* Nico?'

100

She gave a shrug. 'He is younger. *Mi señora* complains that he needs to settle down, marry his girl. He adores the children. He doesn't visit Montevideo as much as she wants.'

'What does he do?'

She shrugged. 'Maybe wine. Something like that.'

Alejandro had sped off into the distance. Manu watched him, leaning her head against the chain links.

'Manu, the people who told you to speak to me. What did they say to you?'

'They said to answer all of your questions, or I would never see my grandson again.'

★★★★★

From the playground he returned to the apartment, slamming the door on entry. Becca glanced up from the sofa. He'd tried not to think about their kiss at Las Colinas, how good her mouth had felt on his. Though they were still sharing a bedroom, the gap between them at night under the covers had grown wider. She had moved to the furthest possible point on the mattress, teetering on the edge without actually falling off it. The kiss itself had not even been mentioned, not even minutes later on the night itself once they'd managed to slip noiselessly back into Jan and Katrin Schaus's spare bedroom. Not the following day, when the key fob for the car had miraculously worked on the first attempt and they had said their grateful farewells, driving all the way back to central Montevideo in silence. Since then, Becca had developed a habit of averting her gaze, avoiding any conversation with him unless entirely necessary.

'So?'

Anil was like an eager puppy in the kitchen, desperate to know the results of his conversation with the maid. 'Can she get us a key or what?'

'No,' Tom stated, yanking off his coat.

'*Faaack*,' Anil said, throwing his arms up into the air.

'There is a chance we could copy one,' Tom said. 'If we can steal it for long enough.'

Ray gave a frown. Even Becca now gave him her full attention for the first time in about a week.

'It would be a long shot. Sabina Cordero has a brother, Nicolás, the maid called him Nico. He keeps a key to the door on a keyring with his own house keys.'

'How do we get to him?' Anil asked.

Tom found himself looking at Becca, only this time she didn't look away. 'We would have to go back to Buenos Aires,' he said. 'Which right now is probably not a good idea.'

'Why not?' Ray piped up. 'What happened to you two?'

Tom was still looking at her. She got to her feet. 'What's the other option?' she asked.

'We don't have one. Sabina Cordero wears her own key around her neck at all times. The maid says she locks the door at night and every time she goes out.'

Anil whistled.

'Tell us why you can't go back to Buenos Aires,' Ray said.

'It's complicated.'

'Becca? Why can't you go back?' Ray asked.

'Because I put a knife in a man's leg.'

'You what?' Anil blurted.

'It was my fault,' said Tom. 'Those people came for me.'

Ray shrugged. 'So we change location. We get a new apartment. How would they, whoever *they* are, even know we were back in the city?'

'Federico has eyes everywhere.'

'Who's Federico?' Anil asked.

'We can do it,' Becca said in his direction. 'I'll wear a wig the moment we touch down. You can change your appearance too.'

'If they find you—'

'They won't find me,' Becca declared. 'I say we go back to Buenos Aires. Track down this Nico Cordero.'

Ray rubbed his hands together. 'I'll go ahead of you. Find us an apartment in a different area of town.'

It should have felt like a bad idea; instead it felt like they were finally getting somewhere.

'OK,' Tom agreed. 'We go back to Buenos Aires. We go after the key.'

Chapter 11

Buenos Aires

Anil puffed out his cheeks then yawned, rolled the back of his head on his shoulders, working out invisible knots. Becca noted that his stubble was now a full-blown beard.

'Four days,' Anil repeated. 'Four fackin' days in this apartment. I've got cabin fever, man.'

The new apartment was in a loft space bordering Chinatown, known locally as Barrio Chino, in the loftier area of Belgrano. From her room – Holt had his own for a change – she could see all the planes coming in to land at Aeroparque. Belgrano was an upper-middle class area, all nice handbags, boutiques and leather goods.

'It's called lying low,' Tom said. 'We only head out if we absolutely need to. Ray says he can handle it.'

'Do you trust him?'

'I trust his belief in his own experience.'

'I told you I'm a dab hand with the ol' locks, don't make it true.'

'Except it is true, Anil. Otherwise you wouldn't be here. Give him one more day.'

She enjoyed watching them butt heads over dinner, her own appetite non-existent. In her mind, she couldn't stop replaying the last conversation she'd had with Tom in Uruguay. Side by side in the bed, not touching, tension thick like treacle, memory of their kiss still lingering. She'd never been kissed like that. Not by anyone. She could count the sexual experiences she'd encountered on one hand, none of them noteworthy or even vaguely pleasurable. Until she had ordered Tom Holt to kiss her, it had never occurred to her to mind.

'Not to pile on the pressure,' he'd said in the darkness, 'but this going to Buenos Aires to get the key... it's all on you. You know that, right?'

It had taken her several moments to respond. 'I target things, not people. The person, their manner, their behaviour, it's all important but it's secondary. I'm an opportunist. Leave a wallet hanging out of your backpack, I will swipe it.'

'So stop thinking like an opportunist and start coming up with a plan of attack. Without those keys, we are nowhere. We might as well go home.'

Awkward silences continued after that, even on the ferry across to Buenos Aires. Sitting together as would-be fiancés, sensing the ginormous gulf separating them. An onlooker might have believed them strangers at best. There had been no physical contact since that night.

Becca knew she had to get close enough to Nicolás Cordero to ascertain whether or not he was carrying a set of keys, remove them from his person, get them to Anil then get them back onto Nico's person without him knowing they were missing, all within the briefest of timeframes. She knew her fingers were quick. Not that quick.

Back in Uruguay, Anil had started digging, brain seemingly wired for finding information. Apart from two young Argentinian footballers, he'd manage to locate three individuals bearing the name Nicolás Cordero, two of whom worked in the Argentinian wine industry and who were possibly one and the same. A search on Facebook of Sabina Cordero's friends quickly provided them with an answer: Nico's own Facebook page, complete with photographs and the name of the company he worked for. That was where Ray came in.

'Leave it to me,' he'd announced, and they had, for five days. Every evening, Ray returned, saying nothing, shovelling food, shutting himself away in his room, making some phone calls before slumping in front of the TV watching BBC news or some Latin telenovela. The wait didn't bother her – sure it bothered Anil – she had used her time wisely, stocking up on wigs, different outfits, new pairs of shoes, high tops, heels. Whatever she needed to get close to him, and more than once, so Nico – or even one of Federico's beady-eyed henchmen – never had the chance to see the same woman twice.

Ray entered the apartment. Tom looked up, eager for news, Anil not quite as optimistic as their dear leader. Ray took his time, shrugging out of his coat.

'Anything?' Tom asked.

'Tomorrow,' was Ray's answer.

She used the phone tracking app to pinpoint Ray's location, creeping out of the house whilst Tom was in the shower, Anil still in bed. She found him loitering on a park bench inside the Plaza San Martin, an unlit cigarette poised between his lips. He was standing within view of an office block across the street, behind him a bench covered in pigeon shit.

'Hey there, Ray,' she said as he looked up.

His eyes softened, offering her a smile. 'Alright?' he said. 'I wondered if you might show your face.'

'Find Nico yet?' she asked.

'Found him three days ago,' Ray confirmed.

'Any reason you didn't mention it?'

'I always did like police work,' Ray mused. 'Before I threw it all away. I was good at watching people. I liked the slow pace of it.'

'Don't let Anil hear you say that.'

Ray scoffed, eyes still on the office building and the revolving glass door entrance. 'That little prick can think what he bloody well likes.'

'So where is Nicolás?' she asked.

'He takes an extended coffee-break around ten-thirty. Goes to a café called La Galette around the corner. Two days ago he had lunch with a glamorous blonde and then later took a cab back to his apartment. Yesterday he spent his coffee break with a different female, a brunette, and afterwards they walked from here to an apartment building called Torre Madero, overlooking the Port. He stayed there for two hours before walking back to his office over there. I have my suspicions but need more time to be sure.'

'That's impressive, Ray.'

'Anything that gets me back on home soil by the end of the year.'

'Is it daughters that you have?'

'Four. The little one has red hair like you.'

The wind whipped up, sending a flock of pigeons flapping. Becca pulled her coat more tightly around her.

'Think you can get the keys?' he asked.

She followed Ray's gaze towards the office building. 'You show me Nicolás Cordero and I'll get you those keys.'

'Suspicions?' Tom asked Ray back at the apartment, Becca having persuaded the former copper that it was time to dish his information.

'That the blonde female from two days ago is the girlfriend and that yesterday's female was the mistress.'

'There's a blonde with him online, she's in all the pics,' Anil piped up. 'Definitely a girlfriend, partner, whatever. She's tagged as… hold on.' He fumbled around for a scribble pad, flipped through some crumpled looking pages. 'Mallorie Siciliano.'

'So we know where he lives,' Becca said.

'Good work, Ray,' Tom nodded. 'Now we know his home and his place of work we can start to track him.'

Ray said nothing.

'Today is Thursday,' Tom continued. 'Ray, you should watch Nico tonight, see where he goes. Try and keep tabs on him this weekend, find the places he hangs out before we introduce Becca into the equation.'

She avoided eye contact, forced a smile. Ray was already pulling his coat back on. She thought of Richie, how excited he would have been by this job, how he saw every moment as an opportunity, never a challenge.

She was still thinking about Richie a few hours later, standing in front of the bathroom mirror, avoiding Tom's presence. He was alone in front of the TV. She heard the door slam, muffled voices, Tom asking questions, Ray grunting responses. She wandered out.

'He was with the girlfriend,' Ray was saying. 'Didn't leave her side. Tomorrow, we need eyes on Cordero's apartment first thing.'

Ray nudged past her. 'I'll see you both in the morning.'

He disappeared down the corridor. After his door had closed, she was left facing Tom in the smouldering light of the TV.

'How far should I go?' she asked. 'If it comes to it.'

Tom took a step closer. Becca felt her chest rise and fall, fingers making brief contact with his. He went to lower his head. She closed her eyes.

'Get a room, you two,' Anil's voice grumbled as he emerged from nowhere. She opened her eyes and Tom was gone.

★★★★★

Three weeks, no progress.

The sense of frustration welled up in Tom's chest daily, a feeling of impending failure in the pit of his stomach. Nico Cordero, a hamster on a wheel, went to work, went to lunch, visited his mistress at Torre Madero then went home to his girlfriend. Two weekends in a row Nico went to dinner with Mallorie, sharing a bottle of wine, going home to sleep. Becca, the chameleon, morphed into diverse caricatures, different outfits, wigs, always on hand to get close. Yet it was never close enough. The chances were zero.

He questioned whether they had set the bar too high:

steal the keys, copy the correct key, return the set of keys. A simple enough task on paper. He trusted Anil's assertion that he only needed a period of a couple of minutes with the key in order for it to be copied at a later date. Tom didn't ask how; he had a fairly good idea. It was creating the right opportunity that Cordero wouldn't notice the absence of his keys for a matter of minutes which had so far eluded them. If he thought them stolen he could inform his sister Sabina back in Uruguay, who in turn could change her lock, if the maid Manu was right and she was that bothered about someone breaking in.

On a Saturday morning in late August, they followed Nico from his apartment. Alone, he entered Ninina, a spacious Palermo-based bakery. Tom followed shortly after, wearing a wool jacket, black-rimmed glasses and carrying a newspaper under his arm, taking an available seat at the next table and shaking open the copy of *Clarin*, the beard he had been cultivating for weeks neatly trimmed. On the inside, Ninina had a single wood-panelled wall, wooden floor and copper lampshades suspended from the ceiling, tables bustling with hipsters.

It was after ten. Nico had a smartphone in front of him on the table, taking his time to peruse the menu. Anil and Ray were outside, lingering at a nearby petrol station. Tom watched the door. Becca entered wearing knee-high boots, a wool coat and a black bob wig, taking a seat three tables down from Nico on the opposite side.

He was smarmy: wavy hair, a streak of grey, longish at the back, *de rigeur* for a man-about-town in Buenos Aires.

Nico had full lips, all over stubble and a sprinkling of chest hair visible under his rugby shirt, a dense look about him. He wore chinos and loafers with no socks, one ankle resting on his knee. Reminded Tom of every other Latino *hombre* in Gabriela's circle of friends, the ones – like Federico – who used to look at him and wonder how a young English prick had managed to snag himself a gangster's daughter.

A waitress came over. Nico ordered Eggs Benedict. Tom ordered coffee from the same girl. Moments later, Nico was rummaging in his pocket, pulling out a second mobile phone that was ringing. He tossed his set of keys onto the surface of the table.

Tom stiffened.

It wasn't a large keyring. Four keys, all standard, bar one slightly unusual key, larger than the others. He raised his eyes. Becca had seen it too. A sense of urgency passed between them and with it the excruciating comprehension that there was not a single thing either of them could do but avert their eyes. Tom cleared his throat, folded the newspaper.

He watched as Nico was joined by a second male at his table, a similarly-dressed Argentine with equal amounts of body hair to Nico but with a couple more chins: a greaseball. The greaseball snapped his fingers at a different waitress, barking at her to bring an Americano and a croissant.

'*Así que te unirás a nosotros esta noche para la cena?*' the greaseball said. Tom struggled to hear everything over the background din. Something was happening that night. '*Máximo va a traer algunas putas. Pueden coger, eh? Sus chicas están fuera de la ciudad no?*'

Both Nico's ladies out of town: the mistress and Mallorie.

111

The greaseball wanted action. Someone called Maximo bringing some girls. Tom watched the warm smile spread across Nico's features. '*Siiii,*' he grinned.

The greaseball slapped his hand against the too-tight chinos covering his thigh. '*Perfecto. La mesa está reservada a las diez.*'

'*A dondé?*' Nico asked.

A table had been reserved for ten o'clock that night.

At the bar, a different waitress dropped a coffee cup, sending it smashing across the tiles. Tom, Becca, Nico and the other man all looked up. Tom nudged his folded copy of *Clarin* off the table and bent down to pick it up, determined not to miss the name of their meeting venue.

'La Colorada,' the greaseball said.

Chapter 12

Thiago Gonzalez knew all his nicknames. They called him 'El Chaparro', the Short, 'El Grasa', the Fat, as in grease, 'El Feo', the Ugly, on account of his mother throwing him out when he was still a kid, sometimes even 'Maradona', the latter not for his skill with a ball. He'd worked hard to gain his current one: 'La Rata'... The rat.

Most evenings he loitered on the same corner of Florida Street, wearing a *Boca Juniors* football shirt stretched out over his ample belly, muttering *'Cambio, cambio,'* to tourists bustling by. Most days he had little success, his frizzy mane, bulbous nose and crooked smile putting many off exchanging their dollars to pesos at the rate on the street. To the *gringos*, he looked like a common lazy Latino. Yet Thiago had a network, from Palermo to La Boca. For the last three years he had worked the streets for 'La Almendra', Federico Hernandez himself. The Bullet.

He had been called to dinner short-notice on the fringes of Caminito, a touristy corner of La Boca. Thiago sat at the farthest end of the table, watching Arturo Baresi's teenage niece, Mariquita, squirming in his boss's lap, arms draped about his neck. She wore a white vest cut low, thick hair tumbling in waves down her back. Envy lined Thiago's stomach like a festering ulcer. Girls like Mariquita barely gave him the time of day. It would have been nice if one woman, with curves and a bit of ass – one who didn't look like the back end of a bus – could pay him the slightest bit of attention, maybe let him take her home so he could get his dick wet once in a while.

To console himself, Thiago took a long swig of beer. On the table, his phone vibrated. He swiped it up, answering with a grunt.

'*Él está de vuelta*,' the voice said at the other end. *He's back.*

Thiago spluttered beer down his shirt, wiping his mouth with the back of his hand. His first thought was for Baresi, and to ask after the red-headed woman, the one who'd stabbed Arturo in the ass in Palermo. It was lucky she hadn't hit an artery.

'*La coloradita*,' Thiago asked. 'Is she with him?'

'*Sí*,' came the reply.

'Where?' Thiago demanded.

'Belgrano. I got a call from one of my guys in Barrio Chino.'

'We know the apartment?'

'Not yet. We'll keep looking.'

'When you find it, have that place covered.'

'Got it, *Jefe*.'

Thiago hung up, got to his feet, forehead gleaming with sweat. The move garnered a few disdainful looks. No one was supposed to hold court down in La Boca except for The Bullet.

'*Fede!*' Thiago shouted, loud enough for the entire table to fall silent. The Bullet dragged his gaze from Mariquita's breasts. It was obvious to everyone, including Thiago, that the interruption was unwelcome.

'What is it, *Ratita*?' Federico hissed.

'*El chupa pija Inglés…* ' Thiago said, holding up his phone, '*está de vuelta.*'

The English cocksucker is back.

The next thing Thiago knew, Mariquita was sprawling face down on the floorboards, pert ass in the air. Fede ripped into his comrades, ordering them to pipe down. '*La Ratiiiita,*' he breathed. 'I knew there was a reason I hired you. Where?'

'Barrio Chino,' Thiago said.

'*Y la coloradita?*' Baresi shouted down the table.

'*Si. Ella también,*' Thiago confirmed.

Fede called for quiet again. He clicked his tongue as Mariquita struggled to her feet. He reclaimed his chair, yanking her back into his lap.

'*Sabes qué hacer,*' he said. *You know what to do.*

★★★★★

La Colorada, Palermo, his back to the door. Red walls, red seats and ceiling, red and bloody cuts of beef. A table reserved for a small group near the back in front of a semi-open kitchen. It had to be the one.

He'd lobbied the waiter hard in Spanish for their table, even got him to move a *reservado* sign to somewhere else. Tom faced the entrance, Becca what he hoped would be Nico's table. Any other engaged couple on an intimate date. He had shaved off the beard.

He glanced again at his watch. It was after 10 p.m., the restaurant only starting to fill up. Across from him Becca wore a blonde wig, a green satin plunging vest and heavy make-up.

'You're staring,' she said, his concentrated gaze not shifting from over her right shoulder.

Tom finished his Malbec, refilling both their glasses. He was thankful for the relaxed service, their meal taking its time to arrive. Anil and Ray were parked in a hire car outside on the street.

'Are we ever going to mention what happened at Las Colinas?' Becca said. It was the first time she had brought it up.

He shifted in his seat. 'We did what we had to do.'

'Have you thought about it?'

He let himself stare, at her this time. Other than Nico Cordero, he'd thought about nothing but kissing her. 'I've thought about it.'

She cocked her head to one side, took a sip of wine.

'We're different, you and me,' she said.

'How so?'

She opened her mouth to answer, the response cut short by her phone vibrating with a message.

'Nico,' she whispered. 'He's outside.'

He looked to the door. 'Alone?'

'Two other men, three women.'

He heard them before he saw them: three men, already half-cut. The greaseball in a black shirt, his arms draped around two of the women, both in their forties. Nico in a white shirt and jacket with his hair gelled back, swaying a little, looking oddly uncomfortable. The third man had a closely shaven head, wearing a trilby and a thick turtle neck, like he'd walked out of a jazz recital.

Under the table, Tom felt Becca's high-heeled shoe make

contact with his shin. He signalled a waiter, ordered a second bottle of wine.

Their steaks arrived shortly after. He tried to force down a few mouthfuls, anything to keep up the charade. Nico was facing the kitchen, jacket slung over the back of the red chair, less than a metre from where Becca sat. It was the best position they could have hoped for.

The greaseball was holding court at Nico's table. He'd ordered four bottles of wine off the bat and was now regaling his companions with a story about a trip he'd taken to Colombia and a run-in he'd had with two *gringos*. Anil and Ray had entered the restaurant, taking a seat at a table eight metres in front towards the entrance. Tom chewed diligently on his *bife de lomo*, attempts at small talk getting more pathetic by the second.

'I need you to complain about your steak,' Becca blurted, keeping her voice low. 'Get the waiter over, send it back, don't make a fuss.'

Tom nodded, did as he was told. He signalled their waiter over, lifting his plate and explaining in Spanish, labouring the point that he had ordered the meat well done and not medium rare.

He didn't witness exactly what happened next, only heard the smash of glass as an entire bottle of wine hit the floor, shards of glass shooting in all directions. Becca's chair scraped backwards as she shot up, the napkin in her lap stained burgundy, seemingly every Argentine in the near vicinity looking their way. Even the greaseball reacted with an '*ay caramba!*' before cackling like a hyena as a second waiter appeared with towels, proceeding to get to his knees and wipe the floor. Nico was talking to the woman next to him, seemingly oblivious.

The next thing Tom knew, Becca was reclaiming her seat. A third waiter brought more wine to their table. When she looked across at him, the waiter unscrewing the cork, she had a face like thunder. She swiped up her phone, typed something. In his pocket, his phone vibrated.

Tom kept the handset under the table. Glanced down at the text:

Both pockets empty. No keys.

His stomach performed a little flip. They waited in silence for both waiters to leave.

'I have an idea,' Becca said.

*****

She'd handed him the engagement ring.

The WhatsApp video from Anil came through at 1.40 a.m. It took minutes to download, the data capability on his phone substandard at best. The visual was fuzzy; the audio distorted by thumping bass, yet it was clear enough to tell what was going on. Becca and Nico were sat at a bar, Becca facing outwards, elbows rested on the surface, face tilted close to Nico's, his hand resting on her stomach.

Tom was sat in an all-night café – the kind that had the chairs attached to the tables – selling *empanadas* and foul-tasting coffee.

'What is it?' Ray asked, opposite him.

A muscle ticked in Tom's jaw. He passed Ray the phone, tried not to grimace.

The second video didn't take so long to download. This time, there was no denying the visual.

★★★★★

Becca lay on her back in the dim light; head nestled into the gentle grooves of the pillow, every muscle in her body tense, brain screaming for her to run.

Get out.

His left leg was over hers, pinning it down to the sheet. It was the hairiest leg she had ever seen. Nico had hair everywhere. He radiated heat. Shifting her eyes down, she could see a line of drool trailed along his bottom lip, face inches from hers. She'd been listening to the air whistling through his nostrils for an eternity.

Her eyes closed. *Be cool, be cool.* The wig had started to itch.

Outside she could still hear the rumble of the Saturday night traffic below the window, in the distance the hum of a forlorn saxophone.

She thought about the others. *Would they know? Had they seen her leave?* They'd been banging their heads against a brick wall, and now she was *inside* his apartment. In the shadows there was a picture of Mallorie on the dresser, with beautiful straight white teeth. There were discarded clothes on the floor. *Hers? Mallorie's?* There was makeup beside a mirror, a jewellery box, another woman's treasure trove. Tom's words in her head: *it's all on you.*

Keys.

She moved to her right, paused. Nico still snoring. A little further, moving from her hips, she extricated herself from the solid tree trunk, hair-covered leg. He groaned; a sleepy, alcohol-fuelled moan then rolled over. Becca slid lithely out, hitting the rug on all fours, allowing herself a breath.

She crawled around, locating her underwear before standing beside the bed, watching him for a moment. Nico Cordero was snoring, arms wrapped amorously around a burgundy-coloured quilt.

Underwear on, she wriggled into her green vest, checked the pockets in the tight trousers that he had dropped by the bedroom door, fingers still trembling. They were empty but for a business card and some loose pesos. It had been obvious in the bar he was already aroused. Yet by the time they got back to his apartment, the amount of wine and spirits he had consumed had permeated his brain and he wasn't quite the lothario of twenty minutes earlier, managing to get her to the bed but subsequently struggling to perform. She had escaped with a hand job, which to her mortification had taken some time to complete, his body finally slumping onto damp sheets.

She tiptoed out of the bedroom. Nico's keys were on a keyring, on the surface of a glass table next to his wallet. She swiped them up, located her phone in her handbag and locked herself in the guest bathroom. Pulling down the toilet seat, she sat down, mind reeling.

This hadn't been part of the plan. Anil was the plan. Get the keys to Anil and he would do the rest. Flipping through the keys, it was obvious which one she wanted. Anil had shown her the type: a long key, oblong in shape, a series of minuscule drilled holes along its shaft in a unique pattern.

She felt a little sorry for Nico. She had spent the week stalking him, doing a pretty good job of it too, not that he seemed to have noticed. Brunette wig with biker boots, a blonde one with heels, the same brunette in a suit, each time a different look. This look had done it, as it turned out: maybe the green top. She hadn't anticipated him being the one to approach her, hit on her in the bar, start asking about her background and flirt with her in half-decent English. Her fingers trembled again. She reached for her phone by the sink. A series of close-ups of the key ought to do it. Only nothing happened, the phone out of battery.

Shit, shit.

She opened the door, peered out into the darkness of the apartment. Light from the street flooded the room. She crept out, rifled through a pile of papers on a breakfast bar leading to the kitchen.

There was no Anil. She needed to copy the key herself.

She found a notepad and pencil, the vague recollection of completing a brass rubbing at a cathedral during a school trip in her youth entering her mind. Locking herself back into the bathroom, she crouched down, removing the key from its ring and placing it flat on the tiled floor. Placing the piece of paper over the top, she pressed down, working from one end, rubbing the edge of the pencil over the metal shaft, careful not to perforate the paper with the lead tip. It took her enough time that the backs of her legs began to ache. Picking up the key, Becca bent the paper round its shaft, ensuring she captured the exact width with the pencil. Once finished, she repeated the process on the other side, holding the paper up to the light, examining her handiwork.

There was a soft knock at the door.

'Lisa?'

Becca stiffened. She'd lied about her name. Lisa from England: a student of architecture on a study exchange to Argentina. He had seen her at La Colorada. She'd laughed it off, told him she'd escaped a really bad date.

'*Momentito!*'

She stood, heart in her throat, deftly sliding the key back onto its ring. Slid the rubbing of the key into the back of her underwear, leaving the notebook and pencil on top of the cistern. Removed her top again and checked her reflection, straightening the wig.

She opened the door a crack, raised her eyes coyly, offering him a shy smile.

'Hello,' he said, in a heavily accented baritone voice. He'd put on some underwear but was still a little drunk. Nico Cordero spoke enough of a level of English that had allowed them to flirt at least.

'Hi,' Becca smiled, the green top balled in her fist, inside concealed his set of keys.

She slid out of the door, his eyes on her bare breasts.

'Wow,' he said.

She leaned in, kissed him. He had slug-like lips that kissed her back. She put one hand against his chest but his fingers encircled her wrist, guiding it away.

'I hate to do this,' he said. 'There is… someone in my life. I would hate for her to find you here.'

'It's OK,' she breathed. 'I can leave.' *I got what I came for.*

'*Gracias*,' Nico said, pushing the hair from his eyes. 'I'm so sorry.'

'Let me get my things,' she said, sliding past him back into the bedroom. Bending, she rifled through some clothes on the floor, locating her trousers, allowing the set of keys to slide out onto the carpet. Would he know that wasn't where he'd left them? She was prepared to take that risk. Standing and pulling on her trousers, she turned to find Nico walking into the room, clutching his wallet, eyes scouring the room for something else. In a moment he had kicked a shirt aside, swiped up his keys, placing them both on the dresser.

Becca fastened her bra, pulled on her top. At the door, he helped her with her coat sleeves.

'Good luck with your studies,' he said.

'Thank you. It was nice to meet you.'

'Will you be alright, getting back to your hotel?'

'Of course.'

'This area of town can be dangerous at night. Juan Antonio on the door downstairs, he can help you into a cab.' Nico opened his front door. '*Buenas noches.*'

'*Hasta luego.*'

There was a moment of awkwardness as she walked to the lifts, glanced back, allowed him a flicker of a smile. He had closed his front door even before the lift came, wanting her gone so he could wallow in his own guilt.

As the lift doors closed, she wanted to collapse into a heap. Reaching down into the back of her trousers, she pulled out the piece of paper with the copied image of the key, studying it for a moment, praying that she had done enough before sliding it into her pocket.

Downstairs, outside the lobby, a large removal van had parked on the street. Two men were carrying furniture inside to one of the lifts in Nico's building. Feeling elated, Becca wondered why anyone would want to move house in the early hours of the morning. Exiting the building, she ignored their looks and tugged off the wig.

She breathed in the fresh air after Nico's stuffy bedroom. Hoped Tom would be pleased with her efforts at least. A few weeks ago, she would not have cared an inch what he thought; now she found herself craving his approval. She slowed her speed, glancing around on the street for a cab. She knew she wasn't too far from the restaurant, La Colorada, wondering if the others had made their way back to the loft apartment.

In the back of a cab she asked for Barrio Chino. In the early hours it was less than a ten-minute journey. In Belgrano she got out at a set of traffic lights, paid the driver in pesos. Turning a corner towards the apartment, she caught sight of a lone male lingering on the street, pacing back and forth. On seeing her, he seemed to straighten a little. Something about him made her heart race. She put her head down and turned back, started pacing. Behind her, the man was making a phone call. He wore a football shirt stretched over a bloated belly.

A black van pulled up ahead. Becca halted. The man behind was gaining on her. The door of the van slid open and two men appeared; one in a leather jacket, the other carrying what looked like a length of rag.

She dropped the wig, turned and ran into the road, straight into the arms of the van's driver, who grabbed her, pinning her arms to her sides. Becca kicked out with her feet. A moment later, the rag was stretched inside her mouth, yanking back the corners of her cheeks, cutting into her flesh and denying her the chance to scream.

Chapter 13

Bar after bar. Her phone: dead. They had lost her.

Tom had covered a large area of turf around the restaurant, La Colorada. Taken the gamble to move to Palermo Soho, searching in vain the more high-class venues. On the street outside the Verne Cocktail Club, he wondered where to try next. Anil had clocked her leaving with Nico around 2.15 a.m. Now it was gone four. Tom had instructed him to follow but the Hackney thief had lost them soon after, still in Palermo. He ordered Anil to get to Nico's apartment, find a spot where he could wait with eyes on the building. Ray took a cab back to the Belgrano apartment. Tom scoured the bars, should the pair simply have moved venues. Like looking for a needle in an Argentinian haystack.

He knew first-hand that Becca could handle herself. That wasn't what bothered him. In his eyes, Nico was scum.

He remembered the words he'd said to her, back in Uruguay. *This is all on you.* Thought about them now with a pang of regret. This was probably their last chance to copy the key. Yet the idea that Becca was having to do what she had to do, alone, without their help, left a nasty taste in his mouth. If he was completely honest, the thought of Nico undressing her was enough to make him want to punch the Latino's lights out.

His phone rang. He stared at the screen, heart skipping a beat. Ray.

'She's not here,' Ray said. 'I'm going to walk the streets a bit. I'll check back here in thirty minutes.'

'Fine. If she's in his apartment, she could be there all night.'

'Keep faith,' Ray said before hanging up.

Tom dialled Anil.

'Fuck, man,' Anil spat. 'Some dude rolled up in a removal van and parked right outside the building. I can't see shit. I might miss her if she leaves.'

'You won't,' Tom reassured him. 'Hang in there; I'm coming your way.' He threw out his arm to a yellow and black cab, slid into the back seat.

It was a quick ride. Anil loitered on the opposite side of the street to Nico's apartment building. The removal van was vast, covering the entire entrance lobby. It felt darker than on the bustling streets of Palermo Soho.

'Nothing, man,' Anil said, shivering.

Tom looked down. Ray was calling again. It had to be good news.

'Have you got her?'

There was the sound of an engine revving, a car speeding down the street. In Ray's voice, an urgency that was hard to make out. He was out of breath.

'I saw her... she was grabbed... outside our apartment, they put her in the back of a van. I'm in pursuit, in the back of a cab... We're heading south on Libertador.'

His mind reeled.

Someone had her. *Who? Nico? The greaseball? No, no...*

Federico. It had to be.

How was that even possible?

He knew instinctively where the van would be going, where they would be taking Becca. He had been once or twice with Gabriela, and she had talked about the place enough. He'd once been told what a lunatic he'd been for turning down the offer of tickets to see a football match at the stadium known as La Bombonera. There were murals there dedicated to Maradona.

They called it La Boca.

★★★★★

When she came to, her head was pounding. There was a sharp pain above her left eye, the last thing she remembered, kicking and screaming in the back of the van, frantic dialogue between the driver and her three assailants then – *bam* – something, or someone, had struck her and everything had gone black.

The now soggy rag was still stretched between her teeth. She tasted blood at the back of her throat. She was on a bed, face down, hands tied together, feet secured at the ankles, a bedside lamp near her head. Orange-yellow walls. The windows were open, a cold breeze swirling around the room. Two, possibly three men conversed in Spanish, out of view. More like grunting at one another. *Está yendo,* she kept hearing. Found herself wishing she'd paid more attention when Tom had thrust a Spanish text book in her face.

Memories flooded her mind of thrusting a knife into the man called Baresi's thigh during their last visit. Had Federico's men been watching the entire time?

Shit, shit.

Tom, Anil, Ray, they didn't even know she had the key, or a copy of it anyway. They didn't know where she was. *She* didn't know where she was. All she knew was that no good ever came of being face down on a bed with your hands tied behind your back.

She remained still, going over in her mind *if, how, when* she could attempt to move. Whether they would leave her there, tied up. Then a mobile phone rang, a mumbled conversation taking place.

'*Cinco minutos*,' one of them said. Her entire body tensed. Something happening in five minutes. Somebody else coming? Would they beat her? Rape her? Fuck, *fuck*, she had to move.

Not for the first time that night, she froze in fear, a shadow looming over her.

*****

Come on, come on… go.

The yellow and black cab was travelling at breakneck speed, south down Avenida 9 de Julio towards La Boca. Ray had confirmed the direction of travel. Tom willed the clapped-out vehicle to go faster. Both he and Anil were getting tossed around in the back, two tomatoes in a salad spinner, the driver navigating his way through the traffic with no seatbelts. Traffic was light, yet if Fede had Becca, they didn't have much time.

Ray, plaudits to him, had stayed on the van's tail, and in La Boca, witnessed Becca being dragged out – unconscious, he thought – from the back of a van up into a low-rise building on a dirty low-lit side street near La Bombonera stadium.

On the radio, commentary from an earlier football game: Boca Juniors vs San Lorenzo, a friendly according to the driver. '*Boca jugó para la mierda esta noche,*' the man complained, slamming the quality of the match. Tom looked across at Anil, the Hackney thief holding on for dear life.

The driver pulled up within the shadow of the stadium wall, the street brightly lit. Tom thrust him a scrunched up pile of pesos, getting out, Anil following. Opposite him was a cheap looking replica statue of Lionel Messi wearing a blue and white *Bocas* shirt. Discarded pamphlets and ticket stubs littered the ground. He called Ray.

'I'm on the south side of the stadium, near a kids' playground. Two guys got out of a car, went inside the building. One had a leather jacket, the other a limp.'

Tom was on the move now, crossing the road, phone to his ear, Anil still tailing.

Away from the stadium the streets were poorly lit. The sound of tango was in the air, somewhere close by a bar still open. Tom spied Ray lingering close to a graffiti-covered wall, concealed in the darkness. Anil bent over double, clutching his knees, catching his breath.

'Up there,' Ray pointed at the run-down building on the opposite side of the street.

'How many?' Tom hissed.

'Three guys took her in. Two more just arrived.'

'Who are they?' Anil asked, looking to Tom.

'One of them will be Federico Hernandez. The other, the

130

one with the limp, his name is Baresi. Becca put a knife in his leg the last time we were in Buenos Aires. They must have picked up on our scent somehow.'

'Holy shit,' Anil said.

'They armed do you think?' Ray asked Tom.

'Definitely. Fede runs a network of guys in BA and beyond. Small time crooks mainly.'

In the darkness, something was glinting. Ray cocked a weapon.

'Take this,' Ray said. Tom felt cold metal. There were no questions in his mind. Given the choice between shooting Fede or leaving Becca behind, he would do what he had to.

'I bought two here, before you ask,' Ray said.

He didn't plan on asking. Watched as Ray reached into his pocket, pulled out a second revolver and cocked it.

'Jesus fuck, we got a plan of action, yeah?' Anil said, a quiver of panic rising in his voice. 'In case you'd forgotten, like, we are supposed to be breakin' into a safe in Uruguay, which is not even the same country we are in.'

'How much money have you got?' Tom asked, ignoring Anil's protestations, the three of them suddenly rifling in their pockets and wallets. The total was a little under two hundred dollars in pesos.

'We need vehicles,' Tom said, looking to Anil, handing him the cash. 'Round up three different cabs, use the money to get them to wait around that corner there. The word for 'wait' is *espere*; use it, don't say why. If we manage to get Becca out, you take a cab to the apartment, grab our passports, meet us at the Aeroparque terminal.'

'We're going to the airport?'

'It's the last place Fede can follow us. Plus it's the only place still open tonight and crawling with security.'

'How is that a good thing?'

He raised his voice. 'You want to die tonight, Anil?'

Anil swallowed. 'Got it. What about the key?'

Tom had forgotten all about the key. 'We hope that Becca did her job. And if she didn't, we'll have to find another way in. Either way, we're getting out of Argentina on the next flight we can. All four of us.'

They exchanged looks. Tom's heart *thud-thudded*, lips gone dry.

'Five against two,' Ray said, as though it were a challenge.

'Let me do the talking,' Tom replied.

Fuck you, Fede, he thought to himself as he crossed the street.

This ends now.

★★★★★

Becca's world tilted. She was still woozy. Upright, she was being tied to a chair, head throbbing. She allowed everything to come back into focus. Two men had entered the room as two more were leaving. Three left behind. She realised in part-horror, part-fascination that the second man was Baresi. He walked with a definite limp. In the first man's eyes, though, was a dangerous malice. He wore a leather jacket and jeans, a grease-stained T-shirt underneath. She recognised a third man as the one from the street as she had been grabbed: ugly with corkscrew curly hair, missing teeth, a football shirt and fat fingers.

'*Arturo*,' the man in the leather jacket started to chuckle, '*No me dijiste que te acuchillaba un niño.*' She didn't know what that meant. He leaned down, face close to hers, wiping his fingers over her hair and down her cheek. She flinched, jerking her face away from him in defiance. '*Hola, señorita*,' he said. '*Yo soy Federico.*'

He straightened, paced up and down a little in front of her, looked to the other two. '*Habla español?*'

The fat one in the football shirt gave a shrug. '*No lo sé, Jefe. No ha dicho una palabra.*'

Damn right I haven't said a word.

Fede stopped still. Becca stared up at him with gritted teeth, biting down hard on the rag. Her ankles were still tied but she was within kicking distance.

'Did you ask her?' he said, in English.

The man in the football shirt shuffled his feet and looked the other way.

Fede had dark features, eyes a fraction too close together, bottom lip more pronounced than the top one. His hair was uneven, as though cut by someone who didn't know how to cut hair. Even his beard was patchy.

'You know who this man is?' Fede asked her, still talking at her in English. He was pointing at Baresi. 'You put a knife in his leg and now he walks like my mother. Then just like that… poof… you are gone.' He flicked five fingers in the air for effect.

The rag made it impossible to speak.

'The Englishman, Mr Holt, where is he?' Fede asked.

She kept her silence.

'*Fede*,' Arturo urged before speaking more words she didn't understand.

133

Fede leaned down to her, face barely a few centimetres from hers, so that she could smell the unpleasant aroma of his last meal on his breath. '*Entonces, mi coloradita*. My friend here would like some special time with you. Call it returning a favour. I hope you are ready to – how do you say… ' He stopped himself, took her chin in between his fingertips and whispered, '*Sufrir.*'

She swallowed, tasting blood mixed with snot at the back of her tongue. Fede straightened, looking to the fat man. '*Thiago, en la cama,*' he barked, '*Arturo, sé rápido.*'

Panic rose in her chest as Federico stepped back, allowing the other two men access to her. She knew shouting would do no good, but there were sounds in her throat – screams – trying to escape. Arturo went behind her. Thiago, the fat, toothless one, had reached into his pocket, was pulling out something that looked like a shoelace. A garrotte. He pulled it tight between clenched fists, lunging at her as Arturo untied her from the chair. Struggling, she ducked underneath the cord, hit the ground hard, legs kicking out. Two pairs of hands were on her, lifting her face down onto the bed. She protested, hips bucking. Thiago's sweaty fingers were on her neck before he was bearing down on her, scrabbling with the garrotte to make a circle. When it tightened around her oesophagus her entire body went rigid, the panic in her chest exploding, no sounds in her throat now. Arturo growled something at Thiago and she was flipped over onto her back, one arm pinned under his knee, forced to look up at him. He was grunting. The sweat from his forehead dripped onto her face. She felt a cool rush of air, as out of her view her trousers and underwear were ripped from her legs. She hadn't even noticed the removal of restraints around her ankles. She kicked out, trying in vain to twist away. Fighting for air, somewhere in the fog, what felt like imminent death, she thought she saw her brother beckoning her.

Half-naked, exposed and on the verge of being violated, Becca thought of Richie, alone in Wandsworth Prison.

*****

Two thugs down. Ray had them in the bottom of the stairwell, thwacking one over the head with the butt of his revolver, knocking him out cold, a gun on the second. Pretty slick for an old man. Gave Tom the nod to proceed upstairs.

Tom hugged the wall up both flights. On the other side of the wall in a room, a scuffle was ensuing, unclear who or what was being attacked. For all he knew Becca was taking them all down. At the top, the nearest door was open a couple of millimetres, enough for him to get a view inside.

Nothing he had witnessed in his entire life prepared him for what he saw.

Federico was at the foot of a bed, arms crossed, still in his jacket. Arturo Baresi was tearing off Becca's underwear, unfastening his belt, ready to inflict his own brand of physical and psychological pain no female would ever forget. Then another, a third, a hulk of a man – the Punisher – another greaseball in a football shirt, was bearing down on her, throttling her.

Sweat poured off him. He had no knowledge of who was armed and no choice but to act. He nudged the door. It made no sound. Three steps forward and the butt of his gun made contact with the back of Fede's skull.

Fede stiffened.

'Call off your dogs, Fede. Or you die.'

The other two men didn't hear, carried on regardless. Fede raised his arms.

Rage erupted in Tom's chest. 'DO IT NOW!'

Arturo looked up in alarm, froze, splayed out his fingers. The Punisher rolled off Becca, hit the floor, air knocked out of his slovenly body, the interruption catching him off guard. Becca shot into a sitting position, tearing the cord from her neck, gulping air through some kind of gag, fingers seizing her neck. She was bleeding above her eye, still wearing the green top she'd worn to dinner in La Colorada, a meal that for Tom felt like a lifetime ago. She scrambled off the bed; fell onto her remaining clothes, covering herself. Back against the wall, Tom could see from the corner of his eye she was regaining her composure. His breath was shallow, shaky.

Nobody moved. 'You alright?' he raised his voice to her, eyes on the room.

Becca nodded, saying nothing.

'Get dressed,' Tom said.

She scrambled into her clothes, sliding out of the makeshift wrist restraints.

'*Thiago*,' Fede hissed, looking toward the Punisher. '*Tu arma.*'

Your weapon.

Tom watched the Punisher raise his eyes to Fede. Thought he could see a look of guilt in his expression. In the briefest of moments, the Punisher glanced to his left, to a coat slung over the back of a chair. Becca saw it too, the pair of them lunging for it at the same time. She won the race easily,

136

swiping up the jacket, locating a small firearm, some kind of Glock. Tossing the coat, she cocked it like a pro, levelling it on the Punisher's bulbous features. He swallowed, spread out his arms.

Tom nodded to her, passed her his gun. She didn't flinch, took it and levelled both weapons at her assailants.

'*Arrodíllate!*' Tom said to the men. *On your knees.*

Both Baresi and the Punisher did as they were told. Only Fede didn't move.

Tom reclaimed his gun from Becca, walked around Fede so that he could face him. It had been years since he had looked into those eyes, yet the memory of Fede stumbling across him and Gabriela in the stables at Rosario was fresh as seven years earlier. Placing the butt of the gun barely a centimetre from the bridge of the Argentine's nose, he didn't speak until he saw perspiration.

'This ends now, Federico. You and I, we are done.' He nudged the barrel forward, so that cold hard metal came into contact with human flesh. Fede closed his eyes. 'On. Your. Knees.'

Fede sank to the floor. It took five minutes for Tom to fasten the three men's wrists to the bed frame, using the various cords that had been used to control Becca. Fede found his voice again, spouting profanities at the one he called Thiago as he was being tied up, channelling his anger in that direction rather than at Tom or Becca: '*CUANDO TERMINE CON VOS, TU MAMÁ NO LA VA A CONTAR UNA MIERDA, VAS A DESEAR NUNCA HABER NACIDO!*'

Tom blocked out the sound of Fede cursing. Satisfied

that none of them would escape, he walked behind Becca, unfastening the rag from her mouth. The blood-stained material fell to the floor.

'Thank you,' she whispered, wiping her lips with the back of her hand.

'Let's go,' he said.

Becca swiped up her shoes. He followed, backing away to the door.

'*Vas a morir por esto!*' Fede spat at Tom. *You will die for this.*

'Be thankful I didn't ask her to blow your brains out,' Tom said, in English, as he shut the door behind them.

Becca was already on the stairs. Ray was still at the bottom, two Argentinian thugs piled up in the corner of the stairwell. For a split second, Tom glared at them in horror, two lifeless bodies. *Were they dead?* He looked at Ray, confused. He had heard no sound of gunshots.

'Go, go,' Tom said, pocketing his weapon, watching Ray do the same.

On the road behind the building, Anil was waiting with three yellow cabs in convoy, engines all running. As soon as he saw them, he sprang into action, opening the passenger side doors.

'Get to the apartment,' Tom ordered him, pushing his gun into Anil's hands. 'Get the passports, any money, phones, anything relating to Uruguay. Leave anything else. Use this if you need it. I don't know who's watching us now. We'll meet you at Aeroparque; call me when you get there. Go, now.'

Anil nodded. 'Got it,' he said.

Ray was already getting into the first cab, barking

instructions gruffly at the driver. Anil headed for the second as Becca lowered herself into the third cab. Tom followed, slamming the creaking door shut behind them.

'Aeroparque,' he said, and the driver hit the gas.

They didn't speak. Exhaustion washed over him. He sank down in the cracked leather seat, hoped to God Fede hadn't sent more goons after them. He would leave his gun in the cab.

The traffic had cleared, even the late-night revellers collapsed into their beds. The sun would soon be up.

He looked across at Becca, staring from the window at the streets rushing by, hugging her waist. Him asking her if she was alright seemed flippant.

'How did you find me?' she asked, moments later, voice hoarse with emotion.

'Ray,' Tom told her. 'He was on his way back to the apartment when he saw you snatched on the street. He followed you. We were trying to track you down from the moment you left the bar with Nico.'

She went quiet again. Looking at her profile, eye swollen, sides of her mouth crusted with dry blood, he couldn't bear to ask her what had happened with Cordero. She was shifting in her seat, lifting one hip, pushing her fingers into her trouser pocket.

She passed him the small slip of paper without a word. Tom looked down to his hands. It was hard to see in the darkness. Light from the street would momentarily flood the interior of the vehicle, disappearing as soon as it came. Tom held the paper up to the window.

As the car halted at a set of traffic lights, it was some moments before he realised what he was looking at. Clasped in his fingers, outlined perfectly, was two sides of the same key.

Chapter 14

The message from Tom Holt came through when Denham was in the back of a London black cab.

> Back in Uruguay. Key copied. Need to get a message to Manuela to test it.

A mixture of relief and satisfaction washed over him.

He checked his watch. It was approaching 2 p.m. A sealed brown envelope lay in his lap. He had sent a message to Tatiana earlier saying he had to work late: another lie. Not that it mattered; they were better off out of one another's company. He thought about Capricorn, how pleased he would be to hear Holt's news. Outside the window, the cab was speeding up a rainy Drury Lane. Years ago he would have bust a gut to get word to Capricorn within a couple of minutes of hearing some good news. These days… it could wait a few hours.

She had requested the Waldorf. He had offered her the Grange Hotel in Holborn. No chance of him running into anyone he might know there. She had protested. He had argued she wasn't his wife anymore. He would take his *actual* wife to the Waldorf. For some reason she'd found that comment amusing and he had got his way. He hadn't seen her for three months. The next few hours would feel like a holiday.

Denham collected the key at reception and took the lift to the third floor. Anticipation pumped through his veins, sweet and delicious. He felt like a teenager again. The 'Do Not Disturb' sign had already been hung over the door handle. He let himself in, the door lock beeping twice in quick succession as he pressed the key card up against it. Inside, he turned and closed the door behind him with his foot, tossed the envelope onto a round table, shrugged out of his coat, loosened his tie. The air was tinged with her expensive perfume.

'There you are,' she said, raising a glass of champagne to her lips.

Belinda Channing – the first Mrs Albert Denham – was sat on the bed, back against the headboard, naked but for an open robe, legs crossed, hair glistening wet. Over fifty, in his mind eternally twenty-six. Shoulder-length highlighted blonde hair, a healthy Mediterranean tan, dead-straight nose, a slight upturned pout: a society girl all grown up. Behind him, Sky News was on the TV. Denham moved to the foot of the bed, pulling his shirt from his waistband and yanking off his tie.

'How long do you have?' she asked in a raspy tone.

He looked for somewhere to hang his shirt. Tatiana paid attention to the laundry. 'Long enough.'

With one hand he loosened his belt, kicking off his shoes. When he was on the bed, on all fours, she said, 'The socks, the socks. Please.'

'Jesus, woman,' Denham muttered, standing up again, removing his socks. 'Anything else?'

'Champagne?' she asked.

Denham had always enjoyed the feel of her; trusted her

implicitly, despite their divorce. She was the reason behind his decision to write a will. Because if anyone in his life was ever going to defend him from whatever emerged from the business with Capricorn – and he was convinced that one day, it would all emerge, even if he was in the ground – it was his first wife, and possibly his only true friend.

Half an hour later, he lay with his head against the headboard, naked, sheet up to his waist, her head nestled on his chest, fingers in his chest hair, legs entwined, watching Sky News. How it used to be.

'I have something to give you,' Denham said.

'Does it sparkle?'

'Not in the slightest. There's an envelope on the table over there,' he said.

She looked over at the point to which he was referring. 'Does it contain money?'

'Not that either. It's a copy of my will. If anything should ever happen to me—'

She lifted her head. 'Stop. Your *will*? Where are you going with this? You're scaring me.'

'*If*,' he emphasised, 'hypothetically, something should ever happen to me... I get knocked under a bus or have a coronary or I disappear into thin air—'

'Is this something to do with *him*?'

'Let me bloody finish, woman. If something happens to me, I want you to have a copy. My solicitor has the original. I've left most things to you.'

She pulled herself up, staring at him, aghast. 'Why would you do such a thing?'

He stroked her hair, cradled her face in his palms, kissed her, wishing he never had to leave. 'Because you are the single best thing that ever happened to me. Sometimes I think you are the only good thing in my life.'

'Al,' she whispered, kissing him.

'There is a letter inside for you too. Promise me you won't open it,' he added, 'unless... ' His throat constricted, no desire to finish his sentence.

'I promise. Now stop talking this way.'

Denham thought about making love to her again. He didn't have long. Sky News had gone to a break: an advert for the charity Elate International, heart-rending images of lives destroyed by natural disaster, flood and famine. 'Lift up the world,' the celebrity-endorser of the charity was saying, Elate International's familiar slogan, as the memories of a night he so desired to forget came creeping back into Denham's psyche.

'Why now?' Belinda snapped. 'Are you in danger?'

He looked for the TV remote control, let out a sigh. 'No more than I ever was,' he began, thinking it was both an easy and a hard thing to explain. 'But when I do depart this world, I want it to be with a clear conscience.'

★★★★★

1992

The Christmas party at the offices of corporate law firm Metlock & Wick had been going for two hours. Al Denham leaned up against the surface of some unfortunate's desk, on his fourth cocktail. House of Pain's 'Jump Around' blasted over the sound system, brought in by his close friend and co-worker, Guy Deverill. The bass line pounded in his chest.

Lately, colleagues had been congratulating him on his engagement to Belinda Bosen, a society girl from Putney, a barrister's daughter.

Two lawyers were dancing crazily between two desks: head-banging, hedonistic. Al found himself glancing across the room at Alice Shales. She was twenty-seven or thereabouts, one of the secretaries, known to all the guys as the hottest piece of ass in the M&W offices.

You're engaged, you fuckwit, he thought to himself, but the alcohol had infiltrated his veins, making him feel invincible. Alice was smiling at him.

Would anyone know? At Christmas, would anyone care?

He stood up, sauntered over, all secretaries batting their lashes. He was the one there with the most talent and didn't they all fucking know it. He made a beeline for Alice. Out of the corner of his eye he could see Guy Deverill watching him, wordlessly egging him on.

'Merry Christmas, Al,' she said. 'What do you make of the party?'

He wondered if she knew he was engaged. 'I'm glad we banned the Christmas tunes. If I hear Band Aid one more time—'

'Oh my God, I love this song though,' she giggled.

'I hear Alan Briers bailed so they're going to trash his office later,' he replied, licking his lips. 'I heard that his wife's about to leave him, that's why he's not here.'

She said nothing. He inched closer. 'Want to check out his office with me? See what dirt we can find?'

Round the corner, Al placed his hand against her back. Briers' office was open, the blinds down. He was on her the moment the door closed, drawing her close, her lips plump. At the desk, he stopped, removed the cocktail from her hand, put it down on the filing cabinet. Slid his hands up her shirt but she batted him away, laughing nervously. He lifted her up, sat her behind on the surface of the desk. Parted her legs, pushing himself between them so she knew the extent of his arousal as he slowed the tempo of the kiss. The music throbbed to The KLF's '3 a.m. Eternal'.

'Maybe we should… ' she breathed, 'go back… '

'Come on,' he urged her, 'we don't have to be long.'

He trailed kisses down her neck, felt her tense, squeezed her breasts, moved his fingers between her thighs. She clamped them together.

'Look, I don't know about this… ' she murmured. 'Briers is a senior partner, Al. I don't think we should.'

'It's Christmas. This is what everybody does at a Christmas party.'

He kissed her again. For a moment she seemed to respond, before turning her head away.

'I'm going to go,' she said, trying to move.

'Jesus, Alice, why are you going all frigid on me?'

'I need to get back.'

He stood in her way. Without thinking, he was grappling with her skirt.

'Al, stop it, please,' she was saying, but he couldn't hear

146

her. He turned her, nudged her forward, so she was bent over the desk. He blocked out her whimpers, hands wrestling with his. His fingers seized lace fabric. In one swift move, he had unbuttoned his trousers.

Her pleas were like a snivel, like the young lawyers who started work at Metlock before realising the bosses weren't shitting them when they said they had to work for their bonuses. He convinced himself that she would change her mind, once he was inside, pleasuring her. Put one hand on the back of her head, felt her expand, encompass him. Within a minute, the strength had drained from his body.

Out of breath, he glanced up. He found himself staring at a red blinking light, at the security camera mounted on the wall in the corner of Alan Briers' office.

*****

His arrest, at thirty-one years old, came on Christmas Eve, followed by a two-hour police interview. The same day, he was informed of his suspension from Metlock & Wick. Belinda called off their engagement. He was charged with aggravated sexual assault. Though grainy and lacking any discernible audio, Denham knew that the video stream from Briers' office was enough to secure a conviction.

Everything he'd had, he had thrown away.

Three weeks following his suspension, he lay on his mother's sofa at her house in Sydenham, South East London, staring vacantly at the television screen. His mother, barely coping with her own shame from one day to the next, had gone out.

He ignored the first knock at the door, the persistent sounds of the doorbell that followed soon after. The noise continuing, Denham opened the front door a fraction. The man standing on his mother's doorstep was tall and wiry, in his mid-fifties with a haggard face and a crumpled suit. Could have been him in twenty years.

'Are you Albert Denham?'

'Who's asking?'

'My name is Daniel Benedict. I'm a lawyer.'

'I already have a lawyer.'

Denham went to close the door. He saw Benedict's long fingers reach out, plant a hefty palm against the paintwork, stopping it in its path.

'I know what you've been charged with,' Benedict said. 'I'm here to tell you I can make it all go away.'

*****

Denham woke in a sweat. Tatiana snored, talking in her sleep. He missed Belinda already. Afternoons spent in her company always caused him to reflect on his life, the things that haunted him, that had spurred him to write his will. He had seen for himself how swiftly life could be eradicated.

He stared at the ceiling. Self-protection was futile. He should have been the first person to acknowledge that.

The sexual assault charges against him were dropped in February, 1993. Stunned, his mother hadn't asked how or why. He had taken a train to Putney, to the flat Belinda shared with her society girlfriends, where he spent the afternoon begging for forgiveness through Belinda's letterbox. Six months later they married in a civil ceremony on the borders of Richmond Park. Her parents refused to attend.

He started his own firm as he had been instructed to do. Occasionally he would hear from Daniel Benedict, until the impromptu calls stopped coming. Naively, he hoped that was that.

In the October, sitting in his office overlooking the Isle of Dogs, his secretary, a willowy spinster called Orla Drake knocked on the door, clutching a package.

'This arrived for you a few minutes ago,' she said.

Denham took the envelope, studied it. It felt light. On it was his name and office address, handwritten. There were no sender details.

'Who brought it?'

'A courier on a bike,' Orla shrugged. 'He was wearing leathers. Didn't even bother to remove his helmet.'

He waited for Orla to leave the room before tearing off the strip and reaching inside, pulling out a copy of the *Evening Standard*. He skim-read the pages, finding nothing unusual. He started again, paying deliberate attention to each individual article.

On page four, in the bottom corner, was a small article, five centimetres worth of copy, about the body of a male who had been found in marshland north of Teddington Lock, three days earlier. The article stated that the victim's name had been confirmed by the Metropolitan Police as Daniel Benedict, a lawyer; the cause of death determined as suicide by hanging.

Orla knocked on the door. Denham scrambled to re-fold the paper.

'You have a call on line one,' she stuttered. 'The man is refusing to give his name.'

He'd known it was coming. Ever since Benedict had told him that he was clear of the charges, ever since he'd been a free man.

'I'll take it,' he said.

She left. A red light flashed on his phone, the caller on hold.

He stood, picked up the receiver, cleared his throat. 'This is Albert Denham.'

There was a silence. The line crackled.

'You saw the news?'

'Who is this?' Denham snapped.

'My name is Solomon Capricorn,' the voice said. 'I believe you owe me a debt.'

Chapter 15

Tom waited in the shadow of the graffiti-covered church that looked suspiciously like a crack den, hands shoved deeply in his pockets, breath turning to vapour in the night air. A single street light gave him a view north, the park where he had sat on the swings next to Manuela hardly visible close to midnight.

Arriving back on Uruguayan soil from Buenos Aires, the first decision he had made was to get the hell out of central Montevideo. Ray had found them a house to rent short-term, situated in the district of Canelones, fifteen kilometres east in Ciudad de la Costa, a rabbit warren of dirt tracks, modest housing and ramshackle shops and businesses. The area lay nestled between the *Interbalnearia* – the motorway – and the long stretches of beach lining the River Plate as it flowed out to open ocean. North of the motorway, across two kilometres of rough terrain lay Aves de Las Colinas: the two settlements like the haves and the have-nots.

The Canelones house was a bungalow, common for the area, open-plan, brickwork painted butter yellow on the outside, fenced with a lockable gate to keep thieves and muggers out, a garage and swimming pool in the spacious rear garden, the latter so lacking in chlorine that the water was moss-green with algae. There were tall trees too at the back, sealing them off from view. They'd found an old treadmill covered by a dust sheet in the garage. Inside, undersized windows let in little light, not helped by a low-beamed, dark wood ceiling and terracotta floor tiles. Uruguayan building techniques did not apparently involve plasterboard: paint had merely been layered onto the bricks outside and in. Nor did they seemingly involve drainpipes: the house suffering from both damp and humidity. The only plus point: he had his own room.

The second thing he had done on his return was to ask Ray to procure him a gun. The former copper had given him an *I-told-you-so* look that had been followed up by the appearance of a 9mm Beretta, now concealed in a shoebox at the back of the wardrobe.

Tom squinted. In the far distance, at the crossroads up ahead, a figure appeared riding a bike. Alejandro. He couldn't see Manu. The boy cycled in a familiar figure of eight pattern, disappearing in and out of shadow. His heart was thudding again. All he needed to hear was a 'yes', a '*si*'; anything to confirm that the key that they had laboured so hard to copy had worked first time.

He heard the sound of tyres against dirt, as Alejandro braked hard on his BMX, skidding to a halt, sending up dust in the darkness. He held up the key, dropping it at Tom's feet.

'*Mi abuelita,*' he grinned, '*Ella dijo noooo.*'

He laughed then, a childish cackle, putting his feet back on the pedals and speeding off into the night.

Tom drove the Vitara back to Canelones. The street where the house was situated, north of Avenida Giannattasio – the area's main artery – was pitch black. He pulled up, unfastened the chain around the padlock on the gate in the metal chain-link fence. If there was one thing he was sure of, it was that out here they stood out.

He slipped a small key inside the padlock and popped it open, the gate whistling as it opened. He got back in the car, crawled forward, before closing the gate behind him, securing the lock in a similar fashion.

When he entered the house, the three of them surrounded the coffee table, huddled together as though in prayer in near obscurity next to the fireplace, where they had managed to ignite a minute fire.

Anil shot to his feet. 'Well? What she say?'

Tom reached into his pocket, tossed the key onto the main dining table where it landed with a clatter.

'Doesn't work,' he confirmed.

Anil hung his head, cradling his temples between his palms. '*Faaaaack*,' he muttered. Ray got to his feet, kicked a metal bucket, sending a pile of firewood across the floor.

'I'm sorry,' said Becca. 'I should have done a better job.'

'No,' Tom replied, 'you did the best you could under the circumstances.'

'We'll try again, yeah,' Anil said. 'I'll go back to the locksmith. Get several copies cut. Manuela can test them all. We've got enough detail that eventually one will work.'

'And what if none of them work?' Ray spat, 'We might as well kiss goodbye to that safe.'

'Easy,' Becca scowled at Ray, motioning him with her hand to calm down. 'Anil is right, we can try again.'

'It's a setback, simple as that. We plough on,' Tom said.

153

'Our only way into Las Colinas right now is through a waste water pipe. Ray, get out there and play a few rounds of golf. Look at the level of vehicle security. If we can sneak in in the back of the car, we should. Find us a different way in. If we are going through that water pipe then we best start living on a diet of protein and salads. No more late-night fast food binges.' He looked to Ray. 'That goes for you too.'

★★★★★

Tom slept for seven hours, awoke to silence. He was on the treadmill when the garage door was thrown open, sending shafts of sunlight running into dusty, spider-filled corners.

'Get that other one open,' Ray barked at Anil, who was already drenched in sweat from a forty-five-minute run on an incline. Anil unhooked the other door. Tom reduced his speed, slowing to a halt, still out of breath when he turned to see the sandy-yellow monstrosity Ray had picked out. It had four doors, an aerial sticking out of the bonnet, a damaged spoiler.

'What in God's name?' he asked.

Ray wiped sweat from his brow. '1985 Ford Tempo. Only car I could buy for cash. They're in good supply here.'

'Those wheels are the same age as me, man,' Anil commented, shaking his head.

'What good is a getaway vehicle if it breaks down whilst you're trying to get away?' Tom asked.

'I took her for a test drive,' Ray said, closing the gate to the driveway. 'She runs fine. We can do some work on her. Paint her a less conspicuous colour.'

'Can the suspension handle those dirt roads?'

Ray yanked open the driver side door. It creaked under the strain of ageing steel and rusty hinges. Tom concealed a grimace. Ray got in, started the engine, which coughed a few times before humming into action, black fumes swirling out of the Tempo's exhaust and filling the garage. He rolled it forward, stopping shy of the treadmill.

'We get caught, we are fucked,' Anil said, shaking his head again, returning to the house.

Ray disappeared for a round of golf. Tom was sat in the garden in a deck chair with his shirt off when Becca came back clutching two large plastic blue containers, both visibly heavy. She stopped short of the swimming pool's edge, setting them down. Returning to the kitchen, she was back seconds later wearing a pair of yellow gloves and sunglasses. Unscrewing the tops to both containers, she managed to pour the contents into the pool by tipping them over onto their sides, allowing the liquid to spew into the murky water.

'You do know that chlorine is acid, right?' Tom asked. '*Aciiido?*'

Becca straightened, didn't bother looking up. 'I find it aggravating how you ask me a question in English then add on some Spanish at the end, because you can. And yes, I do know that chlorine is an acid. I also know that's why by tomorrow this whole pool is going to be crystal clear.'

He opened his mouth to respond, but no words came. She was wriggling out of her skinny jeans and top. Underneath she wore a black bikini. She pulled up a sun lounger and relaxed into it, without even giving him a sideways glance.

He pondered on the idea that if, had she smiled at him, flirted with him a fraction, he would have wanted her less. In that moment, watching her lie by the pool on a banged-up sunbed, he couldn't have desired her more. Most of the time her mood was toxic, yet there were glimmers of something underneath, a *soul* even, someone who actually cared about her own destiny.

He got up, adjusting himself before walking inside to the fridge and helping himself to a drink. His phone vibrated in his pocket. Denham. He walked to his room before answering, kicking the door shut.

'The key,' Denham demanded at the other end of the line. 'Did it work?'

'We're working on it,' Tom replied.

There was a pause. 'My client is concerned.'

'About what?'

'I told him not to question your commitment.'

'My *commitment*?' Tom repeated, moving the window, twitching the curtain to see what Becca was doing outside and if she had moved. She hadn't.

'How much longer do you need?' Denham asked.

'I didn't know there was a time limit on your little *project*.'

Denham sounded awkward. 'There isn't. My client is keen to retrieve the contents of the safe as soon as possible.'

'Mr Denham, with respect. Tell your client we're going as fast as we can.'

'My client needs you to move faster.'

Denham hung up. Tom cursed under his breath. Through the gap in the curtain he could see Anil in the garden hovering over Becca. She was smiling up at him, laughing even.

'Shit,' he said, at no one. '*Shit.*'

They sat in silence over dinner. Becca had cooked, Ray having returned from a round of golf at Colinas. It was becoming obvious to Tom that Denham was getting updates from more than one source. He was unsure whether Anil or Becca were in direct contact: he doubted it. Ray was always on the phone.

'Ray,' Tom said, as the three faces around the table looked up. 'Care to give us an update?'

Anil put down his fork. 'We're not gonna get in and out of there in a car,' Ray began. 'Every car is searched on entry and exit. Even residents' cars sometimes, I noticed.'

'So how do we get in and out?'

Ray shifted in his seat.

'Did you see the water pipe?'

'I did.'

'Did you see any other way in?'

Ray reached for an open bottle of wine in the centre of the table, filled his glass and took a healthy swig. 'No,' he said, at length. 'Much as I hate to say it, that pipe may be our only hope.'

Tom gritted his teeth. He'd lost his appetite. 'That rust heap you bought parked in the garage… does it have any petrol in it?'

Ray nodded once. Becca was looking at Tom.

'Finish your food,' Tom said, getting to his feet. 'We're going out.'

He'd studied the Google Earth images. There were two routes leading to Las Colinas from the *Interbalnearia*. One was on the well-lit narrow concrete road, lined with eucalyptus trees, a route along which drivers would play chicken with one another as to who could overtake the vehicle in front fastest, without getting crushed by oncoming traffic. Sometimes, in a place like Uruguay, as many drivers appeared to learn to their peril, the gamble wasn't worth the risk. The second route was on a dirt track, directly adjoining the main road, the only landmark a makeshift warehouse selling marble kitchen surfaces for prices scribbled on a chalkboard. At night, the route was eerie and unlit, leading off into inky oblivion.

They set off around eleven under the cover of darkness, wearing black clothes, except for Ray who wore jeans and polo shirt. Ray was in the driver's seat; Becca next to him up front. Tom was in the back seat with Anil, knees pressed up against the fabric of the front seats, huddled down so as not to be seen. Ray had driven the route a few times. He was the only one with any experience of it. Soon after the turning, there was a small *estância* on the left, followed by a bottled gas distribution facility on the right. Then there was a long section of road for about a mile where there was nothing but wilderness on both sides: bulrushes and thick scrub. The car juddered and shook as the tyres crunched over the uneven surface.

'The road dips up ahead here,' Ray said. 'That's where I'll drop you. You can't be seen from the house on the hill there.'

'What's there a house on a hill doing out here?' Anil asked.

'It's some kind of quarry,' Becca said. 'We have to bypass

the quarry on foot to get to a marsh. On the other side of the marsh is the back fence of Las Colinas. And the entrance to the pipe.'

'You sure you wanna do this?' Anil asked Tom.

Tom looked out of the window. There was nothing out there, only pitch dark. He looked up at Anil who was staring back at him hopefully, as if pleading with him to change his mind.

'Ray,' Tom said. 'Kill the lights.'

Chapter 16

Becca was beginning to wish he was still sleeping in her bed. For the eighth night in a row she'd woken up trembling, cold and alone, thrusting invisible hands from her body, grappling with Argentine Thiago's sausage-like fingers crushing her oesophagus. Every night she had pleaded with her brain to erase the memory, sobbing into her pillow. And every night she'd resisted the urge to go to his room, to crawl into bed with him and seek solace in his embrace, because she knew that if she sought comfort from him, he would provide it. Every night she wanted to hate him. Federico and his men had come from Tom Holt's past, not hers.

She was sat up front, Ray in the driver's seat hunched over the steering wheel, a cross between a squint and a scowl on his face. With no headlights, Ray had nothing but the vague outline of the bulrushes by the side of the dirt road to guide him.

On a night like this, Richie would have been in his element. Sometimes they'd cross over, Richie walking out the door as she came home with her day's take. He would wait for the clubs to empty, trawl the night bus stops and lift a man's wallet right out of his kebab-grease-stained fingers. He was that good, until the day he wasn't. Richie had been an optimist to her pessimist, the *yin* to her *yang*. As long as they weren't taking a life, they'd reckoned they weren't doing anything wrong. He talked about taking wallets like they were on long-term loan, as if one day he was going to go back and return them one by one to their owners. She wondered what he thought about, all those hours spent in prison, if he had managed to remain positive. Or if the death of an innocent man, caused unwittingly by his hand, had started to grind him down.

She snapped to attention. Ray had rolled the Ford Tempo to a halt. In the back, Tom got out, Ray rolling down his window. Becca opened her door, following Anil to the shadow of a tree by the side of the road. Tom was studying his watch.

'Back here, one hour,' he whispered, reminding Ray of an agreement they had made at the house. 'Half past midnight.' Ray nodded once, rolling the car slowly forward, rubber crunching on grit.

They watched the car disappear. When he was far enough away, Ray would switch the headlights back on. Tom approached. She could barely make out his or Anil's faces. Anil yanked up his hood, pulled on a small backpack. She tugged up the zip on her black jacket, wearing her usual skinny jeans and military-style boots, covering her red hair with a beanie hat.

'Let's go,' Tom said.

He led the way. She followed him, Anil at the rear. Though her eyes had adjusted to the gloom, the long grass made anything at ground level impossible to distinguish. As she took another step the soil came loose and she tripped, tumbling headlong into Tom's back. His frame blocked her fall and she straightened, whispering her gratitude, Tom reaching for her hand, gripping her fingers as they edged forward. His skin felt warm to the touch. The ground grew steeper before they found themselves crawling upwards on hands and knees. At the top of the incline, Las Colinas came into view, a hundred and fifty metres up ahead. They huddled in a line, three soldiers perched on top of a trench, scoping out the enemy. The ground smelled damp.

'There she is,' she breathed.

'Hard to miss,' Tom said.

Light filled the air above Las Colinas, steadily dissipating and turning the sky a paler shade of grey. Floodlights lined the perimeter, inside facing outward, the entire chain-link fence lit up like it was the Emirates Stadium. On the other side, the manicured grass on the fairway was clearly visible, and the houses beyond it. She looked to Tom, who was already looking at her. They held their glance, to her a confirmation of the uneasiness they were both feeling.

Anil was rustling around in his bag. He pulled out a pair of binoculars.

'We need night-vision, yeah,' Anil said, lifting them to his eyes. 'But these will have to do.'

Becca waited in silence, conscious of Tom's hand resting on the small of her back. She pushed it off.

'There's a guard in a hut, halfway down,' Anil whispered.

'What else?' Tom asked.

'A whole lot of light,' Anil said. 'Doesn't matter if we get through that pipe, the lights are gonna get us if the dogs don't.'

162

'Can you see the pipe?' she asked.

'Nah, not close enough,' Anil mouthed.

'Keep going,' Tom said, pulling himself up. 'Watch for rockfalls.'

Edging along the top edge of the quarry, the only light to guide them was from Colinas. Progress was slow. She watched Tom check his watch, the one that had the word 'Papercut' engraved on the back. She estimated they had been gone about thirty minutes since leaving Ray. No one spoke.

Tom clicked his fingers at Anil, raising finger-binoculars up to his eyes. Anil passed them over.

'What can you see?' Becca whispered.

'I can't see shit,' Tom said, lowering them again. 'There is water around here somewhere.'

They had reached the end of the quarry. The ground dropped sharply leading down to a barbed-wire fence. All that was left separating them from Colinas was a sparse group of trees and an invisible marsh. She slid nimbly under the fence, coming out the other side. Tom followed, albeit with a little less grace. Anil did the same, landed flat on his face. She helped him up. Behind the next row of trees they came to the edge of the marsh, pond scum covering a large part of it, the floodlights bouncing off its lime-coloured surface.

'That way,' mouthed Tom, pointing around the edge of the marsh. 'We stick with the line of the trees and get as close as we can.'

A few minutes later they were huddled together, listening to the sounds of their breathing. Becca saw the pipe for the first time. It wasn't so much a pipe as a gap at the base of the chain-link fence that had been lined with a concrete slab on the top and sides. It was questionable whether a human could get through. It was a run-off, the pipe leading to what looked like an entry point, a small dam separating a body of water.

The problem was the six or so metres of wide marshland between the line of trees and the entry to the pipe, the grass a mossy lush green under a beaming floodlight, ground that could flood easily depending on the amount of local rainfall.

Anil took out his phone, took some photographs. She watched in silence for a few minutes, waiting for movement. A lone guard ambled down the perimeter path, an Alsatian tethered close to his side, nose in the dirt. The building next to the body of water, twenty metres back from the pipe, let out a constant low hum.

Tom rubbed his eyes. 'We need a diversion,' he whispered. 'Something that allows us enough time to cross that gap.'

'You're thinking too much,' Anil said. 'We need to cut the power.'

'Because that's so simple,' Becca hissed.

They backed away soon after, walking in convoy, Tom in front, away from the lights, retreating into blackness. The outside temperature had plummeted. Climbing back up to the quarry, Becca eyed the house on the hill, where the lights were all on.

'Whatever is in that safe better be worth all this bullshit,' Anil muttered, striding back into a section of open ground.

Neither she nor Tom offered him a response.

'Wetsuits,' Anil then blurted from behind.

'What?' asked Becca, keeping her voice low. Both she and Tom stopped, turned around to look at him.

'Think about it. We should wear wetsuits, yeah? They're like camouflage in the dark, they'll reduce friction inside the concrete pipe, and they'll stop us from getting hypothermia once we're out of the pipe and in the water. For this job, we should wear wetsuits.'

'Anil, you're tripping,' Becca laughed.

'You got a better idea?'

She watched as Tom muttered something under his breath, carried on walking. Becca shook her head, followed. 'Wetsuits,' she chuckled, picturing them all in scuba gear, complete with flippers.

She kept walking. It was only the tiniest sound – a penny dropping in a puddle – that made her turn her head a degree. Anil had disappeared from view. She stopped dead, turned a full one-eighty, sweeping the area. 'Anil?'

He could have moved into shadow; it was hard enough to see anything. The wind blew. There was nothing. He was gone.

Louder now. 'Anil?'

She said Tom's name; started striding back over the ground she had covered, looking left, right, down onto the ground.

Tom was at her side, both of them searching. 'Anil? Where the fuck are you?'

She stopped still. Squinted, tilted her head to one side. *Was that…?*

'Oh, Jesus.'

She dropped to her knees, plunged her arm down into the wet mud, into the crevice filled with water, less than two metres wide.

'Anil?'

Panic rose in her chest. Tom was doing the same, reaching down as far as he could into silty, muddy water, feeling around for anything to grab onto.

Tom had stood up and was kicking off his shoes, tearing off his jacket. She watched him quickly lower himself in, gulping a breath and disappearing under the sludgy water, which seemed to engulf him. She was shaking then, all alone, arm shoulder deep in mud, feeling around in darkness, grabbing at nothing.

She pulled her arms out, braced each side of the crevice. Waited, stomach in knots.

'Tom?'

A giant bubble rose to the surface, mud splattering as it burst, followed immediately by Tom, arms around Anil's torso, both covered in wet mud like melted chocolate, the only thing visible the whites of his eyes.

Becca grabbed onto Anil's body, yanking as hard as she could, Tom allowing her to take him so he could pull himself up and out. Together they dragged Anil from the sinkhole. Becca manoeuvred Anil onto his side, slapped him hard on the back, opened his mouth, wiped the mud from his eyes using her thumbs. Anil convulsed, vomited water then fell onto his back, still coughing.

'What happened?' Becca breathed, tears stinging her eyes as she tried to cradle Anil's head. Tom was on all fours, still coughing and spitting, wiping thick mud from his face and lips.

'Not a c-c-confident fucking s-swimmer, am I?' Anil managed.

'I could have done with a wetsuit just then,' Tom said with the merest flicker of a smile.

Anil got the joke. There was laughter in his gasping for air, humour in his rolling into a ball on his side and whimpering. She found herself laughing with him.

'How long 'til Ray's back?' Becca asked, grabbing onto Anil's hand.

Tom raised his wrist, wiped his watch face. 'Ten minutes,' he said. 'We need to move. You still with us Anil?'

'Still breathing,' Anil murmured. 'Just. Thanks man, you may have saved my life.'

Becca looked at Tom. He was looking right back at her with a mud-stained face. It dawned on her that she'd never thanked him for coming for her in Buenos Aires.

'Don't mention it,' he said.

Becca stoked the fire for Anil. He was clean and showered, wearing a white robe she had found in one of the wardrobes. Ray sat down on the sofa, passed Anil a glass of whisky with a single ice cube.

'Drink it,' he ordered Anil. 'Don't argue.'

Anil took it, clutching the glass with both hands.

'How do you feel?' Becca asked.

'Like I fell down a sinkhole and couldn't escape,' Anil said.

'You did escape. You were pulled out.'

'Few seconds longer, man... ' Anil shook his head, sipped his whisky. 'Thought I was a goner.'

She left them, walked around to Tom's bedroom, the door partially closed. He was sat on the far side of the bed, freshly showered, wearing only a towel, back to her, his head bowed. She walked over, lowered herself to the mattress.

'Are you alright?' she said.

'I've had better days.'

'You saved his life.'

'Could have been any one of us. You would have done the same.'

She reached for his hand, glancing down at his fingers entwined with hers, her thumb tenderly stroking his skin. There was a moment, when she raised her eyes to his face, noses millimetres apart, when she knew he planned on kissing her. He lingered for a minute, their breaths mingling, didn't move before lowering his head. The moment his lips brushed hers, she closed her eyes. She saw one face staring back at her, and it wasn't Tom's.

'Not here,' she whispered, despite every protestation in her mind.

Tom pulled back, eyes searching her face.

'Every move we make, Ray reports it back to Denham,' she said. 'Ray's worked for Denham for years. And anything that gets back to Denham goes to Capricorn.'

He was frowning at her. 'I don't know what that is. What is Capricorn?'

Becca glanced back at the still open door, keeping her voice low.

'Capricorn is the client. Capricorn is the one who wants the contents of the safe. His name is Solomon Capricorn. He's the one I work for.'

Chapter 17

The beast of a man was chewing open-mouthed on a *chivito* – the Uruguayan take on a burger – consisting of four ounces of beef, sliced hard-boiled eggs, ham, tomatoes, cheese, mayonnaise and olives all piled up and oozing between two sides of a white sesame bun. Juices from the sandwich ran down his chin. He would occasionally wipe them away with the back of his hand. He had black curly hair, shaggy to shoulder level and long stubble covering his chin, not quite yet a beard. Heavy black brows to rival Denham's. He wore a white shirt, open collar, chinos and loafers, no socks. In the ten minutes Tom had been sat opposite him at the table, the beast hadn't uttered a word.

Tom had called Denham. He didn't bother mentioning the business with Anil and the sinkhole, aware now that Denham was briefed on everything anyway, courtesy of Ray. So he had got down to business, kept it simple. What they required was a power cut: for the floodlights of Las Colinas to go dark long enough that they could crawl through the pipe and get inside the compound, and to get out again with the contents of the safe.

'You didn't find a better way in?' Denham had asked, sounding incredulous.

'Every vehicle into Las Colinas is searched on entry and exit, unless you are a resident.'

'So make friends with a resident.'

'You want a trail leading back to your client or not?' *Capricorn*, whoever he was. 'Who was it who found us Manuela? Maybe I could speak to them?'

Denham had given him the address of the *chiviteria* in the Tres Cruces neighbourhood, not far from Montevideo's central bus terminal. Instructed him to go alone. Tom had arrived early to find a black and white Boston Terrier tethered on the street outside the door, every now and then letting out a high-pitched whine, shifting its front paws side to side, restless for the presence of its master. Inside, the hulk of a man now sat on the other side of the table, back to the wall, was the restaurant's sole customer. Tom had ordered a cola and sat down. There were no pleasantries.

In the silence, he played through his list of questions in his mind. Added one about how Albert Denham had come to have contacts in even the darkest corners of Uruguay. Or perhaps Denham was doing as he was told by the client, Solomon Capricorn.

'*Habla espanol?*' the man grunted out of the blue, bits of the sandwich still stuck between his teeth.

'*Si,*' Tom replied, taking it that his burly companion did not speak any English.

'Are you British?' the man then asked, in English, throwing Tom off guard.

'Yes.'

'I despise the fucking British,' the man continued in English. 'My brother died on Las Malvinas,' he added, using the Argentinian word for the Falkland Islands.

Tom's heartbeat quickened. 'You're from Argentina.'

The beast pushed the last bite of sandwich into his mouth, packing his cheeks.

'I'm sorry about your brother,' Tom said.

'I'm not. He was the son of my father's whore. She was a dog. And everybody in my family hated the product of their screwing. Tell me, what it is that you want? I get no indication these days.'

He was wiping greasy fingers on a wad of serviettes.

'I need someone who can create a power cut,' Tom said, lowering his voice.

The big black menacing eyebrows drew together. The beast ran his tongue along his teeth, sucking up the final remnants of his *chivito*. 'What kind of power cut?'

'The power to the perimeter floodlights at Aves de Las Colinas in Canelones. It's a gated community.'

The man flicked his fingers at the waiter, indicating that he required the bill. 'I know what it is. For how long do you want this power cut to take place?'

'About ten to fifteen minutes. A short enough time that it doesn't raise alarm bells. But long enough to get three people into the complex. And then another fifteen minutes a couple of hours later, long enough so we can get back out again.'

'Unless you get caught.'

Tom's eyes shot up. The Argentine was gulping his drink. As the bill arrived he opened his wallet, pulled out a pile of pesos, counting some out onto the surface of the table.

'You and I will see each other again,' he said, getting up.

'You didn't tell me your name,' Tom replied, growing impatient, the dog doing circles and yelping.

'You don't need to know my name.'

At the house, Ray was making lunch.

'Where are the others?' Tom asked.

'Anil went to collect the new key. Becca's outside.'

He went out into the garden. Becca was in the glacial pool in her bikini. Since the night of Anil's near-drowning incident, she had taken on a whole other layer of fascination for him. Who was this Solomon Capricorn character? How did she come to be working for him? And for how long? What exactly was it that she did for him? His name hadn't been mentioned again. He had promised her his silence.

The thought of almost kissing her had sent his mind into a kind of frenzy. But adding to the sweetness of the torture: he knew that *she* knew that he wanted to get her all tangled up between the sheets. He had played his hand, and now she was making him wait.

She emerged glistening from the water, pulled herself up onto the edge, resting on her elbows. Water dripped from her nose and lips. He was enjoying this *frisson* between them.

'What happened?' she breathed.

Tom squatted down, took off his sunglasses, brought his face close to hers, keeping his voice low. 'There's an Argentine. Big guy, maybe six three, black curly hair. Big chest. Denham knows him, I don't know how.'

Becca's eyes flitted to Ray, who emerged from the house. She looked back at Tom. Her expression warned him off.

'Do you know who he is?' he asked.

Becca said nothing, shook her head: no.

'Where are you going?' Becca asked him from her place on the sofa, Anil trying to light a fire. In the evenings, the temperature went south.

'For a run to the beach and back. I'll be an hour.'

In the morning he and Anil had hit the treadmill under the light of a single bulb dangling from the ceiling on a dusty cord, blasting Anil's favourite tunes – various spins on Punjabi MC's 'Knight Rider Bhangra' – through Bluetooth speakers, egging one another on to go harder, faster, before doing it all again in the afternoon, whilst Ray relaxed in the garden or took a nap. Anil had coined it 'the wetsuit diet'.

'Don't forget to call Manuela, yeah?' Anil said.

'When I get back.'

Closing the gate behind him, he ran in the pitch black, down makeshift gravel roads, eventually reaching concrete again at Avenida Giannattasio. He continued south, walked over La Rambla, which was tranquil, before picking up the pace again at the empty car park leading to Lagomar Beach. Street lights filtered onto the waterfront, enough that he could see the waves from the River Plate crashing onto the shore, his running shoes sinking in deep and kicking up coarse sand. He pushed himself harder, until he could feel his heart slamming against his ribs, until it felt like his chest would explode from the sheer exertion. He tried not to picture the Argentine, the man from Tres Cruces, the man with no name.

The beach went on and on, twinkly lights from

Montevideo's skyline in the distance, compared to the inky blackness at his origin. He thought about the morning that Denham had come to see him in North London, how he probably should have closed the door on him then and there. It was greed that had made him say yes, though he would never have admitted to it back then. The same arrogance and greed that had got him fired from his company. And when this was all over – and he hadn't ended up incarcerated – what then? What did he have to go back to?

He slowed to a halt in the sand. Bent double, caught his breath, hands rested on his knees, allowing his heart to cease pounding between his ears.

On his route back he saw a hazy figure, standing in the shadow, waiting motionless near the *guardavidas* hut in front of a grass-covered dune, alone. He slowed to a halt, recognising Becca's stance. She was hugging her waist, wearing her skinny jeans and a hooded top.

He carried on walking, coming to a halt two metres in front of her, looking into her eyes. He thought he saw tears there, or the remnants of them.

'What's wrong?' he said, out of breath.

'Sancho Belosi,' she said. 'That's his name. That's all I know, I swear. I've never met him.'

'Does he work for Capricorn?'

She nodded. 'He has done for some years. I don't know how they met.'

'Is he dangerous?'

'I don't know. If he works for Capricorn... then yes he probably is.'

He took a step closer, checking there was no one around

to watch them, wishing suddenly that he wasn't covered in sweat and grit. 'Thank you,' he said, and reached for her hand.

Standing above him, heels dug into the silt, she was the perfect height. It occurred to him then that it had taken this long for them to find the right moment, albeit in the dark on a frigid beach, the roar of the waves behind them. She lifted one hand, resting it at the base of his neck, eyes fixed on his. His kiss was slow at first, building in intensity, bodies coming together. It took him back to the night outside Sabina Cordero's house, when she'd kissed him and he had been left wanting so much more. He placed both hands at her waist, sliding his fingers under her top, stroking her skin.

She pulled back, breathless, and as though reading his mind, met his gaze. The *guardavidas* hut was less than eight metres to their right. It was rickety, made of crumbling planks and rusted metal struts, the shell of a ramp leading to a hollow yellow shack. She offered him a look of silent acknowledgement. He helped her up to the platform first, wood slats barely holding together, weathered by years of salty beach air. He followed, hauling himself up, using one knee as leverage. Inside the hut the floorboards were equally rickety, enough space for two lifeguards to sit inside and stare out of the gap at the front with binoculars at the choppy waters of the Plate. He took in his surroundings. It would not be comfortable, not that it mattered. In the fuzzy glow from the street lamps outside, a used condom had been left shrivelled over the threshold of the hut. Becca bit back a half-smile, half-look of revulsion. They would not be the first, it occurred to Tom, and they wouldn't be the last.

This time Becca made the first move, unzipping the hoodie and discarding it before removing her vest underneath. He could hear the sound of the waves, the sound of their shallow breathing. He removed his top, damp with sweat, kicked off his shoes. Becca did the same, shimmied out of her jeans, unhooking her bra until they were standing face to face, naked except for the shadows. He paused then, looking around, as if wondering how logistically to proceed. Tom lowered himself to the floor, back to the wall, buttocks on rough wood, reached for her hand and guided her down towards him. Their kiss was more urgent then, Becca on top, knees on wood, sliding against his sweat-covered body, guiding him inside her. She set the pace, slow at first, grasping at the wall behind his head, finding her rhythm, leaning back, coming forward, returning to his kiss to the sound of the waves melting away.

Feeling around in the shadows for clothes, they escaped the confines of the *guardavidas* hut, dropping back down onto the sand. Tom took her by the hand, kissed her one last time, had to stop himself from undressing her again.

'Go back alone,' he said. 'I'll run further up then see you at the house.'

Becca nodded, unravelled her arms from around his neck. He didn't want Denham to know, didn't want Ray to know; didn't want anyone to know. Walking backwards, Becca bid him a wordless farewell, made her way back up the sandbank to the path before disappearing from view. Tom carried on running, only this time his mind was on her.

He was still asleep in his bed when Denham called at 8 a.m. He fumbled around for his phone, grunted an answer.

'Our friend would like to see you again,' he said. 'Do you have a pen? I'll give you the address.'

Becca was in the kitchen with Anil, sitting on the counter top, Ray not yet up. A fleeting look passed between him and Becca, nothing more. She had slept in her own bed.

'You gonna see Manuela today?' Anil blurted.

'Can't. I have to see the man from Tres Cruces. Says he has something for me.'

'We need to test the key, man,' Anil replied. 'Come on.'

'Later,' Tom said, placing a reassuring hand on Anil's shoulder. 'I'll do it, I promise.'

The address Denham gave him was in a low-rise neighbourhood known as Barrio Sur, east of Montevideo's old town. In the drizzle, Tom took in his surroundings, decided swiftly that it was best to keep his head down. It was no place for tourists or the like. Buildings were run down, others colourfully painted yet still wasting away. Cracks and graffiti covered the external walls. Everywhere there were bars on windows, rusted, crumbling, in desperate need of renovation.

He located the door, knocked hard. Across the road, a vagrant squinted in his direction. It wasn't long before the door opened a few centimetres, the Argentine's face visible. He opened the door a little wider, beckoning Tom inside.

He followed the man he now knew to be Sancho Belosi up a dilapidated staircase, two flights. The inside of the building was unoccupied at present, but looked to be a sometime crack den, judging by the graffiti and paraphernalia covering the decaying wooden floorboards. At the top of the stairs, Sancho used a key to enter a room, standing back to allow Tom to enter first.

Tom paused. He could hear a whimpering. He glanced towards Sancho's expressionless face before stepping inside.

In the centre of the floorboards, across from a boarded-up window was a man in his thirties, overweight, blindfolded and gagged, wearing some kind of uniform, wrists tied coarsely to a chair. Blood oozed from a head wound, seeping through the blindfold, down his cheek and neck, through the gag and onto his white collar.

Belosi shut the door behind them. Their prisoner flinched at the sound, raising his head. Tom swallowed, looked down, in that moment noticing the trail of urine travelling rapidly down the chair leg and spreading across the floor.

Chapter 18

Dusk. The stench of blood everywhere.

Denham tasted bile, couldn't drag the image of the young girl from his mind, dead on the staircase inside the small country cottage, on her back, up-turned tutu-style skirt revealing pink underwear. He looked on in disbelief in the study at the very determined looking man – dark-haired, slicked back, with a squashed, rugby player's nose, at least ten years his junior – now standing over the body of a woman, shot twice in the back through her cashmere cardigan. The man was grappling with some blue plastic sheeting, wearing a pair of blue medical examination gloves, exactly like the ones Denham had been instructed to wear at the door. Facing him, a set of crosshatch windows looking out onto a wooded area were spattered with blood.

Not long married. Belinda at home keeping the bed warm. A call out of the blue from Capricorn telling him to get to an address in Kent.

'You Denham?' the man barked at him. He had the trace of an accent.

'Yes,' Denham breathed.

'My name is Anton,' he said. 'Try not to look at the body. Did you leave your shoes at the door?'

Denham nodded, looked down at his striped socks, too stunned to do much else.

'The guy who let you in, that's Morris. We've got less than two hours to clear out. You can start by cleaning those windows. Don't leave any trace behind. Get in all the cracks. Cleaning stuff is over there. Go, get started.'

'Wh— Who are these people?' Denham asked, unable to disguise his horror.

Anton paused, straightened back up. 'He was a driver, I believe. Or used to be.'

'This is his family?'

'Two kids,' Anton said. 'The boy's upstairs.'

Denham stifled the urge to vomit.

Two hours later he was still trembling. All the lights in the cottage were switched off. He helped Anton carry the last of the bodies into the back of an unmarked blue van, wrapped in heavy-duty plastic sheeting. He'd carried the girl himself, flesh still warm. The bodies had been stripped of their clothes, which Anton had placed in a separate bin liner, he said, for burial elsewhere.

'Walk with me,' Anton said, and Denham followed him back inside as Morris closed the doors to the van. Anton switched on the light, handed him a camera. 'Photograph every single room. Capricorn wants to see what's left.'

Denham did as he was told. Anton had opened all the windows but the smell of bleach still lingered. Denham wondered what would happen next. The family would be reported missing. The police would find no trace of them, certainly not at their exceptionally clean house, which would only have a roll of carpet mysteriously missing from their set of stairs. The blood from the girl's wounds had been too deeply set into the fabric. Anton said he'd had no choice, despite what Capricorn would say. No one had thought the girl would bolt so quickly.

Denham didn't ask who had carried out the shooting. He had seen no weapons at the scene. And despite the air of menace that surrounded Anton, Denham wasn't one hundred per cent he was the killer, simply the guy who cleaned everything up afterwards.

Anton and Morris drove the van for three hours in darkness, keeping to the speed limit, across the Kent border into East Sussex, ending up on the M27 towards Southampton. Denham followed in his black Mazda, petrol tank perilously close to empty. He thought about Belinda the entire journey, what he would tell her, if anything. She would be losing her mind by now. And if he turned up and told her nothing of his whereabouts... He'd worked so hard to get her back, to have her as his wife, to win her trust.

Solomon Capricorn had a lot to answer for.

On a country lane, the night was all-consuming. Denham followed the van's tail lights as they turned down a ghostly wooded track. The Mazda did not fare well off-road. He felt himself being thrown around, tyres bouncing over uneven layers of caked mud. They came to a stop at a nearby clearing, surrounded by trees. The van went dark. Denham switched off his engine, kept his dipped headlights on, a tight lump in his throat.

Anton was opening the back doors to the van, the four plastic-wrapped bodies concealed in rolls of old carpet, including the blood-stained one from back at the cottage. Anton motioned to him to get out of his car.

'Let's go,' he said, as Denham emerged.

The forest was dense, with no real path save the initial driveway leading to a clearing. Denham struggled to support his end of the carpet, knowing what was inside.

'Stop there,' Anton ordered, and Denham did as he was told. They lowered the carpet to the ground. Anton pulled out a torch, flashing the beam briefly over a pit, an abyss with no discernible bottom, with mud walls carved out in the undergrowth. Denham guessed it was over three metres deep.

'We put the bodies in with the plastic, then the carpets on top,' Anton said, pulling out another pair of surgical gloves from his pocket and handing a pair to Denham. 'Then we refill.'

They manoeuvred the carpet into position at the top edge of the pit. Anton placed one hand on the long edge, ordering Denham to do the same. He gave the roll a rough shove. The carpet unravelled, sending the body of the woman – the one from the study – sprawling inelegantly into the soil at the bottom, still partially covered by the plastic. In the dim light, Denham could make out her shape. She'd landed on her back, head twisted to one side, one knee drawn up at a right angle to her body. Denham was still examining her when Morris dumped another roll of carpet on the top edge of the pit. There followed the same procedure, Denham watching the body of the young girl being tossed away into the chasm, landing with her head on her mother's stomach, legs still tied up with plastic.

It took a little over an hour to bury them completely, an entire family of four. Denham couldn't take his mind off the image; twisted, blood-stained corpses, connected by their various body parts. The pit had been well-covered. Denham sensed that it was not the first time Anton had buried bodies in the woods.

'You understand, don't you,' Anton said once they had finished, 'that this is what will happen to you too if you speak to anyone about this? Even that society wife of yours?'

Denham opened his mouth, stunned at how or why Anton would know anything about Belinda. 'Who are you?' Denham asked.

'I am the same as you,' Anton replied.

'I want to meet Solomon Capricorn.'

'He doesn't want to meet you.'

'Tell me what I have to do to meet him. I'm done. I won't do anything else until I've spoken to him face to face.'

'You're sure about that?'

Denham held onto his car door, knees weak. In the darkness, Anton was looking at him like he'd wished he had gone to the effort of putting him in the ground with the rest of them. Denham swallowed. 'Positive.'

Anton nodded once, turned and got back into the van. Morris started the engine. Denham waited beside his car door as they reversed out of the clearing at some speed.

Alone, he dropped to his knees and sobbed like a baby.

★★★★★

Denham closed the front door and tossed his keys onto the table. It was almost eight. Two weeks after he had helped Anton bury the bodies, Belinda appeared in the hallway at their basement flat in Clapham wearing a loosely-fastened

Kimono, clutching a drink. She handed the glass to him, kissed him on the cheek.

'It's non-alcoholic, sorry,' she said, with a characteristic flick of her hair. 'I don't want to kill off all your swimmers.'

She sashayed off back down the hallway. 'Want to shower first? Or just ravage me on the sofa?'

'Shower first,' Denham grunted, looking down at an envelope with his name on sitting on the hallway table. He put down his drink, tore it open.

Inside was a compact disc, unmarked inside a sleeve. Belinda reappeared.

'A man came to the door with that for you. I thought it must have been work-related,' she said.

'What man? What did he look like?'

'Tall, kind of gangly. Had an awfully crooked nose, poor chap.'

Denham stiffened. 'What else did he say?'

'Nothing. He gave me the envelope and left.'

'He didn't try to come in?'

'No. He was perfectly pleasant. Why?'

'Nothing. I need to look at this.'

She cocked her head to one side, disappointed. 'Al. I thought we were going to—'

He slid one arm around her waist, captured her lips roughly in his own. 'And I fully intend to. I need to see this first. It won't take long.'

In the second bedroom, which functioned as his home office, Denham powered up the laptop, pulling off his suit jacket and tie. Closing the door, he slid the disc into the machine.

It was a moment before anything happened. Denham took a seat, heel bouncing restlessly off the carpet.

He opened the video file. He heard the soundtrack before there was a visual, a woman's voice: pained, scared. 'I need to get back, Al,' it was saying. 'Please stop it.'

When the visual appeared, there were tears in his eyes. Denham buried his face in his hands. It took him back to his police interview, when his world had finally crumbled.

There were no threats, no words, no warnings, yet Capricorn's message was clear:

You are a free man because of me.

I saved you; I gave you your life back.

You work for me now.

Friday 22 September, 2000

Denham finished his eighth pint of ale, alone at the bar in The Gun Pub. The TV played the day's highlights from the Sydney Olympics. Booze had been his only solace for the last nine months, since the moment Belinda had walked out. Her father had pushed for their divorce proceedings to be expedited, throwing a ton of money at a Kensington-based family law firm, so that he never had to see his rapist son-in-law again.

Denham knew there had been two issues in the marriage: the first, his inability to get Belinda pregnant (his fault, according to the fertility doctors, not hers) and second, his inability to tell her anything about what he was doing when he disappeared, sometimes for hours at a time. The trust had died long ago. Denham had heard through a friend that she was now expecting a baby with her new boyfriend, some kind of architect, a man who could actually hit the proverbial target.

Denham belched, walloped his chest with a clenched fist, pushing a pile of crumpled notes into the bartender's palm. It was dark by the time he stumbled out into the street in Poplar. Knew he was going to vomit so didn't bother hailing a cab. It was early enough that he could still catch the Docklands Light Railway back into central London. Outside, inhaling late summer air, he had a vague notion of a lone man lingering close by. At Poplar Station, behind a concrete pillar that supported the tracks, his stomach clenched and he brought back his last couple of ales, the ones that had made him feel numb to everything.

He didn't like to think about the bodies. There had been more of them, too, together with shredded papers, destroyed emails, and new-found knowledge on illicit finance. Now he was keeping tabs on two young strays too: a redhead and her brother.

'Go easy,' he heard a voice say, feeling a hand lay flat against his back. He shot up, stumbled backwards, wiping his wet mouth. He hadn't seen Anton in a year or so. He still had the same unmistakeable bulbous nose squashed against his face. If anything, it seemed more crooked now, uglier, as if Anton had taken a few more knocks and it was even more bent out of shape. His hair now fell in a dead centre parting, half covering his eyes, as though he had decided to dispense with the usual gunk he used to put in it to keep it slicked back.

'What are you doing here?' Denham said over the rumble of the train overhead.

'Seems your time has come, Al,' Anton replied. 'The boss is ready to meet you.'

'And what if I don't want to meet him anymore?'

'You still scared? After all this time?'

Denham almost vomited again. 'I've given that man the last seven years of my life, someone I've never even met... Why the fuck would I want to give him anymore?'

'Cry all you like, Denham,' Anton said. 'He's coming for you.'

Anton pushed his hands into his pockets, walked away, crossing the street, disappearing into the night.

'When?' Denham asked out loud, raising his voice, shouting for no one, 'When?'

He drank all day on the Saturday. Whisky, wine, vodka: whatever he could lay his hands on without leaving his new bachelor pad in Streatham Hill. He wallowed in memories of Belinda, picturing her with a rounded belly, pretending it was his, stumbling from the sofa to the toilet bowl and back.

Anton was back at his door on the Sunday morning, hammering loudly. 'You look terrible. Get dressed. We're going to see Capricorn.'

Denham stumbled around, doing as he was told. He pulled on some crumpled, unwashed, clothes from the bedroom floor.

'Where does he live?' he asked Anton in the car.

Anton puffed on a cigarette, the window rolled down. 'Belgravia.'

'Is he married?'

'Yes. One daughter, two years old. His wife is pregnant again.'

Denham thought about another faceless male and his ability to hit the fertility target. 'What does he want from me?' he asked.

'Nothing. You have demonstrated your loyalty. He wants to shake you by the hand.'

The house on Egerton Crescent had four storeys, window boxes bursting with fuchsias. Denham took in his surroundings. It was one of the richest streets in London.

A sense of uneasiness bubbled up in his chest as he followed Anton across the road. He'd always imagined Solomon Capricorn as someone of significant means and wealth, yet he had usually pictured a dark and shady character, living under a rock in an East London warehouse. Not someone with a young child living in the borough of Kensington & Chelsea.

Anton rang the doorbell, stood with his feet slightly apart, a soldier standing to attention.

Denham watched as a woman of a similar age to him opened the door. She stood in bare feet, wearing a black dress, with dark hair and fine lines crinkling the skin around her eyes. She reminded him of Belinda, but her countenance was not as gentle. In fact, her gaze was hollow. She looked familiar. Anton seemed uncomfortable in her presence.

'I'll fetch my brother,' she drawled, without bothering to look Denham's way.

A minute later, Solomon Capricorn walked into the light.

The bubble that had welled up inside Denham's chest burst like a firework exploding in the sky.

'Mr Denham. We meet at last,' Capricorn said, holding out his hand.

'I know you,' Denham stuttered, taking a step back, stiffening, recognising the face from countless press interviews, business journals and from the man's prominent position as the CEO and owner of one of the UK's largest corporate firms: Elate International. 'You're Charlie Ebdon.'

Chapter 19

All this was wrong.

He could have had a normal job by now: commuting every day to a new office, maybe in Oxford Circus, heading up security for a City firm, or in somewhere upscale like Bloomsbury or Marylebone.

It had been a bad moment. A blip. The day Denham had knocked on his door he had been in a kind of funk, bitter that Hendrick Van de Vlok had decided to kick him out and not demote him to a lowly, trivial back office job as punishment. The bitterness would have passed. He would have picked himself up. The online gambling, the websites, they were a way of killing time, a way to make a quick buck whilst he put together his CV and applied for normal jobs. Not this.

It was raining. Tom waited in darkness inside the Vitara, the PVC hood up, within view of the playground for Manu to show, a newly cut key for her to test out tucked securely in his pocket. He hadn't eaten since breakfast, growing used to the hunger pangs, reminding himself to like it.

The street was empty that he could see, his vision blurred by the rain.

He felt certain now that Sancho Belosi was the man who had contacted Manuela in the first instance; the man who promised to take away her grandson Alejandro if she did not comply with his demands. Believed it too.

He hadn't yet been able to shake the image from his mind, of Ernesto 'Nesto' Suarez, thirty-something, blindfolded and trembling, blood seeping from a head wound and still-warm piss covering the floorboards, seeping down into rotten wood. Nesto Suarez, who flinched and sobbed and drooled each time he was threatened by Belosi. Nesto Suarez, who Tom now considered to be the missing link in their plan, provided Anil's second key could be successfully tested by Manu. Nesto Suarez, who had been so terrified of the sadistic animal who had tied him to a chair he would have agreed to about anything in that moment, so long as it secured his freedom.

Tom shifted his position in the driver's seat, turned the radio up a notch. Aerosmith's 'Angel' merged into Cher's 'If I Could Turn Back Time'. The Uruguayans had a natural affinity with the eighties. People in Montevideo seemingly didn't like change.

He checked his phone. Almost eleven: still no Manu. The rain hammered. He had no clue where she lived, how far she would have to come. He wanted to go back to the house, make love to Becca, in a bed this time, not fumbling around like two adolescents hiding from their parents.

There were things he knew he didn't understand. Was Belosi a hired thug? How did Denham know Belosi? How did Becca know Capricorn?

He tried in vain to set his mind on Becca, to avoid thinking about the events in Barrio Sur that morning. In the room that had resembled yet another crack den, Belosi was wielding a cheap-looking stun gun as he encircled his victim, the latter drooling freely through the gag. The scent reminded him of a place he couldn't picture – or had perhaps blocked from his mind – of some ramshackle buildings on the outskirts of Lashkargah, shelled to shit, the stench of blood and rubble in the air.

Belosi had yanked off the gag, causing Nesto to gasp for air.

'Who is this?' Tom breathed in Spanish.

Nesto went quiet, sensing another presence in the room, blindly searching. Belosi circled him, looking to Tom. 'This is your power cut,' he said. 'This is Nesto Suarez.'

'What does he do?'

'Tell him, Nesto!' Belosi bellowed, 'What is your job?'

'I—, I—, I work for Usinas y Trasmisiones Eléctricas,' Nesto stammered in Spanish. 'I am a senior engineer within the company.'

'U... T... E...,' Belosi repeated slowly, for Tom's benefit. 'The Uruguayan state-owned power company. Nesto has a unique position within UTE, don't you, Nesto? Want to tell me about it?'

Nesto was shaking all over. 'I—, I—, I— control p-power supplies to the whole grid.'

'And you know what that means?' Belosi said.

Tom nodded once. He felt sick.

'Nesto here will do whatever it is you want him to do. He has the authority; he doesn't require prior permission from his superiors. And he knows what will happen if he doesn't comply. Don't you, Nesto?'

Without warning, Belosi swung round, jabbing the plastic stun gun into the rolls of Nesto's ample belly. Nesto let out an excruciating cry, writhing in his seat, followed swiftly by more sobbing. Tom took a step back, a knot of anguish in his stomach. Belosi was truly a psychopath.

'Tell me, Nesto,' Belosi repeated. 'What will I do?'

'You will go after V-Valencia,' Nesto stuttered.

'*Siiii, correcto.*'

'Who is Valencia?' Tom asked.

'Nesto has a girl. He's going to marry her. She works in a bank in Carrasco.'

'Please,' Nesto begged. 'Please don't hurt her.'

Belosi was looking at Tom, dark eyes questioning. 'Well?'

Tom nodded once, continued in Spanish. 'Nesto. Do you know Aves de Las Colinas? It's a secure complex on the other side of town.'

Nesto was nodding frantically.

'We need a power cut, Nesto,' Tom said, approaching him. 'To the entire compound, at very specific times. Can you do that for us?'

Nesto kept nodding his head, whimpering, eyes pleading. Right now, if someone told him the only way out of this situation was to shoot himself in the head, he would probably have done it.

Tom looked to Belosi, gave him a single nod of approval.

'Nesto!' Belosi said, raising his voice but keeping his eyes squarely on Tom. 'It looks like you are free to go today.'

'To go?' Nesto whispered.

'I will be watching you, Nesto. You try to run, I will drag you back. You aid her escape, I will drag you both back. You call the police, you will both be dead, is that clear?'

Nesto nodded.

Belosi approached Tom, firing off a crack of the stun gun.

Nesto bolted upright, bracing himself. Belosi leered towards Tom. 'When you are ready, get a message to the lawyer. Nesto will be at your service.'

He could tell by her shuffle, the way her boots splashed through the puddles, that it was Manuela. She held onto a broken umbrella, clutching it low, her head not visible to him as she approached. Tom stepped out from the car, began walking towards her. The rain had eased slightly. It didn't matter to him. They stood facing one another on the fringes of the playground.

She apologised for being late, thinking he would have waited until the rain stopped.

Tom reached inside his pocket before pressing the new key for the security door into her palm. She looked down at it.

'*Una vez más, por favor*,' he said. *One more time.*

She nodded, wrapping her fingers around it and tucking the key inside her coat. '*Mi señora*, she tells me today she is taking the children away in January. They go to Argentina and to Brazil. Señor Feliciano, he will go with them. They will give me the dog to take care of. The house will be empty for one month.'

She spoke quickly, as if regurgitating what Sabina Cordero had told her that day, word for word. Though it was dark, he could still see the guilt of betraying her employer etched all over her face.

'That's very good, Manuela,' Tom said. 'Thank you. I need one more thing.'

She looked at him, eyes pleading.

He wiped rain water from his face. 'I need you to get a

look at the safe. Tell me what it looks like. How big it is. If it has a make or a brand name on it. If it has a keypad or a dial.'

She nodded in mute understanding. They stood in silence, all business transactions complete.

'Tomorrow night,' Tom said, pressing some pesos into her hand. 'Send Alejandro with the key.'

For a long while he sat in the driver's seat of the Vitara, listening to the radio playing a Spanish ballad. He turned down the volume, switched it off altogether, inside of the vehicle reverberating to the sound of the rain.

A working key was one of the final pieces of the puzzle. Up until that point, he had been cocky enough to believe in their guaranteed success, that the job could not possibly fail.

His mind swirled. The sight of Nesto had unnerved him. The notion of what Sancho could do to any of them and the possibility that Capricorn never intended to let any of them walk free whether they handed over the contents of the safe or not.

★★★★★

'Let's start with what we know,' Tom said, standing in front of the assembled easel, complete with a hand-drawn sketch map of Las Colinas and the surrounding area: Becca, Anil and Ray assembled on the sofas surrounding the fireplace. 'Manuela told me that Sabina Cordero and her husband are going away in January. The house will be empty for the whole month. That gives us plenty of time to prepare. That is, if the current key works.'

'It's gonna work, man,' Anil piped up. 'No doubt.'

'As you know, the Argentine has secured us some help from the power company. We tell him when we want the power to go down, and when we want it to come back on again, giving us enough time to get into the compound through the pipe.'

'In wetsuits,' Becca added.

He remained unconvinced by Anil's choice of attire. 'In wetsuits,' he repeated. 'Ray will drop us off here, on the far side of the quarry, around midnight or shortly after,' he continued, pointing to a red spot on the map, indicating the same point on the same road that Ray had left them the last time. 'We make our way across the quarry, before the power goes down. Then, blackout. We go through the pipe, over the barrier, wade through the water to the strip of land between the plant and the lake. We need to get to that point before the power goes back on.'

'What?' Ray blurted. 'You're switching the power back on? While you're inside?'

Tom ignored him. 'We stay in the shadow, make our way around the backs of the houses, down the side of the ninth hole, to house 8024 and Sabina Cordero's back garden.'

'With the power on. With the lights on,' Ray repeated, incredulous.

'If we don't switch the power back on quickly enough, the guards will increase their patrols on foot around the perimeter. Keeping the power off indicates a serious problem and warrants investigation. We'll give Nesto a timeframe; have him switch the power back off again a few hours later. There's no CCTV on the inside of the compound, remember.

Once we get past those houses we'll be covered by darkness.'

'And if we don't manage to crack open the safe within the given timeframe?' Becca asked.

'Let's say we get to the house around 1 a.m. We break in *and* access the study where the safe is within thirty minutes to an hour. We'll then have less than three and a half hours to get the safe open before we need to get out of there. We need to get out before the power goes back off again, with enough time to get back to the water and the pipe. If we don't manage it in that time... '

The group fell silent. Ray chewed his nails.

'Then we clear out like we were never even there,' Anil said.

'Agreed,' Tom reiterated.

'Clean up a break-in?' Becca frowned.

Tom ran his fingers through his hair. He didn't have an answer.

Becca shook her head. 'You make this all sound so easy.'

Anil sank further down in his chair. 'Easy, schmeazy. I'm not gonna need three and a half hours to get into a metal box. My money is on the family owning a cheap Chinese-made safe they bought from the supermarket. All I need is a magnet. Failing that a power drill and a crowbar. The safe part is not something you should be worrying about. That's my domain, yeah?'

Becca rolled her eyes.

Tom heard his phone ring in his bedroom. Glad to escape the tension in the room, he shut himself away, swiped up the handset. Denham.

'We need to talk,' the lawyer said.

'We can talk now,' Tom said. 'There have been some developments.'

'We can talk tomorrow. Let's have lunch. I'm in Uruguay.'

'I'm sorry, what?'

'I said I'm in Uruguay. Brought my wife for a beach holiday. Arrived a few hours ago. We're staying in José Ignacio, it's up the coast.'

His mind was reeling. 'I know where it is.'

'Good. Meet me at La Huella restaurant. Tomorrow, 1 p.m. It's on the beach. Look it up.'

'It's pronounced *Hu-ay-ja*. It means footprint.'

'I don't need to hear the benefits of your private education, Holt. Don't be late. And bring Becca with you.'

'Becca?'

'You heard me. Bring her with you.'

It was after eleven. Back in the car, parked up next to the playground in darkness, facing the opposite direction this time, with a view in his wing mirror looking north up Costa Rica street. Insisting on accompanying him, Anil was in the passenger seat, jittery. They waited for Alejandro.

Denham was in Uruguay. He'd come all this way to tell Tom something he couldn't say over the phone. And Becca too, Denham wanted to see her. Did he know about them? Had Ray said something? Ray could have guessed something had happened but he wouldn't have known anything for sure. They'd given nothing away.

Alejandro came into his wing mirror, riding style so distinctive that Tom didn't flinch.

He switched on the engine, used the controls to lower

the driver's side window to halfway. Anil straightened in his seat. It wasn't long before Alejandro drew up alongside the vehicle.

'*Qué dijo, Alejandro?*' Tom asked. *What did she say?*

Alejandro raised his hand, pressing the key wrapped in a slip of paper onto the inside of the lowered window pane for Tom to take. Without looking at Tom, for even the briefest of moments, the boy kept his eyes on the road looking north.

'*Si, Señor,*' he said, before adding, '*la clave funciona.*'

Moments later Alejandro was gone. Tom raised the window, unfolded the paper.

On it was written three things:

Negro
Teclado numérico
Guardia Duro 20L

Anil was looking at him hopefully. 'Was that a yes?'

'It was a yes,' Tom said, handing over the key and the paper, putting the car into gear. 'The safe is black, has a numbered keypad. It's made by Guardia Duro. You can buy them in the hypermarket down the road.'

Anil punched the air.

Chapter 20

Becca emerged from the house into the garage as Tom was throwing a backpack in the boot of the Vitara, Ray lingering in the driveway. He hadn't said so out loud, but she could tell Ray was peeved that Denham hadn't asked to see him in José Ignacio. That he thought he was being side-lined and left behind, with Anil, no less: who he now saw as the other, *less* important member of the crew.

'Ask him what he's doing here,' Ray was saying.

'It's my first question, Ray, don't worry. I'm as curious as you are,' Tom said.

'He's a man who likes to be reassured.'

'I'll reassure him. You have my word.'

She wore a short cut-off denim skirt and floaty V-neck vest with spaghetti straps. Tried not to dress with him in mind. She'd watched his face carefully, taking note of any reaction when he'd seen her. He hadn't flinched.

'Anything else?' Tom asked, putting on his sunglasses.

'You know it's only a couple of hours drive if that,' Ray said. 'It's not even nine.'

She waited beside the passenger side door, curious to hear Tom's response.

'We'll take it easy along the coastal road. Stop in Punta del Este on route. Might as well see the sights whilst we're here.

Wouldn't want to be late for Mr Denham.'

Becca yanked open the door. If it was possible to be smiling on the inside, it was exactly what she was doing.

She got into the car. Tom removed the padlock from the gate, opened it, handed the padlock to Ray. He got into the car and started the engine, hood already down. They backed out of the driveway, Ray waving them off, closing the gate. Tom drove an odd route round the block as she clasped her hands in her lap. Less than a hundred yards from the house he turned a corner onto a dirt track. He put the car in park, switched off the engine, removing his sunglasses. For a moment, she didn't move, staring forward at nothing through the windscreen. There was only the motion of their chests rising and falling, almost in unison.

'So,' she said. 'What are the sights exactly?'

A small smile flickered across his features. He was on her then, as desperate for her as she was for him. It was a hot and heavy kiss, hands grasping at him, underneath his shirt, wherever space allowed. When she broke away, he pulled her back in.

'We need to go,' she said, between kisses.

'We could stop en route,' he told her.

'Where?' she asked.

*****

'Tell me about Capricorn.'

Her head was resting on his chest, listening to the pulsating rhythm of his heart. The moment he said the words, overwhelming disappointment surged in her veins.

Had it all been a ploy?

The road to Punta del Este, the beach resort about one hundred and thirty kilometres east of Montevideo, had been, for the most part, straight and flat. He'd kept to his word, kept his foot down, sending the wind through her hair. The hood down made conversation impossible, but every now and then he had offered her a smile that had filled her with an unfamiliar sensation, if only for a fleeting few seconds. She felt freedom, from Capricorn, from Anton, Denham, from all the men who exerted some form of control over her life and her decisions, and all that she had left behind. Tom drove with one hand on the steering wheel, the other hand holding onto hers, fingers entwined.

Entering Punta del Este, she'd seen the ocean, rough waves spewing up white foam onto the shore. She'd unbuckled her seatbelt, pulled herself up to almost standing to look over the top edge of the windscreen, breathing in the air. Tom pointed at a building on the road ahead, rising like an iceberg out of the sea. It looked like the grandest hotel she had ever seen.

On arrival Tom had passed the keys to the Vitara to a valet, negotiated with a male receptionist for a good rate on an ocean-view room. Kissed her in the lift, deliberate, purposeful, drawing her close. She'd spent her entire life avoiding eye contact with every individual on the street, to make herself forgettable. When she allowed herself to look up at Tom Holt, it felt like she was exposing him to darkest corners of her soul. In the room, he'd opened the balcony door, the breeze whipping up the net curtain, stopping her when she'd tried to dim the light, ripping off clothes, breathless, aching. So this was what the fuss was all about.

She'd never had a boyfriend, never been with a man for more than a single encounter. And none of those had been worth the briefest time it had taken. She'd never felt this overwhelming ache to be this close to one individual.

And here she was, curled up naked beside him, ear to his chest, listening to the gentle *thud-thudding* of his heartbeat, fingers rested against his collarbone, stroking his skin, the sun through the net curtain sending little shafts of orange and yellow across the room, the blissful, post-coital moment about to come to an end in the time it took him to utter four little words.

Tell me about Capricorn.

She allowed his request to sink in for a split second before pulling herself away, untangling the sheet from her legs, getting out of the bed. Hunted around for her clothes, swiping them up one by one from the carpet. Shutters down.

Tom pulled himself up onto his elbows. 'What?'

'Is that why we're here?' she snapped, wriggling back into her underwear. 'You get me to spread my legs then tell you everything?'

'Those two things are completely separate,' he shot back. 'Us making love and me asking you about something I know nothing about.'

'There's nothing to tell. Capricorn is the client. He's the one with the money. Succeed and you will get paid, fail and you don't, believe me, he has an endless supply of funds.'

'You sound like Denham.'

'Denham's not lying.'

'So why the secrecy? What's the harm in telling me who he really is?'

She fastened her skirt, wrestling her top back on, saying nothing. Smoothed down her hair, looking around for her shoes. Moved to the bathroom, unable to bear the way he was looking at her, eyes helpless, pleading, searching for some ounce of truth in the situation.

She splashed water onto her face, used a tissue to fix her makeup. In the next-door room, he was pulling his clothes back on. She allowed herself one last look.

'Tell me one thing,' he said as she emerged from the bathroom. 'Is it money they're offering you? Or is it something else?'

He had his back to her.

'My brother,' she said, after a moment. 'My brother is in prison. I do this for Capricorn, my brother will be free.'

When he turned around, she noticed the handgun tucked into his belt.

They drove in stony silence along the coast, over a double-humped bridge around a cove to the town of La Barra, a kind of surfer's paradise. Stayed on the coastal road, the landscape suddenly much sparser, sand rising into knife edges on the coastal side. They passed through two minute towns signposted as Manantiales and El Chorro. Occasionally they would pass a single house raised on stilts, surrounded by nothing but sandy wasteland. It occurred to her that a person could live anonymously here; hide under a rock from the rest of the wider world. Out in the ocean there was nothing: a cargo ship, an equally tiny speck on the horizon.

A lighthouse came into view over the waves. In the driver's seat, Tom gripped the steering wheel. The ocean disappeared then, concealed from view by more smooth dunes. José Ignacio was the size of a village, a haven as far as she was concerned, far from anywhere. The type of place she dreamed of escaping to if ever that became a possibility. Seagulls swooped overhead. She felt nervous, as curious about Denham making a sudden appearance as both Ray and Tom seemed to be.

They parked the car opposite a swanky boutique, housed in a glorified beach hut selling marine-themed homewares. Sat in silence for a moment. She contemplated how quickly the mood had changed in the space of four hours. The scent of him lingered on her skin.

'Is the gun for Denham?' she asked.

'No,' he said, as he adjusted the rear-view mirror, checking his hair. 'The gun is in case Fede ever decides to leave Buenos Aires for Uruguay.'

'You think that would ever happen?'

'I wouldn't be carrying a gun if I didn't.'

He moved the weapon to the glove compartment, snapped it shut. Outside there was a light grey-coloured wooden building attracting a steady flow of customers. 'I think that's the place,' she said.

She waited as Tom put the hood up on the car. They kept their distance on approach, walking two metres width apart. Tom was wearing a white shirt with the sleeves rolled up, sunglasses, boat shoes and knee-length pale green shorts. Not bad for a November day. He even had decent legs. Becca swallowed, dragged her mind back to the present, felt her heartbeat quicken at the thought of seeing the lawyer again.

La Huella seemed to be a glorified beach hut, a restaurant buried deep in fine white sand, and a popular joint too. Outside on the veranda was the epitome of salty beach chic: all-white sofas, pale oak weather-beaten chairs. Bottle-blonde-haired women wore denim cut-offs, brown leather sandals and their husbands' white shirts tied in knots at the navel. Becca pushed the hair from her eyes. This was how the other half lived.

Tom enquired about a reservation and they were both ushered inside to deep red walls, past a bustling bar towards the back of the restaurant.

He was sat with his back to them, but she would recognise Albert Denham anywhere: the broad shoulders, brown wavy hair with a copper hue. Tatiana – the wife – was with him. Becca remembered her from the couple's wedding ceremony: the wedding few of those in attendance actually believed was based on any genuine feeling. At the time, she'd been ordered to attend by Anton, the man from whom she received the majority of her instructions. At the table, Tatiana was wearing a halter-neck top with a deep V, bordering on inappropriate, blonde hair parted straight down the middle with a short cropped fringe.

Tatiana nodded her head in their direction, causing Denham to turn around and get out of his chair. He wore a blue linen shirt, falling open at the chest. Tatiana got out of her seat, brushed past Becca with pursed lips as she made her exit without a word, giving her the same look she had given Becca at her wedding ceremony; a look of indifference at another face in a crowd.

He greeted them with a half-smile, shook Tom's hand,

kissed her cheek. She wondered if he could smell the odour of freshly-had sex on her. 'You lost weight,' Denham said to Tom. 'I'm impressed.'

She looked back, didn't hear Tom's response. Tatiana was gone, gliding through a crowded place, one more guardian of Capricorn's secrets.

Becca eased herself into the seat at the table, back to the ocean, copying Tom's lead. Denham signalled a waitress and ordered a bottle of local wine. Tom had looked the place up. According to some newspaper, so he'd said, the town of José Ignacio was the swankiest in South America, a far-flung place where celebrities escaped for a little peace.

'The ruby red Tannat, that's what they call it,' Denham enthused about the wine, brandishing the label. 'French never mastered the grape. Might have to take a bottle back in my suitcase.'

The Denham opposite her seemed coarser than the one she remembered from shadowy London cafés.

'Why are you here?' Tom said.

'Tatiana wanted to go kite-surfing. There's a lake a bit further up the coast. *Laguna Garzon* they call it. Keeps trying to drag me out there. Amazing weather you're having.'

'So you came all this way for a holiday and to pick up a bottle of Uruguayan wine.'

She thought she saw Denham flinch. 'I think you know why I came.'

Becca watched Tom lean forward, keeping his voice low. 'You see, that's the thing about all of this. I haven't the first clue why you're here. I am completely in the dark. I have been from day one.'

Denham mirrored Tom's stance as he leaned forward. 'You seemed happy enough when I saw you in July. You want information, fine, I get that. I bring a message from my client. He wants you to move now. You need to get the job done.'

'What?' Becca blurted.

The waitress returned with copies of the menu, poured the wine. There was a silence as they waited for her to move away.

'My client is not a patient man. He needs the contents of the safe, he needs them now.'

'Are you out of your mind?' Becca hissed again across the table. 'We're not ready.'

This time, she found herself under the scrutiny of Denham's glare. He was deadly serious. 'Then *be* ready.'

Tom shook his head. 'Our timescale is January. The maid says Sabina Cordero and her family go away for a month. We move now we risk fucking the whole thing up.'

Denham's eyebrows snapped together. 'There isn't time. January is height of summer in Uruguay. It starts getting light at four in the morning. Even now the days are getting shorter and shorter. You need to move now whilst there is still a long enough period of darkness at night.'

'We go now, we'll be caught,' she said.

'Becca's right,' Tom echoed. 'We go before we're ready and we risk everything we've worked for. We'll end up in a cell, or worse, shot on sight. You'll never see the contents of that safe.'

Denham's features darkened. 'You don't get this done, you don't get paid. There will be no financial reward, simple as that. And you –' He was staring her down again. Her stomach flipped over, guilty that she hadn't thought about Richie that day, her mind on someone else entirely. 'Well, you know what happens.'

Richie: languishing in a cell. She glared at Denham with gritted teeth, chest rising and falling, grappling with her composure, the urge to dive across the table and grab the lawyer by the throat almost overpowering. 'Why the hurry?' she asked.

Denham relaxed a little, shrugged his broad shoulders. 'It is what it is.'

'That's not a reason,' Becca hissed under her breath, perhaps knowing she was not going to receive a legitimate one.

'Then how do you propose we break into the safe with Sabina Cordero's entire family still sleeping in the house?' Tom asked.

'There are plans afoot to have the entire family go to Buenos Aires for a few days, potentially more.'

'What plan?'

'The brother. Nicolás Cordero.'

Becca shifted in her seat, memories flooding back. She and Tom exchanged glances. 'Nico.'

Denham nodded. 'Nico, that's the one. Nico will be involved in a... let's call it a near-fatal accident. In about five days' time. The sister, Sabina, will want to be by his side, naturally. When she realises the seriousness of his condition, the rest of the family should follow. The house will be vacated.'

She let the information wash over her. Tom sat back in his chair. Outside, the sun was beating down; waves crashing.

She could hear laughter on the white sand, metal chinking on ceramic plates, voices all around her chattering. The waitress was heading back over and she had lost her appetite. She pictured Nico, swarthy and not all that smart, cheating on his girlfriend yet somehow still quite caring and considerate. She even felt sorry for him.

'The Argentine,' Tom stated.

'The man has his uses.'

She pictured Sancho Belosi – as Tom had described him – approaching Nico from behind on a dark street in Buenos Aires, clobbering him over the head with a sharp implement, or mowing him down in a car, sending his brains splattering across the pavement but somehow managing to keep him alive with hardly a pulse. From what Anton had told her, Belosi had a talent for prolonging a gruesome death.

'We'll need him here,' Tom was arguing. 'He's our link to the guy from the power company.'

'You don't need to worry yourselves about that. Our friend will be here. I'll give you the signal.'

Tom leaned forward again. 'Your henchman is no friend of mine.'

The waitress returned and asked if they were having lunch, peeved when Tom answered in Spanish that they were still deciding. She turned on her heel.

'So you should ready yourselves,' Denham began in a lighter tone, raising his glass once she was gone again. 'You have the key to the secure door, you have everything you need.'

She looked to Tom, a look of irritation on his face. Denham had been talking to Ray. They'd both known it was happening, accepting that it would annoy Tom that he hadn't been the one to break the news about the working key. Not that it would have made a difference. Ray had been the spy in their midst from the outset. She might have worked for Capricorn, but she certainly didn't go around telling him everything.

Denham swirled his glass, stuck his nose in and inhaled the odour before smacking his lips in approval.

'I need to talk to Becca,' Denham said, addressing Tom, 'Alone.'

She looked to Denham, then to Tom.

'I need five minutes.'

Tom rose slowly from his chair, an indignant look on his face, as if this invitation-only non-lunch could not have been any more bizarre. Talk of unnamed clients, Argentines, near-fatal accidents and now secret discussions with her. She experienced another wave of guilt, mind flashing back to the hotel room an hour earlier, her naked body writhing against his. Having him leave the table felt like a betrayal.

'I'll be outside,' Tom deadpanned. 'On the beach.'

'Not bad looking, is he?' Denham said when he was gone.

'I didn't know you were that way inclined.'

'Are you sleeping with him?'

Her heart raced. 'Is that coming from you or Mr Capricorn?'

Denham poured the contents of her wine glass into his own, now empty glass. 'I couldn't give a shit if you were. What Capricorn wants to know is, is his identity still a secret from Holt? Or have you managed to give it away?'

'Like a superhero, his secret identity is safe,' she said. It was her turn to lean forward. 'And every day that my brother is still in jail, I get closer and closer to giving it all away.'

'Richie has a parole hearing. Two weeks yesterday.'

Her eyes widened. 'Why didn't you tell me?'

Denham shrugged. 'Capricorn wanted me to tell you in person.'

'Will he get it? Will he get parole?'

Denham took another mouthful from his glass. 'Capricorn wants you home. He's got another job for you to do.'

'When?'

'Now.'

'What? No. I can't, I'm needed here.'

'For what? Moral support?' Denham scoffed. 'I think you've served your purpose. They don't need you here. Capricorn needs you.'

Becca's eyes narrowed. 'He doesn't want to *lose* me, is that it? But the rest of them he can afford to lose? If they are caught and incarcerated, it doesn't matter because I was never here?'

Denham sat back. 'I pass messages. Maybe wait until you get back to Montevideo before you tell Holt, *hmm*?' He was reaching into his shirt pocket for a slimline wallet, pulling out a wad of pesos.

'What happened to you? When did you become such a slave?'

His eyes snapped up, glaring at her. His expression softened as quickly. 'Listen, I'll get this. Why don't you and Holt stay for lunch? I recommend the Octopus Carpaccio, it's really delicious.'

'Tell him I said no.'

Denham paused, looked a fraction surprised. 'Are you sure?'

'I'll come back when the job is done. Not before.'

Denham got to his feet, downed the wine, put down his glass and kept his fingers resting on the rim. 'If that's your decision, then tell Holt I said good luck. You're going to need it.'

Becca remained seated. *Fuck you*, she wanted to say. Denham stood, loomed above her.

'Tell him five days from now, you'll be hearing from me. It's time.'

Chapter 21

'Are you ready?'

Five gut-churning days. Five days of sitting, pacing, waiting for the call to come. Five days of too much rain – three out of the five – the marshland at the back of *Colinas* liable to flood. Manu sobbing in the back seat of the Vitara, remorse etched on her features. *We need the code for the intruder alarm, Manu. We won't ask you to betray your employer again. We don't know if those* maleantes... *if they'll take your grandson, Manu. We don't know what will happen if you don't give us what we want. You have to do as we say.*

Think of Alejandro, Manu. Think of his future.

'Ready as I'll ever be.'

In José Ignacio, Becca had been alone at the table when he'd returned from the beach. She'd told him Denham's demands: that she return to London, abandon ship. On the ride home they hadn't spoken. At El Pinar, the small beach community on the edge of Canelones, a four-kilometre drive from the house, he'd pulled over on a dirt road, switched off the engine.

'He's right to ask you to go back. Your employer. It would

have been his plan all along, I see that now. You've served your purpose here. He doesn't want to risk you getting caught.'

'I'm not leaving,' she'd said. 'I'm not leaving you.'

There had been a pause. A visual acknowledgement that maybe she felt more than she was letting on. She'd kissed him then. He'd kissed her back until they were both breathless.

'Anil and I can go,' he'd said, leaning his forehead against hers.

She'd recoiled. 'When was the last time you broke into a house?'

'I could ask you the same question.'

'Six months before I flew to Buenos Aires. I was tasked with breaking into a detached gated property in West Dulwich to steal a briefcase. And I went in during daylight hours.'

He'd looked at her, feeling like he didn't know her at all.

'So perhaps I should be the one to go with Anil,' she'd added.

'Look, whoever Capricorn is, he sees you as a valuable asset. Whatever he's promised you, for coming here, I am sure he will absolutely take it away if you don't do as he asks. And I'm guessing that means your brother.'

Tears had sprung to her eyes. She fought them off. After a few moments, she nodded, capitulating out of frustration, agreeing to stay with Ray on the night but remain in Uruguay. Those were her terms.

The call came on the Thursday as they were gathered together at the table eating lunch.

'Phone,' Anil piped up, the moment they heard the sound. Becca's eyes shot up. Tom put down his sandwich, chair scraping across the floor as he got to his feet. He walked to the bedroom, pulse racing.

Denham, back in London. 'Nico Cordero's in hospital. Sabina Cordero took an Aerolíneas flight to Buenos Aires this morning. I have eyes watching to see what the family will do. Get ready to move tomorrow night.'

'We need to get confirmation to the Argentine. The guy from the power company—'

'It's in hand.'

'1.05 the power goes out. Not a minute later.'

'There's something else.'

'What?'

'A condition from my client. Whatever you come across in that safe, you're not to look at it. You don't inspect. You do nothing. You seal it all in a bag, you bring it out. And your reward is guaranteed. Do you understand?'

Tom paced in the bedroom. Rolled his eyes, threw back his head, pulled a variety of exasperated expressions. Wished he could look Capricorn in the eye. 'I understand,' he agreed.

He hung up, returning to the table. Becca, Anil and Ray were waiting. Nobody touched their food, looking to him for answers.

'We're good to go,' he said. 'Tomorrow night. Nico's in hospital. Denham thinks the family will clear out.'

Anil whistled, made the sound of an object in a cartoon dropping over a cliff before exploding on the ground in a plume of smoke. Ray ignored him, returned his attention to his food.

'There's something else,' Tom announced. 'Whatever we find in that safe; we're not to look at it. We seal it up, smuggle it out. Otherwise we don't get paid.'

Anil stifled a laugh. 'We're not allowed to look at diamonds and wads of cash?'

'It would seem that way.'

'So I could swipe a coupla dem stones for myself, right? Who's gonna know?'

'Did you confirm the time for the power outage?' Ray asked, spitting his food.

'Five minutes past one.'

'What happened to Nico?' Anil said as a hush descended over the room.

'I didn't ask.'

Friday 11 November, 2016

'Are you ready?'

11.30 p.m. He sat on the bed, bare-chested, legs covered by a black wetsuit up to his waist, staring out at the darkness through the window. Wondered where he would be at the same time the next night, and the one after that.

Sleep had come briefly. In his dreams, he had died in various gruesome ways: mauled by a dog, drowning in the pipe, shot at point blank range in the chest. Always waking in a sweat. He felt weary before they'd even got going, mouth dry, pulse racing.

Sabina Cordero's house at Las Colinas was empty. That morning, Denham had confirmed that Feliciano Ledesma and their children had departed on an Aerolíneas flight for Buenos Aires from Carrasco International Airport. Manu had taken the dog.

'I said, are you ready?'

She was waiting in the doorway, watching him, shoulder leaning against the frame. She'd wanted to come. She was angry, now that she'd been denied the opportunity. Hadn't said as much but he knew it. She closed the door behind her, approached him from behind, crawling across the sheets, wrapping her arms around him.

'Ready as I'll ever be,' he said, resting his hand over hers. 'Never thought I'd die wearing a fucking wetsuit.'

She laughed, kissed his neck. He wasn't sure the laugh was genuine. Wanted to tell her he was serious. Instead he laughed gently along with her in the moment, because it might have been their last, until his fingers came into contact with cold metal.

He glanced down, saw it on her wrist. 'Is that my watch?'

'Took you long enough to notice.'

His head snapped around. 'You took that off my wrist?'

She released the metal clasp, let the watch fall into his palm. 'Maybe I did. Maybe I didn't.'

He fixed the watch on his wrist with a shake of his head. She liked him to believe she was that good.

'Make sure you're out of the house before the power goes down again,' she murmured. 'Give yourself enough time to get out.'

'And if we have nothing to show for it?'

'You get out anyway.'

He nodded, felt her hand at his back. 'Promise me you'll leave,' she whispered.

'We'll get out,' he said. 'I promise.'

11.55. Friday night fading to Saturday. Tom still in his bedroom: sweaty in head to foot neoprene, feeling like he was about to go scuba-diving. He'd packed a small backpack, in case they had to get out of the house quick, left it under the bed. They had spent the day clearing the house, removing any evidence of their ever being there, wiping down surfaces, taking a pile of bin bags to separate locations along Avenida Giannattasio, erasing their existence. The escape plan was last minute, but in his mind, at least they were planning on making an escape.

Anil was waiting in the kitchen when he got there, lights dimmed low, head shaved and also wearing a wetsuit.

'Is the haircut purely cosmetic, or… ' Tom asked.

Anil wiped a palm over his scalp. 'Aerodynamics, yeah?'

'Whose idea was this getup again?'

'Mine.'

'Then when the shit goes down, I'm blaming you, Anil.'

'You'll thank me when we're through that pipe.'

The pipe. One of the many unknowns they would encounter along the way, unknowns that were tying his stomach in knots. Anil was holding onto his bag – a backpack – its contents held securely in double black bin bags for water resistance. They had practiced how long it would take to get inside. Tom knew exactly what it contained: a crowbar, a rare-earth magnet inside a sock inside a plastic container, a pair of gloves, battery-powered hand-held drill, a set of clothes wrapped in a plastic bag. In his own bag – a black backpack with a single cross-torso strap – a torch, a pair of gloves, clothes to go over the wetsuit inside a plastic bag that would then be used for whatever they found in Sabina

Cordero's safe. Finally, the key to the secure door, looped around his neck. He had asked Denham for an approximate size and weight of their intended loot. The answer had come back not to worry.

'Remember we're three nights away from a full moon. Sunrise begins at 4.55 a.m., it will be light by 5.30,' Becca said, addressing them both. 'Power goes down at four-fifteen. That gives you about three hours in the house if everything goes to plan.'

He could tell she was anxious. She'd barely eaten a thing all day. None of them had.

'We went through this already, yeah?' Anil reminded her. 'You're making me nervous. If I can't do it in three then I'm never gonna crack it.'

Tom held out his hand. 'Good luck, my friend.'

Anil shook it. 'Fuck that. You stand or you fall.'

He kept his position low in the back of the Tempo, legs straddling the moth-eaten passenger seat in front, holes in the fabric, disintegrating pink sponge spilling out. Nobody spoke. They had said their good lucks. In the front, Ray drove a steady sixty-five, back tyres throwing up clouds of dust into the night. Tom questioned whether he'd had him all wrong from the start, if Ray wasn't just a decent guy, there to do his best and get paid.

Ray had re-sprayed the main body of the car. Kept it in the garage, dusty and mud-splattered to blend in, sporadically checking the engine was still working. The car was the least of their worries as they crossed at the junction of the *Interbalnearia*, empty of motorway traffic. At the *Marmoleria*, the barn-like structure that sold marble worktop-surface slabs, Ray took a sharp left down the dirt road, disappearing from view into the isolated darkness of the Canelones landscape.

So many unknowns. So much untested. Becca reached up, slid her hand through underneath her headrest. He reached up and grasped it, catching Anil's wry smile in the shadows.

He wondered if they would ever reach the safe or if they were doomed from the start. Thought about his two brothers. Knew he should have called them, got a message to them somehow, his mother too, in case it all went sour. Apologise for the past, in case he never made it back.

They needed more time. Was it Denham doing this on purpose? What was it that Capricorn needed so badly? He tried to focus, mind in a tailspin. Fear crept up from his toes, adrenaline coursing through his veins. The gambler inside him found it thrilling. The security consultant inside was screaming out risk percentages versus threat levels, their chances of getting caught spiralling with every passing second spent inside the fence.

To his left out of the window, over the tips of the bulrushes, he glimpsed the glow emanating from Colinas that came from the floodlights around the perimeter fence, the intensity so bright the sky above the complex was ablaze.

The dip in the road came into view. Ray killed the headlights. Not long after, he braked. They were at the bottom of the slope, in the shadows underneath the overgrown tree.

Simultaneously, he and Anil opened their doors. Tom waited for Anil to move around to his side of the car, taking a second to glance through the passenger-side window. Her face was obscured but he could still make out the whites of her eyes. Becca pressed her palm flat up against the glass. Tom did the same on the outside. If everything went to schedule, he would see her again in a matter of hours.

The car moved off, grit from the dirt road crackling underneath the tyres. He moved deeper into the shadows, kept low, the branches from the tree nudging him in the back, watched the vehicle get smaller and smaller before disappearing from view, reappearing as two red dots when Ray switched the lights back on, the one advantage of a car so decrepit it had no automatic sensors.

No turning back.

Anil followed suit, offering up a nervous glance. *Hold your nerve*, Tom thought to himself, then gave Anil a swift thump on the back.

He was starting to sweat. It was a warm night and he was wearing a thick layer of thermal insulation, a backpack on his back. It hadn't occurred to him to check the thickness measurement of the suit, or argue with Anil that a black, long-sleeved rash guard might have been more appropriate attire for Uruguay in late spring. Making their way around the base of the tree towards the entrance of the quarry, he felt the moisture trickling down his torso.

In the moonlight, the grass *swish-swished* against his legs and the fabric of his shoes. He walked out in front, Anil a few strides behind. The terrain altered, the quarry unfurling like an open stage. It had rained three times in the past five days, heavily at times, yet the mud beneath their feet still kicked up a fine powder in the darkness. He kept an eye out for sinkholes. The house on the hill was shrouded in shadow, nobody home. The only light to guide them came from Las Colinas. Tom glanced at the watch on his wrist, pulse quickening. Fifteen minutes to blackout. He kept walking as far as the barbed wire, crouched down and slid underneath.

Descending to the marsh, the cicadas once more appeared to be warning him off, telling him to turn back, to return to his old life, the life he had supposedly left behind. After tonight, it occurred to him, it might not have even been a possibility.

He felt a sharp tug on the wetsuit zipper pull, yanking him backward.

'Get low,' Anil hissed. They dropped to the ground. Ahead, at the Colinas perimeter fence, a guard patrolled under the electrified wire with a slobbering Alsatian. They were close enough to hear the dog's ragged breaths, could see the earth being kicked up by its paws.

They had reached the marsh that bordered Las Colinas. Tom saw it, drew a sharp breath. The water level was high, much higher than they had anticipated; the run-off from the higher ground. The pipe was there, barely visible, less than ten metres away, almost completely flooded. Tom wiped the sweat from his forehead onto his sleeve, waited for the guard and his canine to pass.

They were going to have to swim it.

He'd had visions of one of them drowning, getting caught in the pipe. Anil couldn't bloody handle himself well in water. He felt nauseous.

Time check: eight minutes to blackout. The guard hut to the west was about in sight, impossible to see if it was manned or not.

There was a small patch of ground where the floodlights didn't quite overlap, reachable along the line of the trees around the edge of the marsh. Anil had seen it too, tapped him on the shoulder and pointed. Tom nodded once in confirmation. They moved along the ground, slithering on their bellies, moving around the edge of the water, Special Forces commandos without the war paint, dragging their bags beside them.

From their new position, barely fifteen metres from the fence, Tom could see no light through the pipe. There looked to be about a thirty-centimetre gap at the top, the water stagnant, only space to draw breath.

Any second now.

He checked his watch again, wished he'd been like Becca and done a few extra laps in the pool, training himself to hold his breath. Wondered what the cut in power would look like.

1.05 a.m.

Any second now.

Heart racing. Adrenaline at Helmand levels.

Any second now. Power gone.

Three-two-one.

Any second now. Any—

He looked to Anil. Another wave of heat washed over him, more sweat, drenching him underneath the wetsuit, the whites of Anil's eyes like beacons under the floodlights.

The floodlights. The floodlights still on, still beaming. *Beaming.*

Checked his watch again.

Any. Second. Now.

Fuck. *Fuuuck.*

Chapter 22

The longer they waited, they more exposed they became. He knew that; Anil knew that. The dogs would likely pick up their scent on the next rotation.

It had been one of his guarantees, not one of the unknowns. He had not anticipated Sancho Belosi messing this up.

Nearly five minutes over time. They had not discussed the question of how long they should wait if the lights didn't go out.

Anil was grabbing at his neck, sweltering in the night air.

'We can't stay here,' Tom whispered. 'We need to move.'

'Now?' Anil asked.

Tom looked at his watch. 'Three more minutes.'

Like waiting for a pan of water to boil, three minutes dragged by.

Watching. Listening. Sweating.

'Do we abort?' Anil breathed.

'We retreat. Just a little. Give it a bit longer.'

They moved back in the direction of the quarry, the cicadas seemingly shouting louder, giving away their position.

Anil was now in front, scouring the ground for somewhere to hide. The pipe was thirty metres away.

Tom glanced at his watch. One nineteen.

Something fluttered against his cheek.

A split second later, the lights went out.

It happened without a sound, the Colinas glow ceasing to exist, extinguished in an instant.

Every nerve in his being stood on end.

He couldn't see shit.

'Anil?'

'I'm here.'

He reached out, feeling around, found his companion.

'Go,' Anil hissed, and they were up on their feet, stumbling at first, Tom realising the need for calm, steadying his pace, still shifting fast, knowing they were up against a clock over which they had no control. The stars of the southern hemisphere were beacons now, the vastness of the night sky enveloping them.

They hit the marsh, tightening bag straps, lowering themselves down into icy black depths. The cold hit him first, then the smell, knocking the breath from his lungs, temporarily immobilising him. There were no sounds emerging from the Colinas compound, not yet. There were bugs everywhere, small ones, fizzing past his ears, mosquitoes perhaps, bouncing off his cheeks. The water was up to his neck, shoes moving through silt, Anil behind. The perimeter fence gave off its own reflection in the moonlight. He followed its line until the pipe came into view and they were both able to paddle closer.

At the entry point, he glanced back, clinging to the top of the concrete. Anil looked like he was making progress. Though not a strong swimmer he was able to wade through the water. Above them, dogs barked in the distance. Somewhere in the night, a voice exchange was taking place over radio, impossible to decipher.

Tom removed his bag, pushed it ahead, watching it float on the surface. The army officer inside, now coming to the fore, bellowed *you're a goner, you're dead, you're dead*. The sound inside the pipe was hollow, his ragged breaths emphasised. Water lapped against his chin. The concrete from the sides of the pipe pressed up against his hips and legs but it was still possible to scrape through, aided by the wetsuit, which he'd mentally thanked Anil and God for the moment they'd descended into the marsh. A simple rashguard could have meant hypothermia. Hitting the treadmill had paid off, and chin tilted up he could breathe. Behind him, Anil's entrance into the pipe sent a wave of water forward. He took in a mouthful, gagged, coughed it back again as silently as he could. Before he knew it there was wet grass underfoot and he was out of the pipe and onto an incline. He'd hit a metal gate, maybe a metre wide. The pipe had got them under the fence but a second pipe, shorter but with a wider circumference, with the gate acting as some kind of miniature dam, took them underneath the perimeter path and into more water.

Tom lifted up his backpack, pushed it over, letting it down slowly so it wouldn't splash. Using the grass verge as leverage, he pushed himself up, head at the level of the perimeter path, managing to slide in between the gap at the top of the gate, feet first into the water. He stifled another gag. It smelt like rotting carcass. As his feet touched the bottom, he heard the sound of voices approaching, of grit underfoot. Hovering inside the hollow alcove underneath the path, water sloshing against the gate, he closed his eyes and prayed Anil had found somewhere to hide, perhaps still inside the pipe. The voices grew closer, a collective groan in Spanish about regular outages in power. They were gone soon after, and with the silence that followed brought Anil's backpack through the gap. Tom took it from him, waited until they were both together in the hollow, barely able to see one another's faces, the only sound audible their uneven breaths.

They had to get to the other side, to the line of trees. Tom checked his watch.

1.35 a.m.

He would go first, as agreed, but this time they would hold onto one another and move across the water as one unit. Any sounds and they would go under, try to keep moving, unless they felt the guards were too close. Three sharp squeezes on the body meant full immersion, and to remain as still as possible.

Four months, seven days.

It all came down to this.

They hadn't gone far when he heard the voices coming back. In the pitch dark Tom stopped moving, started treading water, keeping motion to a minimum so to limit ripples on the surface. Murky liquid lapped against his chin. He stifled another retch at the stench, quashing the urge to swim like hell for the bank on the other side. Mosquitoes, cockroaches, flies – he didn't care to know what – still flitted about his face, flashes in the moonlight, wings letting off a fizzing sound and skimming across the surrounding water. Something crawled up his cheek. He let it, focussed on the job at hand.

The voices were almost on top of them now: two guards on patrol, walking the three-metre-high perimeter fence with cattle-prod sized torches that doubled as batons, the ones he had seen from the other side of the chain-link before the lights went out, the sound edging closer, enough that he was able to make out individual words. He felt Anil squeeze three times on his bicep, the agreed signal, gulping as big a breath as he could manage before sliding down into the icy black, immersing his body completely. He let go of Anil to keep himself submerged, grabbing at anything he could to stop his body from floating upwards, wafting water, lungs beginning to tighten.

Denham's voice echoed in his ears: *You need to move now. You need to get the job done.*

Water seeped through his pursed lips, tiny bubbles of air forced out.

He grappled to maintain focus, his heart, slowing now... *thud... thud... thud.*

Air. Jesus, help me, I need air.

There sounded a distant *bang*, audible under the water, before bright lights exploded above him, bringing the shimmering surface above him to life. The power to Colinas had returned but he couldn't think of that now, couldn't hear the voices, couldn't make out the two individual shapes of the guards... Nothing mattered over his own brain screaming out in agony for oxygen, lungs on the verge of collapse.

Unable to bear it any longer, he found the bottom with his feet and pushed up.

With a loud gasp he emerged at the surface, turning to

face the path, expecting to see two guards and staring down a cold, hard barrel of a shotgun. Light was everywhere. He squinted, gulped air. There was no one. Behind him, the bank, where the line of trees provided some cover was four feet away. Anil came out of the water and within half a second, threw himself onto the verge and vomited into the long grass.

Tom pushed with his feet, darting up the bank, yanking Anil's body into the cover of the trees. Shielded and in shadow, they bent over double, hands on knees, catching their breath, as quietly as one could after a near-drowning experience. The power cut had been brief to say the least. Tom gripped Anil's shoulder, pointing down at his bag. *We need to keep going, get to the house.*

Anil gave a single nod, wiped his mouth. Looked like hell. The whites of his eyes were now bloodshot. Together they unzipped the backpacks, removed clothing from the sealed plastic bags, kicking off shoes, dressing themselves over the top of the wetsuits, jeans and T-shirts, an attempt to look normal, blend in, two guys walking late at night across an upscale housing complex. They had studied the route multiple times, mostly on paper, impossible to know exactly where the light and shadows would fall. There was no CCTV inside the compound, he reminded himself, at least where the houses were situated, so provided the guards stuck to the perimeter they would be OK. It was what he had told himself every night for the last five nights when he couldn't sleep. A power cut could throw all of that into question. Extra patrols, dogs. His heart was hammering again.

Another single nod. *Move.* Their shoes were soaked,

leaking like sponges as they walked. Squeaking. A dead giveaway that something was amiss. Tom pushed the thought from his mind, ploughed on. They stayed close to the line of trees, until they were as close to the end of the cul-de-sac as they could be without walking directly underneath the street lights. So far there was not a soul in sight, only the cicadas making a racket and fireflies blinking in the grass.

They had to do two things: cut across the roundabout, moving up the side of the last house on the edge of the eighth hole before cutting around the back of six other houses, skirting the edge of the ninth on the fairway to meet up with the path that he had first taken with Becca, the night he had first kissed her. He wondered what she was doing now, if she was back at the house, pacing, if she would sleep tonight without them.

They waited. The night was still. About to step out into the well-lit street, Tom faltered, the sound of a vehicle halting them in their tracks. A Las Colinas guard was making his rounds on a motorcycle, using a strong torch, a light beam flooding the air.

Tom reached back, yanked Anil down into grass, light from the torch grazing their heads, and illuminating the grass. It lingered momentarily. Thin blades tickled his cheek, Tom closing his eyes as the sound of the motorbike faded into the distance, climbing back up the hill, the guard disappearing into the night.

Now or never. They got to their feet, kept their pace deliberately casual, resisting the overwhelming urge to run. Across the roundabout, they made it under the street lights, back onto the grass, up the incline. Reached the fairway; the tee-off for the ninth hole.

They walked the line of back gardens, remaining in shadow, passing the party house. He needed water, hadn't thought of that. So much sweating underneath the wetsuit, all that physical exertion had left him parched and dehydrated.

Dogs barked in the distance. House number 8024, almost in sight. The neighbours had security lights. Sabina Cordero's house lay in complete darkness. Manu had warned him about two sensor lights at the front of the house, but at the rear, there was nothing.

They hopped the fence, scrambled up the grass verge, crossing the well-manicured lawn, heads low. The pool in the back garden was covered, a steady whir of the pump audible, the vague lapping of water. Anil slid off his bag, removed the crowbar in one seamless movement. This seemingly crass method of breaking in gave Tom the jitters. Anil had assured him he was well-versed in using it without making a racket. Their biggest problem: making it to the alarm code pad before alarm bells started ringing and all hell broke loose. Manu hadn't been able to say how long they would have from the time the motion sensors picked them up to the call going through to the alarm company. She thought at least a minute and a half, possibly two. She *thought*. He had the code ready in his head: six-seven-six-five.

Six-seven-six-five. Six-seven-six-five. Seven-six-six-five?

'Gloves,' Tom whispered, as they reached the door. He handed Anil one of the two pairs of golf gloves, Anil holding the crowbar between his legs as he tugged them on, tightening the Velcro. Tom did the same.

The door: floor-length glass, white uPVC surround, single, lever-style handle. A few days earlier, he and Anil had got into a debate about the pros and cons of uPVC windows and doors, both from a homeowners' perspective and a criminal perspective. Unplasticized Polyvinyl Chloride – one of the most commonly used plastics in the world. Modern homes were awash with the stuff. Then there were four cam roller locks, Europrofile locks, cylinders, tongues, dead-bolts, lock snapping: words that had featured in both their vocabularies for – previously – wholly different reasons. The one thing they had agreed on: that in lever-style handle, outward-opening doors the dead bolt was often defunct, either worn out or in the majority of cases not properly fitted.

'How long will it take you to break in?' Tom had asked, back at the house.

'I can do it in under a minute, unless they really splashed some dough on the uPVC, which most people don't.'

Anil was running his hand around the edge of the door and lever handle. He seemed to smile a little, one arm high in the air, gripping the top edge.

'Can you do it?' Tom whispered.

Anil reached into his bag. Brought out what looked like a towel, handing it to Tom. He placed the crowbar at the bottom edge of the uPVC, shimmying it upward, wedging it underneath a small lip. Once in place, he signalled for Tom to place the towel on top as a noise-breaker.

Tom braced himself, glancing left and right, heart thumping *bam-bam-bam* against his ribcage.

Anil yanked hard. There was a cracking sound, muffled

by the towel. A second attempt resulted in an entire piece of the panel snapping off, exposing the lock. Anil got to work removing the cylinder.

'Get ready to move, yeah?' Anil said.

Six-seven-six-five.

Anil made quick work of the lock. After a few moments, he lifted the latch, the door open. The alarm panel in the other part of the house rang out, a high-pitched shriek. Tom ducked inside in the darkness, head low, racing towards the sound, past the sofas and across the open kitchen, adrenaline clouding his vision, a faint scent of Bullmastiff in the air.

Blue lights on the keypad. He punched the numbers: six… seven… six… five.

The alarm panel fell silent; the only sound left his ragged breathing. He stood stock still for thirty seconds, half expecting the alarm company to call and ask questions.

'Let's go, yeah?' Anil whispered behind him. 'Key?'

Tom had taken a leaf out of Sabina Cordero's book, secured the key on a silver ball chain around his neck, underneath the wetsuit. He teased it out, yanked off the chain and handed it to Anil, thinking his friend should do the honours.

The security door was at the back end of the kitchen. He pictured Nico Cordero on a hospital bed in Buenos Aires, tubes coming out of his mouth and nose, Sabina Cordero by his side, clutching her brother's fingers in one hand, a rosary in the other, tears streaked down her face. *For what?*

For whatever was behind the door.

Tom pushed away the guilt interlude. Anil slid the key in the lock, turned it twice, two low, hollow clicks. He pushed the handle downward, gave it a shove, let the door glide open. The hinges creaked, interrupting the silence. They stood side by side in the threshold, cloaked in damp clothes in the darkness. It felt like a hallelujah moment, only they were mute.

Tom took one step forward. The staircase led up to his right, a window halfway up, three doors to his left. They had almost made it.

'Middle,' Tom said, taking a step and trying the door. It opened.

He checked his watch. 2.23 a.m. They were inside the study. They had less than two hours before the power went down again, provided it actually happened on time.

Anil followed. Inside, there were floor to ceiling cupboards on both sides of the room, a desk in the corner with net curtains covering a barred window with a view of the main road. Outside in Colinas, nothing stirred.

Anil was opening and closing cupboards as quiet and fast as he could. Tom followed suit, hands hot inside the golf gloves.

'Here she is.'

Four months, seven days.

It all came down to this.

Chapter 23

Anil had opened a lower cupboard, the safe right at the back at floor level.

'I can't see a fucking thing,' he hissed. He pushed a hand in, feeling around. 'Got the keypad, hand me the Maglite.'

Tom zipped open the bag, located the torch, passed it over. Anil eased half his torso into the cupboard, legs resting on the floor, switching on the torch. Tom glanced towards the window. No curtains he could close, only the net. Anil came out again, leaving the torch inside. Rummaged inside his bag and pulled out the plastic container, peeled off the top and reached for the rare-earth magnet, secured inside a sock. Disappeared back down the rabbit hole. Next thing Tom knew, there were some clanking noises. Tom returned to the window, finding himself a position where he could see out but would not be seen. Twitched the net curtain, glanced outside. All quiet.

Anil re-emerged. '*Naah*,' he whispered, panting. 'They bought a Chinese safe, but it's not like the ones we picked up. Magnet's not gonna cut it. Think I gotta crack off the front.' He wiped his brow. 'Should have brought water, man, I'm dying here.'

'I'll get us water, you get to work.'

'You wanna try some random codes first?' What was the alarm code?'

'Six seven six five.'

Back down the rabbit hole. Tom glanced at his watch. They were wasting time. Anil needed to get going.

He heard the sound of four beeps, Anil punching in numbers. Then a whirring sound, echoing inside the cupboard. Followed by the sound of Anil chuckling.

'You are fucking kidding me,' Tom breathed.

Anil wriggled out of the cupboard. 'Told you, yeah,' he grinned. 'All people, you see, we're creatures of habit.'

He handed over the torch. 'You should be the one to look inside,' Anil added. 'You got us here.'

Tom looked at him, in denial that the safe had been opened with barely a moment's effort. Manu had known the code all along. She just didn't know she did.

Still chuckling, they shook hands. Tom crouched down, manoeuvred his way into the cupboard, squeezing his shoulders together. He was larger than Anil.

He moved the torch, hooked his fingers behind the safe door so he could slide it open. Back at the house, when he couldn't sleep, he'd pictured wads of cash, diamonds, jewels, piles of illegal documentation, fake passports, compromising photographs.

Cash won out. Not a great deal by the look of it.

He pushed his hand inside, pulled out neatly bundled wads. Eight in total. American: crisp one hundred-dollar bills. A thin plastic wallet slipped out from the top of them, containing a folded slip of paper. He felt around for anything else. That was everything.

He passed it all out to Anil, who gathered the cash into a pile. Tom switched off the torch and wriggled out.

'How much you reckon?' Anil whispered.

'Looks like eighty thousand,' Tom confirmed.

Anil pointed to the plastic wallet. 'What's that? I mean, I know we ain't supposed to look.'

Tom picked it up, taking it to the window. Inside was a folded document and in the bottom corner, a silver-coloured USB thumb drive.

'Why would you bother to send in a team of people for five months to retrieve eighty thousand dollars?' Anil said.

'Whatever this is, whatever is on this paper, and on this USB, that's why we're here.'

Anil was staring at him. 'You wanna go fifty-fifty on the cash?'

'Anil –'

'Come on man, I can't change who I am. For our trouble, like. As a bonus. Even split, right here, right now. We take that thing, whatever it is, we say that was all we found in the safe.'

His heart thumped. He thought about Becca, about the feeling of drowning, about Capricorn, Denham, and all the unanswered questions.

'Done,' he said.

Anil bent down, swiftly spilt the wads of US dollars into two piles of four, loading them into the separate backpacks, protected by plastic bags. Tom thought about what Denham had said, watching Anil separating the bills.

Whatever you come across in that safe, you're not to look at it.

Still beside the window, he removed the document from the wallet, stood by the curtains and used the light from the street lamps to read it. Unfolded it, ran his eyes over the text. The breath caught in his chest. The paper was cream-coloured, familiar looking, headed with 'Certificate of Birth' in red print, the unmistakable crest, *Dieu et mon droit*: God and My Right. The symbol used by her Majesty and her Majesty's Government. The British Government.

The birth certificate was for a Beatriz Ana Cordero, the date of birth: 26 December 2004.

Listed as the mother was Sabina Izarra Cordero.

Tom stared at the document, blinked hard, squinting at it, thinking momentarily he was mistaken.

The father on the certificate was listed as Charles William Royston Ebdon.

Charlie Ebdon.

Unless he was mistaken, the Charles Ebdon on the document was Head of Elate International, a global conglomerate.

Ebdon was one of the richest men in Great Britain: a businessman, highly respected upstanding member of the community, renowned philanthropist, three blonde-haired daughters in their late-teens, a glamorous wife, a super-yacht or two. He had friends in high places, including Downing Street.

He was also the father of a love-child of an Argentinian mistress, a child born in the UK.

So Charlie Ebdon was the client, and this was what he was trying to hide.

Charlie Fucking Ebdon! Otherwise known as Capricorn. Had to be. Ebdon trying to protect himself.

Whatever you find in that safe, you're not to look at it: else you'll work it all out.

Anil came up behind him. 'What is it?'

'A birth certificate,' Tom said, folding the paper back inside the wallet, sliding it back in with the USB drive.

'For who?'

'I'll tell you when we get out.'

There was a distant hum.

'Get down!' Tom hissed and they dropped to the floor. Another patrol: a motorbike passing on the road outside. Tom glanced at his watch. It wasn't even 3 a.m. An hour and fifteen to blackout. They should have left the power off.

'We need to move,' Tom whispered.

'But we're early,' Anil said.

'We go back as planned. Leave everything as it was except the alarm. Head back towards the water. There're some bushes at the top of the ninth.'

Anil handed him his backpack. There was a pause as he passed it over, a silent pact between them that said no one ever had to know. Not Becca, not Ray. Not Denham, not Charlie Ebdon, not Capricorn. Tom added the plastic wallet to the plastic bag in his backpack, slung it over his shoulder.

Anil crouched down, wriggled into the cupboard space, using the torch to reset the safe with the same four digits. Tom heard the same whirring sound and a double-beep to confirm the device was locked. With the torch switched off, they were back to using the light from the window. Anil closed the cupboard and they backed out, closing the door. Anil moved to the kitchen as Tom locked the security door. In the kitchen, they took a swift drink from the kitchen tap.

Back outside, Anil pushed the door closed, using a small rock to jam it shut. Tom picked up the handle, lock cylinder and the white pieces of plastic panel, tossing them underneath a hedge. Edging their way to the end of the garden, they moved to the line of trees, staying out of the light.

Tom cursed himself, wishing he'd taken a phone. He could have contacted Belosi, told him to issue orders to Nesto to switch off the power. Now they would have to wait, more exposed with every passing minute.

It took ten minutes to reach the top of the ninth over the grass, creeping closer, hugging the shadows. A cluster of trees at the tee-off provided some cover, but there was nowhere to fully hide. The perimeter fence was within sight, less than one hundred metres away, lit up, fully electrified.

They could push on. Get back to the water, to the trees where they had put clothes on over the suits. They crouched along the line of hedges, sounds of their ragged breaths blending in with the cicadas. This was the worst part. If there was a risk of them getting caught, this was it.

'We're fucked,' Anil muttered. 'We need the power down now.'

'Get back to the trees,' Tom said.

They stood, walked side by side on blancmange legs. The urge to sprint was worse on the way back. They skirted around the edge of the cul-de-sac, impossible to hide exclusively in shadow, the risk of them being seen by someone in the guard hut or a patrol at its height.

Then finally, under the sweeping protection of night, they reached the trees once more.

'There,' Anil said, pointing to a space underneath a hedge where there was room enough to lie side by side. Tom clung to his bag, backed himself in, lay on his front, legs entwined uncomfortably in branches. Anil followed. Tom allowed himself a breath. He had sweated so much he felt dizzy. He glanced at his watch. 03.25.

In the silence and the gentle breeze, his mind strayed back to the birth certificate.

Why bother going to such lengths? The official record existed in the system: a birth certificate was simply a hard copy record of a fact. There were other ways for Sabina Cordero to prove that Charlie Ebdon was the father of her child. And why keep the certificate in a safe? Unless you knew its very existence was under threat, or the lengths that somebody would go to get their hands on it. So a powerful British businessman had a love-child. Nothing new there. If the press were to get hold of the news, it would be in and out of the papers within a couple of days: internet fodder. It wasn't enough to affect his global brand, surely, even if Sabina was from Argentina, given the political history. Half the UK population probably couldn't even accurately point out Argentina on a map, let alone Uruguay. Perhaps Ebdon was trying to save his own marriage. That couldn't stop Sabina Cordero coming forward though, if she so desired. Perhaps Ebdon, or Capricorn, planned on silencing her too, like they did her brother? But what would be the point of all of it?

Tom glanced over at Anil. His companion was falling asleep, the adrenaline not enough to combat the sheer warmth offered by a wetsuit on a summer's night. It was like wearing a sleeping bag. He could feel his eyelids drooping too, a wall of exhaustion hitting him. He punched Anil in the arm. They had to stay awake. Couldn't risk falling asleep and missing their window, given Sancho's flawed timing.

03.35.

03.55.

Time dragged.

At four they wriggled out of their clothes, Tom screwing them into a ball and stuffing them into the backpack.

At 04.15 on the dot, the lights went down.

Tom couldn't even see a hand in front of his face. Wherever the moon had gone to, it was no longer in their sights. The feeling of terror returned to the pit of his stomach. The fear of near-drowning again, or being mauled by a dog before they even made it past the fence.

He commanded his legs to move, squeezing Anil's bicep as a form of encouragement, as if to say *see you on the other side*. He wriggled out from underneath the fence, got to his feet, eyes steadily adjusting to the blackout.

Immediately, something slashed his cheek below his right eye: a low-hanging branch or limb, impossible to make out what. He touched his fingers to his face. It had drawn blood, he couldn't tell how much.

Anil nudged him forward, Tom hissing at him to stay low. He lowered himself back into the water, attempting to minimise the number of ripples the movement caused. It was the same vomit-inducing smell as before. Looking ahead, he could make out the perimeter fence, the place they needed to go. He gulped a breath and swam.

He reached the hollow alcove underneath the path. His attempts to get back over the metal gate, the same way he'd come in, were unsuccessful. Anil tried and failed. They looked to one another, knowing they would have to go up and over the path.

They inched back out. Other than the cicadas and the gentle lapping of the water, there were no sounds, not even dogs. No foot patrols nearby, that they could tell.

Tom scrambled up the bank, taking two large strides across the path and dropping back down into grass leading to the pipe. All he had to do was swim out and they would be free. Seconds later, Anil was on his tail.

He willed his body forward, edging back through the pipe, breaths echoing, feeling his hips scrape against concrete. He swam through the marsh, one eye on Anil, ducking through the undergrowth, scrambling up the hill. It was only on the other side of the quarry, into the long grass, behind the overgrown tree that he let himself come to a standstill, doubling over at the waist and gripped his knees. Anil joined him, and after a moment, started laughing.

'*Fackin'* hell,' he spluttered, and Tom felt the relief surging in his veins.

They were free. Behind them, Colinas was indistinguishable across the landscape.

Tom laughed then, felt giddy. Grabbed Anil and gave him a bear hug, finding himself in an embrace, wetsuit to wetsuit, slapping his friend on the back, jumping up and down in muted celebration.

As the Colinas power exploded into action, lighting up the sky, Tom threw his head back, immersing himself in the sense of elation, of release. He walked side by side with Anil, gripped his comrade's shoulder. His entire life, nothing had ever felt quite so satisfying.

On the other side of the trees, Becca and Ray would be waiting for them.

They dropped down onto the dirt road, where the Ford Tempo was parked, headlights off but engine running. The passenger side door opened and Becca's head appeared above the door frame, two hands gripping the edge of the roof. Tom thought he saw a flicker of a smile. He walked around her side of the car, slid wordlessly into the back seat. Becca got back in; Anil closed his door. Nobody said a word. Ray inched the car forward, back towards the *Interbalnearia*, switching on the headlights, keeping an even speed.

'We can talk now, yeah?' Anil asked after a minute.

'You get it? What happened?' Ray blurted.

Becca switched on the light above the rear-view mirror, head appearing between the front seats. She looked his way, expression turning to one of concern.

'You're bleeding.'

His hand shot to his cheek. Felt like a nasty, open gash. He withdrew bloody fingers.

'I'm alright,' he said.

'Did you get in?' she asked.

'We're good,' he said, looking to Anil with a wry smile. 'We're all good. There was only one thing there.'

Ray switched off the light. Becca sat forward. Before long, she'd put her hand underneath the headrest again. Tom reached for it, gave her fingers a squeeze. She held onto him tightly. Outside, to his left, a bright amber light was peaking on the horizon.

The sun was coming up and he needed sleep.

In Ciudad de la Costa, Ray dimmed the lights again. At the house, Becca got out of the car, opening the gate so that

Ray could pull into the driveway. Tom stepped out of the car as Becca was locking the gate. He watched as she went to the garage, opening the door as quietly as she could. Ray pulled forward in the Tempo, Anil still in the back. Tom ducked his head under the door as Becca brought it down behind them, and in the dim light grabbing him by the hand, pulling him in for a rough, celebratory kiss before Ray could even switch off the engine. She pulled away as quickly.

'I need to fix your face,' she said.

Inside the living room, Tom grinned as Anil whooped and punched the air, slinging down his bag. Still in wetsuits, they high-fived, embracing liked two homeboys escaping the long arm of the law.

'Holy shit,' Anil said, breaths still coming in rapid gasps, veins still fuelled by adrenaline.

'That was too easy,' Tom added.

'Easy?' Becca repeated, raising an eyebrow.

'Didn't even need to break the safe, yeah?' Anil said, 'We already had the code.'

'How?' Becca breathed.

'Same as the burglar alarm,' Tom said.

Becca looked genuinely shocked. 'What was in it?'

Tom sobered. Ray lingered in the doorway. 'Not much. A document and a thumb drive.'

'That's it?'

'You would think, right?' said Anil. 'All that work and... that was it.'

Ray stepped forward, in a sombre mood. 'I should take everything you managed to retrieve.'

'No,' Tom said, in a tone stronger than the one he had aimed for. 'I'm looking at the contents of that USB.'

'But Denham—'

'I don't care what Denham said. I want sight of it. Then you can do whatever you like.'

Ray seemed nervous, backing away a little.

'Then we sleep a few hours before making a move,' Tom added.

'I'll boot up the laptop,' Anil said.

'Come,' Becca said. He felt one hand on his arm. 'Your cheek is still bleeding.'

He looked towards Ray, an odd sensation in the pit of his stomach. Allowed himself to be guided by Becca to the table. He was hot again. He unzipped the wetsuit, blissful cool air hitting his back as he sat down.

Anil had done the same. Tom noticed for the first time that Anil had a tattoo on his back. He couldn't make out what. Anil had located the laptop, the same silver-grey model Tom had picked up in Buenos Aires in the corner by the fireplace, and was powering it up.

Ray turned on his heel, disappearing down the corridor to his bedroom. Becca went to the kitchen.

'Can you get me some water?' Tom asked and she returned with a full glass and some damp cotton wool. She remained hovering over him, waiting whilst he downed the water before cupping his chin in one hand and tenderly dabbing the cotton wool over his skin with the other. She moved closer. He slid his hands around the backs of her knees. Tomorrow they would be making the welcome journey back to London. Would she want to come with him?

Anil had unzipped Tom's backpack, removed the plastic wallet and resealed it as quickly. Tom thought he heard the sound of Ray closing the door, the sound of his voice in his room.

'Make it quick,' Tom shot in Anil's direction.

Anil hopped over the back of the sofa and back into his seat, reaching inside the wallet for the USB. Pulled the lid off the drive and slid it into a port on the left-hand side of the laptop.

'What's the document?' Becca asked.

'It's a birth certificate for Sabina Cordero's daughter. The father is listed as Charlie Ebdon.'

'Charlie Ebdon?'

Anil tapped at the keyboard. Ray's voice was raised, coming from his room. Moments later he was back.

'I need the contents of the safe,' he demanded, red-faced.

'You can have them, Ray; we need a minute,' Tom replied evenly.

Tom watched Ray lean against the doorframe, looking to Anil, the former's chest rising and falling, as though battling some kind of inner demon.

Anil punched the keyboard. 'OK, we're good, we're good.'

Tom nudged Becca's hand away.

Ray disappeared again, back to his room. Tom got to his feet, hovered behind Anil, leaning his arms on the sofa. On screen, the drive appeared to contain only a few items.

'Open it up, copy the contents,' Tom said, voice low, 'all of them; do it now. Put them on the desktop.'

Anil did as he was told.

Tom glanced up as Ray came back, holding a gun.

Ray raised the weapon, levelling it with Tom's head.

'Jesus!' Anil blurted and shot to his feet, throwing his hands in the air, abandoning the laptop on the sofa.

'Ray… ' Tom began, slowly raising his hands. It was a handgun, semi-automatic, one he hadn't seen before in Ray's possession.

'Shut the fuck up and do as I ask,' Ray ordered, cheeks flushed, training the gun on Anil. 'Take the USB out of the laptop, give it to me. Do it now.'

'I'll do it, put the fucking gun down, don't be a dick, yeah? Yeah?!' Anil stammered.

Ray held out one hand. 'Give it to me, Anil.'

'I'll do it when you take the fucking gun off me!'

Tom felt frozen to the ground. 'I can do it, Ray,' he said.

Ray nodded, eyes focussed on Anil. 'Do it.'

Tom leaned down, whipped out the thumb drive from the laptop, tossing it towards Ray. Ray caught it in one hand.

There was a silence in the room, only the sound of their breathing audible. Anil was starting to panic.

'You can take the gun off me now, Ray. Don't be a dick, Ray, yeah, take the gun off me, take the gun off me, TAKE THE FUCKING GUN OFF ME!'

Bam. Bam.

Slow motion somehow. Heart in his throat, punch to the stomach, mind reeling. Next to him, Anil's body thrown backwards, slamming into the white wall, eyes wide open.

The body slid down, slumped to the floor, a smear of red blood and brain matter left behind, a bullet wound between the eyes.

As he landed in a heap on the ceramic tiles, doubled over, Tom caught a glimpse of the tattoo on Anil's back: the outline of a dove.

Chapter 24

Two shots fired. The noise sent jolts through her body. She immediately covered her ears, mouth open in a half-gasp, half-scream. Her friend was thrown backwards before he sank down, leaving behind a trail of crimson on the wall: gone in a matter of seconds.

She couldn't breathe for the shock. Ray's jaw: rigid, his body stiff, weapon-arm perfectly straight. For once he looked professional. The arm swung around, the gun barrel alternating between her and Tom.

'Where's the document? Give it to me now,' Ray ordered.

'It's here on the floor,' Tom answered, hands still in the air.

'Get it,' Ray barked.

She watched, still in disbelief, as Tom edged himself down towards the floor, slowly picking up the plastic wallet. He held it out. Ray reached out, snatched it.

'Both of you, in the kitchen, now. Move!'

She flinched, turned, obeyed, following Tom into the kitchen area.

'On your knees, hands on the back of your head.'

Had this been his plan all along? To execute them one by one? Her legs went to jelly, eyes stung with tears, ears still ringing from the sound of the gunshot. Tom went down first. She followed.

'Ray—' Tom began.

'No talking. There's been enough talking.'

Her cheeks were wet. Was Anil alive? Could he have survived? She pictured his face as he fell down to the floor, refusing to believe he was dead, that Ray... fat, lazy, good-for-nothing Ray had done this.

She stared at the oven door covered in stains, at the dark brown cupboards, at the crumbs littered across the floor tiles.

There was a rustling sound behind them, the sound of keys, of Ray's footsteps. After a minute, a door slammed. She looked across at Tom. Ray wasn't in the house. Outside, in the half-light of dawn, she heard the familiar clanging sound of Ray opening the gate. Seconds later, the sound of an engine – the Vitara starting up – the equally distinguishable crunch of the tyres on gravel, and the car reversing onto the road. He had driven away.

She fell forward onto all fours. Tom was on his feet, racing over to Anil. She followed.

'Anil, Anil,' Tom was saying, lifting his chin, shaking his shoulders, desperate for some kind of response. There was none, Anil's eyes, his expression, empty of light, a pool of blood still oozing from his head rapidly expanding over the floor tiles.

Hands covered her mouth and nose. In Anil's immediate vicinity there was a salty, meat-factory stench in the air. She backed away, unable to comprehend what had taken place.

'We need to go,' Tom stated, with a tone empty of emotion. 'We need to move right now.'

He was on his feet pulling at the wetsuit to get it off, yanking the thick fabric down his arms and disappearing to

252

his room. She couldn't move, gripping the side of the sofa for support, unable to drag her eyes from Anil's body.

'Get the backpack, put the laptop in it,' Tom was saying, barking orders from around the corner. 'Find the keys to the Ford.'

When he came back, she hadn't moved. 'Becca, come on!'

He had changed into jeans and a shirt, pulling on a charcoal-coloured grey hooded top. He was holding a different backpack. 'Someone in this street might have called the police. We have to get out of here right now.'

'What about Anil?'

He was looking at her, eyes swollen with sympathy. 'We have to leave him. We have to go. Anil is gone.'

Something snapped inside her. Was it Richie's voice she could hear? She looked down, swiped up Tom's backpack, scissor-kicked over the sofa, closed the laptop, hooked the power cord from the fireplace, loading it all inside.

'Get your passport,' Tom said. The cut below his eye had stopped bleeding. He was rummaging through Anil's backpack. She watched him pull four wads of US dollars from one of the pockets. Didn't ask what they were, where they had come from, went to her room. On autopilot, she threw open the wardrobe, grabbed her passport, jacket, mobile phone, the small messenger bag she'd already prepared, changing her trainers to boots, all the while pale fingers trembling. She pushed everything into Tom's backpack with the laptop, fingers brushing up against something. Looking inside, she found yet more wads of money.

She glanced around, closing the door behind her.

Tom appeared, took her hand, leading her to the garage. He'd grabbed a cap to shield his face. The Ford Tempo was already unlocked.

'I'll drive, you close the gate,' Tom said, lifting the garage door.

She did as she was told, pushed the backpack into the back seat, walked out into the dim light of the morning. The air felt fresh, the sky rose-ginger with a sliver of cloud. In the garage, Tom got into the driver's seat. It took a few attempts to start the car.

He reversed out into the road. Becca slid the metal gate across, secured the padlock. She noted Tom had closed the blinds on the front windows. Anil was alone. The thought made her heart slam up against her ribcage, eyes welling up, still desiring to save him so badly.

Tom was pushing open the passenger side door. She got in, slammed it shut. The car spluttered as Tom hit the accelerator.

Neither spoke. She looked to his wrist, both hands on the steering wheel, at his watch peeking out from underneath the hooded top. It was 05.35. He was concentrating on the road. For the first time she noticed how exhausted he looked.

'Where are we going?'

'If we take Ruta Nine we can be at the Brazilian border in about four hours.'

'Brazil? Are you serious?'

'Brazil is our safest option. We can go to the airport, exactly where Ray is heading, or take the ferry to Buenos Aires. Or we drive west to Argentina and I doubt you want to do that.'

Her stomach did a little flip. Brazil had never even been raised, not by any of them.

'Four hours is a long time. We need to dump this car.'

'This car is all we have.'

Her mouth had gone dry. 'If we drive fast enough, we can get the 7 a.m. ferry.'

Tom slammed his foot on the break, vehicle screeching to a decrepit halt. He stared at her.

'The ferry only goes to one place, Bec.'

'Then once we get to Buenos Aires, we keep moving. Federico never has to know we touched the ground. We get a flight out, or—'

'We cross over into Chile,' he suggested.

His breathing had quickened. She glanced around at the houses on either side of the road, felt exposed, despite the early hour and no sign of human activity.

'We need to get out of Uruguay before anyone finds Anil in that house,' she whispered.

He nodded once.

At the junction with the *Interbalnearia*, Tom paused. A left turn was towards Montevideo and the ferry. The other lead towards Ruta Nine. She squinted. To the right, in the distance, a lone police officer appeared to be flagging down the few cars that were travelling in his direction.

There was only one turn they could make. Tom swung the wheel left, kept his speed steady, leaving the outline of the police car disappearing in her side-view mirror.

A minute later, he puffed out his cheeks.

'You think Denham ordered Ray to do that?' she said.

She saw Tom glance from his window. 'Ordered Ray

to murder Anil? There was definitely a phone call. I don't know. I don't know anything anymore.'

She turned her head away from him, stared out of the window at the road, at the passing trees, blurring to a single green strip. Grappled with her thoughts, going through the motions. Questioned what was expected of her at this point in time. They took the bridge, the one that gave a view of the smooth white dome of Carrasco International. Was that where Ray had gone? Had he already bought his ticket? It seemed hard to believe they were leaving it all behind: Colinas, Ciudad de la Costa, their lives for the past four months. They had done what they came to do. And Anil had paid the highest price.

'What was the money in Anil's bag?' she asked, processing the events of the last hour over in her head.

He was checking his wing mirror now, manoeuvring between the other cars, getting them ahead whilst still obeying the speed limit, checking his watch. It was obvious from the moment she'd opened her mouth that he didn't want to answer the question.

'There was money in the safe, wasn't there?' she said.

He was following signs for central Montevideo, heading towards La Rambla. She'd become quite used to the roads here, knew now that she would never be coming back.

'About eighty thousand dollars,' he said after a moment. 'That's a guess. We didn't count the bills.'

'And you split it between you.'

He glanced across at her, shifted in his seat. 'Until Ray shot Anil in the head, it was never going to be an issue.'

'What else did you find?'

256

'Nothing. There was nothing.'

'But you took the money anyway.'

'I would have told you.'

'Don't lie to me.'

They didn't speak, reached La Rambla, the indicator *tick-ticking* before they took a right, driving along the coastal road and the beaches bordering the River Plate. The muddy waters were tranquil, cargo ships on the horizon, some early morning joggers and dog-walkers kicking up sand. Not a care in the world, getting on with their lives.

She wondered if Anil had felt any pain. If he knew he was dead when he heard the gunshots. Or had it all been too quick, his life snuffed out the moment the bullet penetrated his skin. She wondered who would find him, who would identify his body; if he would ever get a proper funeral. She and Tom, they had abandoned him. Her lip wobbled. So much of her life had involved only her, never other people. Her and Richie. When bad things happened, they didn't affect her, until now.

In silence, they pushed on to the end of the peninsula, to Montevideo's old town, with its cracked paint and ugly-beautiful charm. She had liked living there, even when rain was coming through the roof. Reminded her of the time when she and Richie had first moved to London.

They were nearing the ferry port. It was 6.25 a.m. Tom parallel-parked the Tempo in a small street not far from the Port Market. He got out of the car, reached for the backpack in the back seat, the one containing the laptop. As she got out a man approached them. He had dishevelled hair, wore a long coat, mud-caked trainers with a few teeth missing. He and Tom exchanged a few words in Spanish.

Then Tom was heading for the port, bag slung over his back. She had to run to catch up with him, the other bag slung over her shoulder.

'Give me your phone,' he said, and she reached inside her pocket. He stopped on the pavement, holding both handsets in his hands, tearing off backs, tossing batteries into a nearby waste bin, yanking out both SIM cards and folding them in two. Then he placed both units down on the concrete pavement and crushed them with his heel, tossing the plastic fragments into a nearby waste bin.

The homeless man was still watching them.

'What did you say to him?' Becca asked as they kept moving.

'I gave him the car keys and a fifty-dollar bill,' Tom replied. 'Told him we were never there.'

At the terminal, a stout female informed them that the direct passenger ferry to Buenos Aires, departing at 7 a.m. was fully booked. Tom grew aggravated with her, Becca grabbing him by the arm, urging him to calm down. He had wild eyes, starved of sleep. She pushed her way in front of him, requesting in broken Spanish two seats on the next available service, a slower boat which stopped on route in Colonia, western Uruguay, docking in Buenos Aires in time for a late lunch.

On the half-empty ferry, they sat side by side on blue, wipe-clean faux leather seats, on the back row of the passenger cabin. As it pulled away from the port of Montevideo, Tom removed the laptop from the backpack.

'Not here,' she whispered, purposefully pushing the screen closed. 'You should sleep.'

He pulled away. 'I need to know what it is we went in there for,' he hissed. 'I need to know what Anil died for. And it's not for that fucking certificate.'

'Keep your voice down,' she hissed back. 'Jesus Christ. Can't we get out of Uruguay? Right now I'm just grateful to be alive.'

He was staring at her. The blood had dried around his cut, his face drawn. He needed a shave. He must have been awake pushing twenty-four hours, his aroma not so pleasant either. But he was alive. She placed one hand on his cheek and suddenly he was embracing her, holding onto her tightly, burying his head into her shoulder.

He let go of her then, closed the laptop shut and pushed it back inside the bag. Pulled the cap down over his face.

She watched him breathe in and out. Part of her hoped that Anil hadn't managed to copy anything across before he had been shot and that Tom wouldn't find what he was looking for. Because that would mean a dead end. Nothing to investigate. Nothing to look into. A birth certificate and some shit bad luck. Nothing to make him crave to know more about her past, not the individuals she worked for, or the murky corners she had lurked in during her life. She didn't want him to be able to access those things. It might change the way he felt, and she didn't want that. He'd never looked at her and been disappointed. She looked down at him, eyes closed, wished to God she didn't have to do what she knew she had to. Knowing what was coming made her chest ache.

★★★★★

The Argentinian immigration official looked at Tom, then back down to the two passports in his hands, then to the immigration forms they had scribbled in a hurry, then back to him. There was a frown on his face as black eyes lingered on the gash on his cheek. The official slid his passport into the scanner, typed something on his keyboard, eyeing Becca up and down too. Tom held on tightly to her hand, remained impassive, like everything was normal.

On the ferry they had spread the eight bundles of dollars about their persons, concealing four each in jackets and underwear. He knew the customs limit for bringing in money to Argentina was something like ten thousand.

'*En qué hotel se hospeda?*' the official asked. *Which hotel are you staying in?*

'Sheraton,' Tom lied.

The official typed again before stamping both their passports, handing them back.

'*Bienvenidos,*' he muttered.

Tom hadn't been able to sleep. Every time he closed his eyes, Anil's face stared back at him, blood running down the wall, pooling at his feet. And they had run. They had left him there, left his body to rot to save their own skin.

Becca had fetched him breakfast from the café at the front of the boat: a Coke and two lukewarm cheese empanadas. He had devoured them. She'd said she wasn't hungry. The journey to Buenos Aires took four and a half hours. He hadn't thought about what they should do after that. Find somewhere to rest their heads for the night, then clear the hell out of Argentina, get on a plane. *A plane to where exactly?*

First he wanted to look at the laptop. See if Anil had managed to copy anything from the USB Ray had taken. Second, he needed to speak to Denham, unleash a little hell. They could still be safe: neither Denham nor Ray were aware that he now knew the name written on the birth certificate, or that there was a chance the USB drive had been copied, or that he was even aware of the name Solomon Capricorn. Neither ever had to. Denham could get him and Becca back to England, pay them the rest of what they were owed and they would be squared away, free to do as they pleased. Had Ray not put a bullet between Anil's eyes, the job would have been a complete success.

He thought back to those moments in the house, before shots were fired. Ray had disappeared to his room: Tom had heard him on the phone. Was it Denham who had given him the order? Denham, who would go to any lengths to protect his client's identity, including issuing a kill order? And if he called Denham, would Denham send someone after them to exact the same fate?

In Buenos Aires, they found a guesthouse on Suipacha Street – the Posada del Esquina – in the bustling centre of town above a cigar shop. The elderly woman on the front desk wore a brown polyester dress and looked as though she spent her days puffing on cigarillos. She asked for nine hundred pesos for the night: Tom told her he only had dollars. She gave a shrug, asked for fifty *dólares* and passed him two powder-blue towels, frayed at the edges, and a room key.

Deep red wallpaper, peeling at the edges, covered the walls. It smelled damp. He showered quickly, eager to check the laptop. The bathroom was the size of a cubicle with a frosted window at ceiling height. Opening it caused an intense smell of fast food to waft inside. Tom thought the better of it and snapped it shut, steam swirling around his head. He yanked open the door. In the main room, itself the size of a slightly larger cubicle with a street-facing window, Becca lay on the double bed – more or less a large single – facing the wall. She had said as little as possible since they'd departed Uruguay.

'Shower's free,' he mumbled.

She got to her feet, walked in a zombie-like fashion towards the bathroom, locking it behind her. Over the sound of rushing water, Tom tugged on the only fresh pair of underwear he owned before reaching for the laptop. He sat in the only chair in the room, knee bouncing restlessly up and down as the computer whirred to life.

On the desktop was a folder called 'fghjlkh', named by Anil in a hurry. Tom's fingers hovered over the keyboard, chest rising and falling. He double-clicked on the mouse pad to open it.

The copied contents of the USB contained six items: the first, a video file, named 'Statement'. The other documents were all PDF files.

He double-clicked the video file to open it.

It took a few moments to start. There was a crackling sound. A woman appeared to switch on a video camera, backing away to a grey wall, her face vaguely familiar. She was holding a piece of paper from which she read.

'My name is Clare Rose Buchanan,' the woman began. 'My date of birth is the eighteenth of September, 1970. Today is Friday the eleventh of February, 2005. My address is 14A Sicily Street in Highbury, London. I am currently Head of Elate International Charities Division in central London. This is a video statement I will be passing to police in relation to my work at Elate.'

Tom frowned. Clare Buchanan. He recognised the name.

He paused the video, logged on to the hotel Wi-Fi, open and unsecured. Typed her name into Google, skim-read the results. His heart began to hammer. Clare Buchanan had gone missing in Islington on the night of the twenty-first of February 2005, eleven years earlier. She had last been seen on CCTV getting off a London bus near Angel tube station and had not been seen nor heard of since. He had a vague recollection of her face on the news, resident in North London at the time.

He navigated back to her video statement, continued watching.

Clare Buchanan didn't look into the camera as she spoke. He could see her fingers were trembling, sometimes glancing down at her notes, sometimes appearing to speak ad lib.

'I am making this video,' Clare continued, 'because I can no longer stay silent. I have recently become aware of my company – of Elate International's – financial dealings. In the face of natural disaster, where tragedy strikes and lives are lost, Elate's job has been to raise money from the British public, the British taxpayers, to support local charities across the world and to give funds to those in need. In recent weeks I have seen documents that show that a large proportion of these funds are being creamed off to charities that on the surface look genuine, but in fact do not even exist. I believe the funds are being accumulated by Charles 'Charlie' Ebdon and his company investors, some of whom I also do not believe exist in the flesh. I believe the money is moved into offshore companies, to shell businesses for their own personal gain, and most never reaches the real victims. In recent weeks I have been followed and I believe my life may be in danger.'

She had to recompose herself then. Wiping her palms against her trousers, wiping tears.

'The proof I have at this stage is limited, but I believe it is enough to warrant an open investigation. I will be sending my statement and the evidence I have to the Metropolitan Police and I plan to hand in my resignation from Elate in the coming days. I can no longer work for a company where syphoning off taxpayers' money has become standard practice. I can no longer stand to watch the likes of Charlie Ebdon get rich from tragedy and desperation across the world. I have to speak out.'

There were still tears in her eyes. She stepped forward, switched off the video camera. The screen went black and she was gone.

Tom swallowed the lump in his throat. It made sense now. Why Charlie Ebdon would want the contents of the safe so badly: to claim back evidence of his secret from Sabrina Cordero. Forget that he was the father of her child; he had much bigger skeletons to hide.

But what was Cordero's connection to Clare Buchanan? And how did she end up with the video made by a British woman in her safe? And if Clare Buchanan had died for being a whistle-blower, who was her killer?

His mind reeled. Elate was one of the largest of the UK corporations with a charitable division, the latter's role primarily to raise money to provide aid to other, smaller, charities worldwide in extreme circumstances, such as the Indonesian earthquake and tsunami in December 2004, shortly before Clare Buchanan would have gone missing. Even he had given money to Elate back then. Had he been lining Ebdon's pockets? Like everybody else? And who else knew but Clare Buchanan?

He ploughed on. Opened up some of the other files. They contained separate financial transactions, some names of companies, funds leaving Elate's account. Names he didn't recognise. The other files were the same, except rather than being current they were now eleven years old.

Becca emerged from the bathroom in a swirl of hot steam, wrapped in a towel that barely covered her modesty, hair damp and still dripping water down her back.

'I need to ask you a question,' he said. 'I need an honest answer.'

Becca looked down at him in the chair, her expression hard to read. 'I'll try,' she said.

'Solomon Capricorn and Charlie Ebdon, are they the same person?'

She adjusted the towel, quiet for some moments.

'Yes,' she said, this time averting her eyes.

'Why do you work for him?'

'What did you find?' she asked, ignoring the question.

'A statement. A video statement. The woman's name is Clare Buchanan. She disappeared in London eleven years ago. She claims Charlie Ebdon is making large amounts of money from companies posing as charities. Front companies that don't exist.'

Her expression, unchanged.

'You understand what that means? Like embezzlement but on a grand scale.'

She hovered over him. Reaching out, Becca removed the laptop from his lap, bending down and placing it, still open, on the floor before straddling him, parting her legs and gently lowering herself into the warm place where the laptop had been. She unclasped the knot in the towel and it fell away. Water dripped from her hair, down over her breasts. Tom felt himself harden. When she kissed him, he forgot all about Clare Buchanan and Charlie Ebdon.

He awoke in darkness, legs still entwined with hers. Slid his hand up the side of her body and she stirred. Planted a kiss in the crevice of her neck. Becca inhaled, slowly waking. He glanced at his watch. It was 7.30 p.m. They had slept for about four hours. He felt better, not exactly refreshed, but enough to want to get out of bed to go and find something to eat.

They dressed, walked three blocks south to a small branch of Burger King on Carlos Pellegrini, bordering the main traffic artery that was Avenida 9 de Julio. The traffic hummed. They took three bags of food back to the hotel, passing the same leathery old woman on the makeshift reception desk, keeping their time away to a minimum. Back in the room, Tom closed the laptop, brain too addled to think about what he had seen and read, yet determined to look at the video statement again in the morning.

Becca finished her second burger, the appreciation written all over her face. Tom leaned forward, wiped a smear of ketchup from her lip. Their previous sexual efforts had been brief to say the least, over in a few minutes, both simultaneously crashing into a deep and much-desired sleep. Second time round, Tom took his time, exploring her, keeping the pace slow, Becca on top then, seemingly the place where she took the most pleasure. He'd known for some time that he'd fallen for her; that she wasn't quite like any other woman he'd been close to.

It was around eleven when they drifted off to sleep again, Tom with his back against the wall, Becca curled into him, his arms around her, stroking her skin. Sounds from the street wafted in through the window, their bodies slick with sweat in no air-con.

When he woke up again, he'd moved, now facing the wall, mind hazy with sleep. He thought he heard a noise, the door maybe. He rolled, feeling around for Becca. The bed was empty.

His body stiffened, the sensation washing over him that they were not alone in the room. He felt around in the shadows for the bedside light, located the button and twisted it on.

Chapter 25

His chest tightened, the initial terror-fuelled reaction taking hold. The kind of terror associated with staring into the eyes of a stranger – an intruder no less – slipping in through the door undetected under the cover of darkness. He considered for a moment whether he might be dreaming. The dark-haired stranger was now sat in the chair that earlier he and Becca had made love in. He tore his stare from the stranger's face, up past his shoulder where her hand was resting. Becca's hand. She was stood beside him, fully clothed, unmoving, eyes down, still-damp hair falling across her face.

The realisation hit him like a freight train.

She had let the stranger in.

Under the sheet Tom was naked and sweating, white cotton gathered around his waist and legs. The tightness in his chest increased with every passing second. The stranger had an obnoxious leer, jet black hair parted in the centre, half-beard on a square jaw, the nose of a rugby prop too many times at the centre of a scrum. A weapon – a 9mm SIG-Sauer – was resting on one knee, barrel pointed directly towards Tom's chest.

'Who the fuck are you?' Tom said, after a moment.

The stranger tilted his head. 'My name is Anton.'

'Anton,' Tom repeated, recognising the name from somewhere.

'Bec? What's going on? Who is this?'

She didn't look at him, wouldn't raise her eyes.

He watched her; didn't bother with the stranger. 'So you had sex with me, what, as a stalling tactic?'

The man who called himself Anton inhaled sharply through his bent nose. 'We asked her to,' he said.

'Who's we?'

Still looking at Becca. Nobody answered. He could still taste her on his lips. 'Becca. Look at me,' he said.

She moved her head to one side. He caught sight of her blank expression. The eyes, they were dead, nothing behind them, like Anton was a demon who had sucked out her soul. He knew there would be no explanation emerging from Becca's lips anytime soon.

'How did you find us?'

Anton leaned down, swiped up the laptop, placing it underneath the SIG in his lap, keeping his splayed fingers over the pistol, the barrel firmly aimed in Tom's direction.

'Becca kept me informed of your movements. She sent me a message from Uruguay that you would be travelling to Buenos Aires. Then when you kindly destroyed her phone she sent me an email from this laptop with your location.'

Anton gave the laptop a gentle pat.

Tom ground his teeth. He hadn't seen her send any message. It would have had to have been after he'd argued they should head for the border with Brazil. Her sleight of hand stretched even to sending messages on a phone. She would only have needed to type two characters: a B and an A, and it would have been enough. If Anton had been in Uruguay, he could easily have followed them, perhaps on the next ferry out. And sending an email from the laptop when he had believed her to be curled up in his arms… The *bitch*.

He eyed Becca again. 'All part of your plan, I see.'

'Becca also tells me it was Anil Choudhury's idea to copy the contents of the safe onto this laptop,' Anton interjected, clicking his tongue in disapproval. 'Not yours. She assures me that you haven't looked at it. Not yet. That she managed to *distract* you long enough for me to get here.'

It was a barefaced lie. He couldn't tear his eyes from her, couldn't work her out. Why would she go so far as to get Anton here only to lie about him watching Clare Buchanan's video statement? To stop Anton from slaughtering him on the spot? To make him seem like less of a threat?

'It was my plan to look at it at first light,' Tom spat, the anger threatening to engulf him now that she had still refused to meet his gaze.

'Congratulations, Mr Holt, you saved your own skin. But copying the contents warrants a reduction in your final payment,' Anton said. 'The client will insist on that. If you'd have watched it I'd be putting a bullet in you, like your deceased friend.'

The look of him was chilling. The odd-shaped square jaw, broad shoulders, dressed all in black like some kind of hitman. Becca clearly hadn't told her friend Anton about the cash either, piled in his backpack, a metre away from the hitman's foot. Tom kept his breathing steady, resisted the urge to look at it in case it gave Anton any ideas. He had realised a long time ago that this job had never been about money.

'I want to speak to Denham,' he said, swallowing.

Anton raised his chin. 'Your work with Denham is

finished. Your job here is done. The contents of the Cordero safe are on their way back to London. Becca and I will also be going back to London,' he added, giving the laptop another reassuring stroke. 'With this.'

He wanted to smash the guy's face. The laptop represented the last stand. Any hope for Anil and a dead woman. Murdered. In Anton's hands Capricorn/Charlie Ebdon's secrets were protected. Forget the money, Tom thought sardonically: the truth had much greater value.

'So I'm free to do as I please,' Tom said.

Anton looked him up and down. 'I've a mind to kill you anyway.'

Anton's hand went to the butt of the gun, and with the movement came the first reaction from Becca, her eyes flashing, looking into Tom's for a millisecond before looking away again, her face contorted, the first spark of emotion he'd witnessed since switching on the light.

His heart hammered, chest rising and falling, mind reeling. He pictured his family, Anil's dead body, heard the quiet desperation in Clare Buchanan's voice on the video.

If he died she would stay missing forever.

Anton lifted the gun, leaned forward.

The only thing within reachable distance was the table lamp.

Anton glared, as though making his mind up.

Tom held his stare, stopped breathing.

Bam-Bam-Bam-Bam

The knocking on the door – four quick hammers in quick succession – made them all jump. A sound could be heard, that of the hotel receptionist they had seen earlier, the elderly *señora* in the brown polyester dress.

'*Los visitantes cuestan extra!*' her voice squawked through the door.

Anton's eyes shot to Becca, nodded in the direction of the door. Concealed his weapon up his shirt. Tom watched as Becca took three paces across the room, opened the door a fraction. The two women exchanged hushed words.

'What does she want?' Anton hissed at Becca.

'She wants to charge you for being in our room,' Tom said.

Becca muttered something to the woman then closed the door.

'We need to go,' she turned and announced to Anton, in a tone Tom didn't recognise. 'Right now.'

Tom watched Anton get to his feet, the barrel of the weapon back in his face. Becca was leaning down, picking up the backpack and the power cord for the laptop. She opened it up, Anton sliding the computer inside. She zipped up the bag and slung the strap over her head so that it fell diagonally across her chest. Tom watched as a bystander as the two entities moved in perfect unison. Perhaps that was it. They came as a team but only one had ever been visible. Had Anton been in Uruguay the whole time, like her shadow? Had she been speaking to him? What else didn't he know about her?

He watched her leave. Becca didn't look back, not even for a second, unchained the door, flung it open and walked out in a flash of red hair, carrying the laptop bag and her own small messenger bag, followed at pace behind by Anton, the gun disappeared, concealed somewhere on his person. In the doorway, the receptionist was still standing there as two figures filed past her. He saw the frown on her face as she caught sight of Tom on the bed, naked, sheets entangled in his lap, bare legs. He stood up, keeping one hand on the sheet to protect his modesty, reached out and pushed the door shut in her face.

He was alone.

Several things hit him at once:

He wasn't dead.

The laptop was gone.

He was still naked.

Anton was a murderous thug.

And lastly, Becca worked for said thug, and had walked out of his life without so much as a backwards glance.

An explosion went off, deep inside his gut. It made sense now. She had been told to get close to him, to feed him enough information to build trust, to flirt with him enough to make him think that she wanted him, to build a physical intimacy to break down barriers that he would listen to her. She'd been the archetypal honey-trap and he'd been completely strung along.

Yet she had lied to Anton too, about the money, and about him not viewing the contents of the laptop. She had stopped Anton from putting a bullet in him. Why? And what did that mean?

He searched around for some underwear, yanked it on, going to the window to see in which direction they had gone, leaning over ornate wrought iron railings. Down on the street, Sunday morning sun peaking on the horizon, the pair were nowhere to be seen. Tom bent down, checked the backpack for the money, all eighty thousand in eight bundles inside. Why hadn't she taken at least some for herself?

He swiped up the sheet, tossed it back on the bed. The linen held her scent. It filled him with disgust. He looked around for the rest of his clothes, too angry to think straight. He scoured the room again, beside the bed, underneath it, on the floor, inside the backpack, in the knot of sheets. Then he checked the en suite.

He stood, looking back at his reflection in the mirror of the bathroom cabinet, realising it was gone.

One day, she'd said.

Tom threw a punch against the bathroom wall.

The bitch had walked away with his watch.

★★★★★

London. Saturday morning, 18 Hours Earlier

Denham paced in his living room. Holt was not picking up. He glanced at his phone for the hundredth time. 06.30 Montevideo time, 09.30 in Streatham.

He should have heard something by now.

Capricorn would be waiting. He wanted to give the good news himself then break it to him that this was his last job. Leave on a high. Go back to Belinda. Beg for another chance.

He wished he hadn't been quite such a dick to Holt and Becca in Uruguay.

Please God let it not have gone bad.

He dialled Holt's phone. It took a few moments to connect before the line went dead. He swore out loud, hung up, tried Becca's phone with the same result.

WHAT THE FUCK WAS HAPPENING?

He didn't want to have to make the call. The last man in the world he ever wanted to speak to.

The line took some moments to connect.

'We may have a problem,' he said, as Anton answered.

Anton appeared to be eating something. When he spoke, the call sounded oddly long distance. 'I talked to Belosi,' Anton said. 'He will handle it. Ray's at the airport. He's through security, he's safe.'

Denham stood stock still, aghast, Anton's words a sucker punch to the abdomen. 'I'm sorry, *what*?'

'I thought Ray would have called you.'

'I am waiting on a call from *Holt*.'

'Holt is with Becca. They're on their way to Buenos Aires. Becca says the Indian copied the contents of a USB from the safe onto a laptop. Holt's got it with him. I'm waiting to hear back from her so we can retrieve it.'

Denham's chest tightened; the panic spreading through his veins to the tips of his fingers and toes. 'I don't… ' His hand went to his forehead. He was struggling for air. He suddenly made the connection. 'Where are you?'

'I'm in Montevideo.'

Of course he was in fucking Montevideo. Denham stared at his fireplace, lowered himself onto the sofa, realising in one horrible moment that the rug had been well and truly pulled out from under him. Not only had he been sidelined, but Anton had apparently taken over the running of the entire operation.

'They were successful?'

'Yes. Ray called me. Choudhury couldn't help himself. Went snooping. I told him to do what he needed to do.'

Denham had to control the trembling indignation in his voice. 'Told who?'

'Ray.'

'Ray is *my* guy, Anton. Ray works for *me*.'

'Don't be ridiculous. I asked him to keep me updated from time to time for a little extra reward. He came through. Had to put a bullet in the Indian but it couldn't be helped, you know. Should have done as he was told.'

Denham's hand slid from his forehead down to his face, the tightness in his chest feeling like a full-blown heart attack. Questioned whether he'd heard right. 'Anil Choudhury is dead?'

'Belosi is on his way to the house. We'll know more once he gets there. But yes, he took a bullet to the head. Ray said he hit the deck fast.'

'Does Capricorn know?'

'I told him myself half an hour ago. Ray has everything, all that we hoped would be inside the safe. All being well he'll arrive at Heathrow tomorrow morning. I'm arranging for a car to pick him up.'

'I tried Holt's phone, he's not answering,' Denham said, ashamed at how pathetic he sounded, petty with jealousy.

'Leave Holt to me. Becca's a smart girl. She knows how to handle him. She knows I'm waiting.'

With that, Anton hung up.

Denham sat for a moment, deflated. Anil was dead, shot by Ray, who had been working for him yet been under Anton's sway the entire time. Everything Ray had told him, he had said to Anton.

He scrolled through his contacts in his phone, selected Ray's number.

The rent-a-cop answered immediately with a clipped, 'Yeah.'

'You… *Fuck*.'

'I was about to call you,' Ray said. 'Had to get through security. I'm at the gate in Montevideo, waiting for a flight to São Paulo.'

'You work for *me*, you fat fuck. You want to shoot somebody in the head you run it by *me* first.'

'I was given instructions, I reacted. My apologies, Mr Denham.'

'Anton's ordering you a car to collect you at Heathrow. I don't want you to take it. You come into Terminal 5, right?'

'Right.'

'When you come into arrivals, take the lifts to the top floor; I'll meet you in departures. Do you understand me?'

'Yes.'

'What time do you land?'

'It's a seven-hour wait in São Paulo. Best I could get at short notice. Flight doesn't leave 'til five something p.m. I land at 6.40 tomorrow morning UK time, British Airways. Terminal 5.'

'Switch your phone off. No more phone calls with Anton. Understand me? Do *not* speak to Anton. Tell him nothing.'

Ray sounded peeved. 'Understood.'

'Don't forget what I've done for you, Ray. You owe me that much.'

He hung up, mind reeling. It was hard to keep a grip on reality when the events that mattered to him were taking place on the other side of the world. He questioned then why he hadn't stayed in Uruguay with Tatiana. Why he hadn't made that choice to be close by. He hadn't thought it necessary, when Anton, Capricorn's man, clearly had other ideas. Had Capricorn sent Anton to South America? Had he been sidelined some time ago, without even realising it?

Denham knew what happened to men who were sidelined by Solomon Capricorn.

He swallowed the lump in his throat.

He hadn't been the one to deliver the news to Capricorn.

He would never be in a position to tell Capricorn this was his final job.

Even before his conversation with Anton was over, he had known he was a dead man walking.

Chapter 26

Tom paced back and forth in the fusty hotel room, in as much as the space allowed for pacing. Becca had been gone for ten minutes. He could still taste her, skin clammy with the memory of her undressed body, her flesh against his.

Even the fucking she had managed to fake.

With the realisation had come a certain unfamiliar brand of resentment. The betrayal had left him stung, he didn't deny it. He tasted bile at the back of his throat. So her role within the team hadn't been only to steal things. If Ray was Denham's spy, then she was Anton's: the honey-trap, his infiltrator, and ultimately, betrayer, all in one perfect soulless combination. Had Denham been the one to order her to get close to him? Or Anton?

And yet, she had allowed him to watch Clare Buchanan's statement on the laptop. She'd stopped him from doing so on the ferry to Argentina, but in the hotel she could have yanked him back into the shower with her, done *something* to stop him from viewing it, so that he'd hold off. But she'd missed the chance. Perhaps she'd wanted him to watch it. Had she known about the existence of the video all along?

The only genuine player all along had been Anil. Tom winced as he recalled the moment Ray had pulled the trigger; the moment Anil's body had sunk, lifeless, to the ground. He stopped still, stared at the wall, steadied his breathing. Anil had died for nothing. He had died so a rich man could keep his secrets buried. Clare Buchanan had disappeared off the face of the earth for nothing, for the very same reason.

Anil had been a decent man, despite his chosen profession, or the profession that had managed to reel him back in one last time. Somewhere back in England, his wife and daughter were likely frantic with worry, wondering why their husband and father had stopped calling. Eleven years on, Clare Buchanan's family were likely living with a day-to-day glimmer of hope that one day their beloved daughter or sister might walk through the door.

Without the laptop, Tom had no physical evidence to present to anybody. Without it, their deaths would continue to mean nothing. He was bound by a watertight NDA. Without proof, any allegation he made against Charlie Ebdon was baseless, grounds for libel or some other such shit.

With evidence, he might be at least able to point the finger of suspicion at Charlie Ebdon and a dangerous individual known only as Anton.

An idea was brewing in his mind.

He squeezed his eyes shut, trying to push it away. It was a suicide mission, yet there was a small margin of success if… *if* he could pull it off.

He remembered something Anil had said, the night of the robbery.

You stand or you fall.

He was prepared to try, for Anil's sake, for Clare Buchanan's sake. He had to be.

He looked to the bag containing the eighty thousand. It

was a gamble, one that he had the slimmest chance of winning.

He considered his future for a brief moment.

Anil was a better man than he. Had been all along. The better man was already dead.

London held no future for him, at least not one that was in any way appealing.

He didn't have much time.

Swiping up the backpack, he went to work, knowing the next eight or so hours would probably be his last.

After 8 a.m. he stepped out of the cab in the long shadow of La Bombonera Stadium, wearing jeans and a crumpled white shirt from his severely limited wardrobe. La Boca on a Sunday morning was sleepy. He had travelled light, carrying only a small wad of local cash. He crossed the road to get out of the sun. Even at the early hour, humidity was on the rise. Ahead of him were two young boys, around ten or eleven, messing around on the shabby street corner on their bikes, a mural of brightly coloured graffiti as a backdrop.

Tom approached them. He looked towards the taller of the two, black hair swept over into a side parting, with buck teeth and wearing an Argentine national football shirt. The boy squinted up at him.

'*Hola, chico*,' Tom greeted him. '*Conoces el que llaman La Almendra?*'

The boy suddenly looked nervous, a little frightened.

Tom held out a wad of notes towards the boy, continuing in Spanish. 'I need you to get a message to The Bullet for me. You tell him the Englishman is here and wants to speak to him.'

The boy took the money, looked down at the notes in his hand. 'Can you do that for me?' Tom added.

The boy nodded.

'I'm going to wait down that way, towards Caminito, underneath the figure of Evita on the balcony. Tell The Bullet that's where I'll be.'

The boy nodded for a second time, his friend hanging back, unsure.

'Now go,' Tom said, and the boy scarpered, leaving his bike lying abandoned on the cracked paving stones. His friend hopped on his bike and sped off in the other direction.

Tom waited for a moment, puffed out his cheeks, looked to the cloudless sky.

It was about a two hundred metre walk to the spot he had chosen, the only space he'd been able to come up with under pressure, the colourful *Plaza Bomberos* where a network of smaller streets came together. The balcony was famous, on the fringes of Caminito – home of the tango – a building painted red, blue and yellow, iconic in La Boca. A figure of Maradona was on the left in his Boca Juniors kit, the celebrated number 10 emblazoned on his shorts. Next to him the figure of Evita leaned over, waving regally, wearing a blue suit with her trademark blonde hair and red lips. The other figure was a famous tango dancer; he couldn't recall the name.

He stopped underneath the balcony. Five metres away, two elderly Argentinian gentlemen sat in the sun playing cards, oblivious to his presence. Chest rising and falling, he waited. Instinctively looked to his wrist, only to find a strip of white flesh where his watch should have been. *Damn*.

Fifteen minutes. Sweat poured off him. The position of the sun meant there was no shade. A few locals shuffled by, most of them of advancing years.

Half an hour. His mind skimmed through the alternatives. He could let the laptop go but the image of Anil alone in the house back in Uruguay kept him going.

Shortly after, he noticed the two men emerging from a street behind him to his left at the crossroads. They stopped still and lingered, hands in their pockets. Two more appeared from the opposite corner, still to his left. They greeted one another with a single nod. They were wearing jackets, unusual for the weather, which Tom assumed meant they were carrying. Another pair appeared across the park, this time in short-sleeved shirts, one with a closely shaven head. The fourth pair, to his right, Tom recognised one of the men as Mazzanti, one of the men who had first spotted him in the Chinese supermarket in Recoleta.

Nobody moved. The air was stagnant, not the slightest hint of a breeze. He waited, they watched. Beads of sweat gathered on his temples, dripping down to his neck. The two card players appeared to realise something was amiss, swept up the pack and shuffled off down towards the river mouth.

From the opposite side of the park, a man approached head-on wearing a white short-sleeved shirt and beige chinos. Tom squinted. He walked with a definite limp. He wore sunglasses and had a dark beard: Arturo Baresi. He was flanked by two younger muscular thugs with closely shaven heads, also in shades.

Baresi stopped two metres in front of Tom. Tom recalled the Argentine's face, the way he had sneered at Becca before she had stabbed him in the thigh. His colleague – the fat one with the curly hair, the one they called Thiago – was nowhere to be seen.

Baresi stopped in front of him, removing his sunglasses. Looked him up and down. '*Estás armado?*' *Are you armed?*

'*No,*' Tom replied, holding out his hands wide, as if to show willing. '*Quiero hacer un trato con Fede.*' *I want to make a deal with Fede.*

'*Dar la vuelta!*' Baresi spat. *Turn around.*

Tom did as he was ordered. The two younger thugs were on him then, frisking him, checking for weapons or wires, hands thrusting in his pockets, shoving him roughly against the wall below the balcony. Baresi ordered them to check his shoes. When they were happy he was clean, Baresi ordered Tom to turn back around.

'You'll get your five minutes with The Bullet,' Baresi stated. 'This way.'

He walked to Tom's right. Tom followed, the two thugs on his tail. No sooner had they started walking in convoy, one of the thugs tossed a stone fragment. It hit the back of his neck, below his left ear, stinging his flesh and drawing blood. They kept to Baresi's slow pace, allowing for the two shadows to continue with their onslaught, catching the back of his knees with their boots, causing him to stumble. He gritted his teeth. Par for the course. These were Fede's men. Turning off the main street, he followed Baresi into an alleyway, only a thin strip of sky visible above his head. A metal staircase hung off a windowless building. Baresi stood back, nodded up the stairs. The moment he stepped forward, he felt a sharp elbow come into abrupt contact with the top of his spine, sending his arms flailing. He didn't have a moment to think before his cheek was planted into rusty cast iron grating. He winced, used his arms to push himself up. He could hear laughter. He touched his cheek. More blood, the wound he had taken on his face in Uruguay reopened and oozing. He kept Anil in his mind. His friend had suffered a worse fate.

He reached the top of the staircase, Baresi close behind. Baresi rapped on the door in a pattern of sounds: three quick knocks followed by two long ones. After a moment, the door opened and Tom found himself face to face with Becca's Punisher, the one they called Thiago, twisty hair and a fat gut. Thiago opened the door wider. It was then that Tom noticed he was missing two fingers on his right hand and there was a weapon thrust into his fraying leather belt, which in turn held up a baggy pair of jeans. He crossed the threshold into a warehouse of sorts, except he was on a balcony, looking down to a shadowy concrete floor below. On the balcony was an old desk, two overturned chairs. A bulb swung precariously from a wire above their heads. Minus Thiago, there were three other men, seven in total once Baresi and his thugs were through the door. Tom kept his shoulders back, head high, legs rigid and slightly apart. He had one chance to persuade Fede that this was worth his time. Except Fede wasn't there.

'You'd better start talking,' Baresi said in Spanish.

'Where is Fede?' Tom demanded.

'He took his mother to church. It's Sunday morning. She likes to talk with God.'

'Maybe we could tell this Motherfucker to talk to God,' one of the men piped up.

'God's too good for this Motherfucker,' said another.

There was another coded knock at the door and the men all piped down. Thiago went to open it. Federico stepped inside, dressed smartly in jeans and a leather jacket, the bottom of his expensive leather boots scuffing against the grubby concrete floor, heels raised to allow The Bullet that little extra height.

Nobody spoke. Tom kept his eyes fixed on Fede, knowing The Bullet would prey on any sign of weakness. His would-be nemesis glanced around, surveying all the characters in attendance.

'I had to cut short my visit to *mi mamá*,' he spat in Spanish, voice echoing up to the rusty corrugated metal roof held up with equally rusted supports, sunlight peeking through scattered holes.

Baresi piped up. 'He says he has a deal he wants to make with you.'

Fede looked Tom up and down.

'Start talking,' Baresi spat.

Tom stood his ground. Fede took a step closer, causing a ripple of panic to spread across the balcony. His crew shuffled uncomfortably, weapons at the ready. Fede held out a hand. Someone put a blade in it. Fede eyeballed Tom, tilting his head to one side.

Fede switched to English. 'Give me one good reason I shouldn't slice you open,' he said, pressing the tip of the blade to Tom's chest.

His heart, fit to explode. 'Because I'm offering you eighty thousand US dollars cash. And because I need your help.'

Fede lowered the knife. Started laughing, a kind of rasping cackle. 'You need *my* help?'

Tom swallowed. 'Gabi once told me that in Buenos Aires anyone The Bullet doesn't know isn't worth knowing.'

Fede contemplated this for a moment. 'What is it you want in return?'

'A laptop. The girl I was with, the redhead, she has it. I need it back.'

Baresi's eyes snapped up. Fede sobered. '*La coloradita,*' he mused.

'There is a condition. The girl remains unharmed.' He was looking to Baresi as he said it. 'You get me that laptop, you let her go, that money is all yours. She's currently with another man, heading to the airport to leave the country. He's dangerous. They're due to fly to London this afternoon.'

Fede's eyes narrowed. 'What's so special about this… laptop?'

'It has something on it that I need. That I can't get elsewhere.'

Fede took a step closer, bared his teeth. 'Last time we met you put a gun to my head. *Me.* I am The Bullet. You don't come into *my* city, into *my* barrio, and put a gun to my head. When you do something like that your days are over.'

The stifling air inside the warehouse grew warmer. He felt the sweat pooling at the base of his spine, Fede's dark-haired crew bearing down on him.

'Once I have the laptop, once I have done what I need to do with it, then you can do what you want with me.'

Fede was silent, black eyes glinting. 'Is that so?'

'You have my word.'

'Where is she, *La coloradita*? Which airport?'

'Ezeiza,' he replied, referring to the international terminal an hour's drive out of town.

'And she has this… computer.'

'One of them has it.'

'Where is the money now?'

'In a hotel room in the city. When I get the laptop I will give you the eighty thousand.'

Fede clicked his fingers. Thiago stepped forward. Fede switched back to Spanish.

'*Bueno. Ratita.* Take him. Take Baresi. Use the *estância* at San Vicente.'

'*Si, jefe,*' Thiago nodded.

Tom was reluctant to allow Baresi along for the ride, given his volatility, on the grounds of wanting revenge for his limp. The Bullet was sending them across the city to somewhere called San Vicente. He was giving orders to Thiago to contact their people.

Fede leaned over to Thiago, kept his voice low. '*Si no obtienes el dinero,*' he said, eyes raised once last time to Tom, '*Entiérralo en el suelo.*'

Thiago nodded in understanding.

Tom understood every word.

If you don't get the cash, put him in the ground.

Chapter 27

In the bathroom, Becca rubbed steam from the mirror and faced her reflection. She felt unable to recall a time when she had physically shed tears. Not after her parents had died. Not when Anton had taken a belt to her back aged twenty-one for failing to steal what she'd been ordered to. Not when Richie had been dragged off to jail.

Now though.

She closed her eyes, refusing to allow the prospect of Anton seeing her like this to become a reality.

The door was locked. Anton had showered first, now sitting on the bed on the other side of the door flipping through TV channels. Inside the pokey hotel en suite bathroom, she reached out, turned the shower up to full power, water splattering onto the floor tiles. She reached into her pocket, teasing out Tom Holt's watch, cradling it in her palm with her thumb stroking the watch face. The time read two minutes past eight. They would leave for the airport in ninety minutes.

The watch felt bulky, the metal strap warm from living inside her jeans. She had removed it from his wrist in the night, right before Anton had replied to her email on the laptop to say he was close by. She'd wanted a memento of him – of everything they had shared, including a bed. It would have to do, until the day she would be free to seek him out again.

She kicked off her boots, unbuttoned her jeans, peeling them from her thighs. Her underwear was damp, his scent still on her body. She closed her eyes, diving again into a delicious memory. She longed to rewind those moments so she could experience it all again, the sensation of his tongue driving her mind to extremes she'd never experienced before. The memory came crashing apart with the memory of Anton in the hotel room, the picture of Tom's face as he'd switched on the light, the realisation dawning on him that she had been the one to let Anton through the door.

She'd known that had she buckled and opened her mouth to speak, to react to his pleas to communicate, that her façade would have crumbled and her true feelings come spewing out. Anton would have realised the truth and he would have murdered them both for it. Without the laptop, and with the selective lies she'd told, she knew she could keep Tom Holt alive. She'd left him with the safe money: it was enough for him to disappear for a spell at least.

It was all the life she had known: Capricorn, Anton, Denham. *Do as you are charged, ask no questions. Obedience and discretion are fundamental to success. The rewards will come and they will be substantial.* Perhaps she could have driven off to the borders of Brazil with Holt but they would have dragged her back. Their *property*. They controlled her, always had. She had done her job first, like she'd always done. She'd been on auto-pilot her entire life.

She removed the rest of her clothes, stepped into the shower. Water hit her back and hair as it ran in streams between her eyes and across her nose, plummeting to the floor tiles from her open mouth.

She felt the tears before they came, flames of guilt licking at her insides. She wanted to go back. To live her days and nights with Tom Holt in a house in the Uruguayan beach town of José Ignacio. To be like those women who wore their husbands' white shirts tied at the naval, expensive sunglasses and who ate lunch at restaurants nestled in the sand. She gripped the wall. Her shoulders were trembling, the water continually washing away tears, the shower loud enough to mask the wretched sounds of her falling to pieces.

Anton was on the bed, legs crossed at the ankles when she emerged from the bathroom, fully dressed in clean clothes, steam swirling out from behind her. She dropped the pile of dirty clothes she was carrying into her messenger bag, the watch concealed inside material folds.

Anton was chewing gum. 'Ray's stuck in São Paulo. Flight was overbooked.'

Becca perched on the edge of the bed and pulled on her shoes. She didn't care about Ray.

'Anil's body… ' she began.

Anton dragged his eyes away from the television. 'Sancho's dealt with it. Body's in the ground. We are done here.'

'Where did you get the gun?'

'What?'

'The gun. You couldn't have brought it on the ferry so where did you get it?'

'Dante Belosi was here to meet me.'

She frowned. Dante Belosi was Sancho's nephew. He had

a twin brother, Rolo. Much like Sancho, she'd never come face to face with either of them and knew them by reputation alone.

'You know I could have left that hotel room. Walked away with the laptop. I could have met you somewhere.'

He cocked his head. 'Upset I put a gun to your boyfriend's head?'

She recoiled on purpose. 'He's not my boyfriend.'

'But you liked him though. Practically jumped out of your skin when I threatened to kill him. Tom Holt needed to know who he's been dealing with. Not fucking Denham. I had to demonstrate to him that you belong to someone else, Becca.'

It took over an hour to get to the airport in the back of a taxi, crawling through some of the areas in Buenos Aires she recognised from before. Looking out of the window, she wondered what Tom was doing at that precise moment. Sancho would have buried all trace of Anil. It occurred to her with a heavy heart that he would forever remain in that house in Uruguay, his eternal resting place.

Compared to the dank and gloom of Aeroparque – the other airport in the centre of Buenos Aires – Ezeiza was positively airy and gleaming. She kept hold of the backpack, still containing the laptop, for which she had given Anton the secure password, allowing him a chance to watch Clare Buchanan's video for himself.

She had never asked what they had done with Clare Buchanan's body. She didn't want to know.

They waited in the queue for British Airways Economy

Class check-in. She chewed the skin around her nails. Anton seemed more relaxed than she was used to, perhaps because he knew it was all over, that Capricorn would be giving him the standard slap on the back and a hefty financial reward for his efforts as soon as they were back on home turf. She worried for the lawyer. Anton had always done his best to discredit and undermine Al Denham. By coming to Montevideo and then to Buenos Aires, he had managed to cut Denham out of the equation altogether. It hadn't entirely surprised her when he'd made contact in the days leading up to the robbery at Las Colinas. It would have been his order for Ray to kill Anil. Unlike Denham, Anton had no qualms with death. Death was Anton's currency.

It took twenty minutes to reach the front of the queue, Becca lazily nudging her bags along the floor tiles with her foot. Anton was in his black overcoat in preparation for the London winter. The Hispanic woman on the check-in had high cheekbones, arched eyebrows and too-thick foundation. She took their passports, typed something into her keyboard and gave a frown. She rose up from her seat, manicured nails gripping the desk, looking side to side down the check-in line, eyes searching for a face.

Without smiling she said, in accented-English, 'We have a full flight today so British Airways would like to offer you both a complimentary upgrade to Business Class.'

Becca raised an eyebrow, looked to Anton whose features had collapsed into a frown. The woman was still looking for another attendant, somewhere in the crowds.

Anton cleared his throat. 'We'll take it,' he said.

The woman pushed their passports back across the desk. 'Someone will be with you shortly. Wait here please.'

Minutes later an airport official arrived. He was squat with greying curly hair poking out of his hat, shirt stretched over his protruding belly. His badge said his name was Rimini. He nodded once, indicating that they should follow. They followed him through the crowds to the far end of the check-in desks. Rimini used his security pass to access a set of white doors. They followed him down a long windowless corridor, no advertising, no cameras, no check-in desks either, only the sounds of their own footsteps, strip lights buzzing overhead.

'Wouldn't they check us in at the desk?' Becca said, thinking out loud.

Rimini's pace slowed. A sensation in her gut said something was off. Anton stopped dead. Becca looked to him, shook her head. He had dropped the gun from Dante Belosi down the hotel's rubbish chute. Her knife she had abandoned in Uruguay. They had nothing but their fists.

It was a moment before Rimini turned around. His features had darkened. Her chest tightening instinctively, Becca wondered whether he was even an airport official.

She glanced over at Anton, the look that flashed between them in mutual agreement that they needed to turn back.

They turned, started walking fast, leaving Rimini for dust. When she glanced back his hands were on his hips, head cocked to one side. When she looked forward again, two more officials appeared from nowhere, shape-shifting out of the walls. They were both armed with handguns, weapons drawn. Becca ground to a halt. She and Anton faced one another, as they had done so often before. Anton gave her a single nod that meant: *by any means necessary.*

The two officials drew near and Becca let her two bags slip. Before they'd even hit the ground she'd dropped low, launched herself at the official on the left, arms outstretched, palms up, hitting him full force in the ribs, sending him tumbling backwards. Landing her body squarely on his stomach, she aimed a clean punch at his jaw and went for the gun. He held on tight with white knuckles, shouting in some indistinguishable Spanish, bucking his hips underneath her, his free hand tearing at her hair. She cried out, head yanked to an awkward angle as she dug her nails into his flesh at his wrist, pushing up with her legs and forward-rolling over his head, creating enough thrust to rip the weapon from his grasp. Pain seared through her scalp, a tress of red hair still sprouting from between her assailant's fingers. Before she could stand, Rimini had launched through the air, sending her backwards, her skull cracking against the tiled floor.

Little grey dots filled her vision before everything went blurry, her limbs floppy. Somewhere close by, she could hear the sounds of Anton in a tussle. Two Riminis floated above her, becoming one before separating again into two men. Her assailant had stood up, helping to subdue Anton. It was rare to find an individual who could match the man who had taught her all she knew. In all the time she had known him she had never once called Anton a friend.

★★★★★

Thiago held the wheel steady. The sedan came from a stock of stolen cars Fede kept parked in two different back lots in La Boca. Fede kept three *hombres* in service working a chop shop. The car Thiago was driving had been robbed from a lot in San Telmo, had been re-sprayed from white to silver then splattered with mud to blend in with local traffic. The shabby interior remained unaltered.

They had made it out of the city onto the flat plains, the northern fringes of the lowlands of Las Pampas, taking the southern route from Buenos Aires on Ruta 1 and 2 to avoid skirting around the airport. At a spaghetti junction Thiago followed signs for Brandsen towards San Vicente on Ruta 6.

He glanced in his rear-view mirror. The Englishman Holt was brooding in the back of the vehicle, probably, Thiago considered, because the bitch with the red hair had gone off with some other *hombre* and some fucking piece of junk laptop computer. He glanced across at Arturo Baresi in the passenger seat before allowing himself a smile.

Motherfucking Baresi. If it hadn't been for the Englishman sitting in the back of his car, he would still have all ten of his fingers. Yet if he still had all ten digits, he wouldn't have gained the admiration from Fede's crew that he now possessed. Forgetting to arm himself on the night that the English *cabrón* had come to La Boca had been the best decision he could ever have made. Losing two fingers had put him up in the rankings to Fede's number one. The crew looked at *La Rata* differently now. They respected him. He even held rank above Baresi, which made Baresi's blood boil. And being Fede's go-to guy had won Thiago attention from the opposite sex. Staring at the road, his mind floated back to the previous evening when he'd been alone with a *señora* known as Carminda. He shuddered, hardly believing his luck.

Ruta 6 was a straight flat road. Thiago checked his watch and put his foot on the gas. The *Estância Genovese* was situated down a private road, about five kilometres east of the small village of San Vicente, with its own lake.

He didn't want to miss the black van that would soon be arriving from the airport.

★★★★★

Tom squinted in the sun, leaning up against a tree and watching at a distance, Anton the first to be dragged from the back of the van. Anton had a sack over his head, wrists and ankles secured with cable ties. He was fighting them: bucking all over the place, until one of the guys driving the van cocked his weapon, thrust it into contact with Anton's temple. He was still after that.

Then came Becca. Tom straightened. He recognised her stance, the same pair of skinny jeans he'd seen almost daily for the past four months. Felt his chest tighten. She too had some kind of sack over her head. She was more placid than Anton. The two men who had been in the front of the van shoved her into a standing position, adjusted the sack over her head and cut the ties around her and Anton's ankles, forcing them to kneel. Their luggage came after that: a larger suitcase – Anton's presumably – Becca's small satchel and lastly, the black backpack. The driver tossed them all down to the grass metres from the two hostages.

Tom looked over at Thiago, who was standing underneath the same line of trees next to Baresi, arms crossed over his belly. Both men looked entirely out of place in the lush fields of the *estância*, an overpowering odour of manure wafting up from the nearby stables, aided by a steady breeze sweeping in from the south. Out here, this was still The Bullet's turf. Whatever happened, there would be no witnesses.

Thiago gave him a single nod.

He hadn't asked who, or how. The fact that Anton and Becca were now on their knees on the grass, wrists bound and gagged, snatched at the airport, was evidence enough of Fede's influence. He felt several pairs of Argentinian eyes on him as he stepped forward. They had agreed in advance on no verbal communication: no way for Anton or Becca to be able to say with absolute certainty who was behind their capture. They would assume he was the lynchpin, of course, but he would be long gone – either that or dead – if everything went to plan.

He made his approach. Crouched down, unzipped the backpack, checked the laptop and power cord were still inside and glanced up towards Becca. She was metres from him. The wind rustled the trees. Her movements were small, body swaying in the breeze. Less than twenty-four hours ago she had seemed like a different person.

He picked up the backpack, walked over to Thiago, offering him a single nod in confirmation, that their work there was done.

Thiago turned, was ready to make orders to depart when Tom heard the voice from behind. One of the van drivers cried out, some kind of warning. He turned in time to

298

witness Baresi advancing on Becca, weapon thrust outwards at the ready, limping as fast as he could down the grass toward where she knelt helplessly. Tom let go of the bag, darted across the grass, Baresi firing a single shot as Tom's heart leapt in his chest. Becca fell to the ground, face down. Tom skidded, torpedoed into the back of Baresi's knees, taking him out, launching himself atop the weaselly Argentine, pummelling him with a series of merciless blows to the face, driven by an unparalleled desire to inflict pain. Baresi hit back, striking a few blows, one to his cheek, then to his eye, forcing Tom to double down. Blood spurted from Baresi's nose. Becca had not been part of the deal. She was not supposed to suffer. Swiping up Baresi's weapon, he got to his feet, brought the barrel in line with Baresi's head, breaths coming in shallow gasps. Baresi cowered, finally relenting, elbows covering his face. Out of the corner of his eye, Tom saw Becca move, the drivers of the van scooping her up. A sound came from her throat: *ummh ummh.*

She was alive.

Baresi's shot had missed. His finger squeezed the trigger. Thiago was looming in his field of vision. He said nothing, dealing Baresi a swift kick to the ribs. Baresi began to whimper. Tom took a step back, lowered the weapon, relief washing over him, watching as Anton and Becca were returned to the van, tossed back inside like scraps, their remaining bags following them before the doors were slammed shut.

'*A dónde los llevarán?*' Tom asked Thiago, gun now lowered at his side. *Where will they take them?*

'*Lejos de aqui,*' Thiago grumbled in return with a

nonchalant wave of his hand, walking back up to the line of the trees. *Away from here.*

★★★★★

They had been driving for some time, over rocky terrain and smooth. In the back of the van, Anton kicked and kicked, stumbling to his feet and slamming his body into the back doors in an attempt to force them open, cursing through the duct tape.

She lay there, on the floor of the van, still trembling. Let the shock sink in, going over the events in her head.

A small hole in the hemp sack over her head meant she had witnessed everything.

Tom – so close to her yet so far – an unbearable look of indifference on his face as he walked away with the bag containing the laptop. The same look she had given him back at the hotel when she'd left with Anton. She could dish it out but, *boy*, she couldn't take it. That look for a single second more would have sliced her open.

Yet he had saved her life.

A second shot from Baresi on target meant they would have been putting her back into the van a corpse.

She had watched him advancing on her, panic rising in her throat, Tom's back to her, oblivious to what was happening. She'd cried out, *ummh ummh ummh ummh*, hobbling from side to side on her knees, waiting desperately for an eternity for someone to take notice. When he'd fired the gun she had recoiled, losing her balance, dropping forward to the grass, only the sack saving her from a mouthful of cow shit. From the small hole, she'd been able to witness the resulting carnage, Baresi on his back, Tom pinning him down, pounding the life from him. At that point, she was either going to vomit or pass out, until her world tipped and she was being dragged back up again, flung back inside the vehicle.

The vehicle came to an abrupt halt, engine cutting out. Anton was still on his feet, muttering something through the tape though she couldn't comprehend a word.

The doors were thrown open, light flooding in. From the bottom of the hood she watched Anton lunge but it was one against two and the drivers grabbed him, flinging him to the ground. She followed, sensing strong fingers on her, a moment of exquisite freedom in the air before she landed with a crack on solid ground, skull whipping backwards, spinning and whirling over arid rocks and grit, the breath knocked out of her.

Her body rolled one last time, coming to a stop. She tasted blood mixed with her saliva. There was a sharp pain in her hip and thigh, as if they'd been gone at with a cheese grater.

In the near distance, she heard the sound of the van starting up, driving away.

Groaning a second time through the tape, Becca pulled herself into a sitting position. Yanked off the hood and squinted in the sun. Her cheeks were still wet. She had no idea where they had been dumped. Anton was ten or so metres away, removing the tape from his mouth and launching into a diatribe of swearing. Next to him was his discarded suitcase and her messenger bag. Both their wrists were still tied. Becca hooked a nail underneath her own tape and yanked it hard, skin smarting as it was pulled taut by the adhesive.

She eased herself into a standing position, everything sore. She could see the road and the endless flat lands that stretched out for miles on the other side. The nearest tree was three hundred metres away. They were in the middle of nowhere.

She hobbled over towards Anton. He had a cut above his left eye.

'Are you alright?' she asked.

'Fine,' he grunted. 'You?'

She nodded.

'There's blood on your lip,' he said.

She wiped her mouth on the back of her hand. It wasn't much. She looked to his suitcase. 'You got a knife in there?'

Between them, they managed to unzip Anton's suitcase, locate a pen knife and cut one another's ties, tossing them aside. She rubbed her wrists, thin skin gnawed by the plastic slicing into her flesh.

'Could you see anything?' Anton asked, doing the same. 'Through the hood, could you see anything?'

'No. You?'

He grimaced. 'Couldn't see shit.'

Anton looked to the luggage. Realised there was no backpack.

'Fuck!' he started ranting again. 'Fuck fuck *fuck*!'

He went over to her messenger bag. Becca watched him swipe it up, knowing it wasn't the laptop bag but he opened it anyway. 'Fuck!' he yelled again. He raised his eyes to her. 'Was this your boy? Was this him?'

She shook her head. The breeze was picking up again, grey clouds in the distance. She had betrayed Tom Holt for the last time. 'I don't see how. I don't see how it could have been. He doesn't know anybody.'

'Then what the hell just happened?'

'We were robbed, that's what just happened.'

'Yes but by who?!' Anton questioned, hurling the leather messenger across rough terrain, then out of frustration, picked up his suitcase and threw that too, sending its contents scattering across the dry, cracking mud, continuing his cursed-fuelled rant.

She gathered up her bag, sealing it up again, thankful that the watch had remained inside. Slung it over her shoulder and hobbled towards the road. Through the corner of her eye she saw Anton's shoulders droop. He didn't like to lose. He'd rarely lost at anything his entire life.

When she climbed up to the road her shoes hit smooth tarmac. She hoped it was only money Tom had offered Fede, and that he was on his way to freedom.

Chapter 28

Sunday 13 November, 2016

Denham turned the key to the gate to the gardens behind Lauderdale Road in Maida Vale, the gate whistling as it opened. A kitchen light was on nearby, illuminating the garden that contained the giant rabbit run that Denham had only ever seen at night. It was too cold out for rabbits. He peered into the all-encompassing darkness ahead.

By the time he'd turned fifty, he wished he had done the time. Pleaded guilty to statutory rape in '93, lost his license to practice law, apologised to Alice Shales for his actions. His younger self had been too arrogant to even consider such a sentence. His career would have certainly suffered, granted, but he would have been free. He believed deep in his heart that he would have won Belinda back, perhaps not so soon, but one day. Children had never been on the cards for them, it seemed, no matter their age. Tatiana would have been palmed off to some other schmuck roped in by Capricorn. He would never have even heard her name. He would never have met Capricorn or Anton and been cornered into doing the things he now had to live with, things that would haunt him for the rest of his days. His arrogance, his self-belief – something he'd had since childhood – these things had been his downfall. Over time, arrogance had shrivelled away to acceptance, and then finally to obedience. It had been a slow, chipping away at his soul. Sometimes he looked in the mirror and didn't recognise himself anymore.

Capricorn was sat on his usual bench under the sprawling beech tree, sipping a glass of wine and wearing an overcoat with a dark plaid scarf. Denham's breath caught in his throat as he caught sight of a corpse hanging lifeless from one of the branches.

'It's not real,' Capricorn's droll tone reassured him, glancing at the body over his shoulder. 'Left over from Guy Fawkes Night.'

Light emanating from the surrounding houses in the triangular-shaped garden meant he could see enough of Capricorn's face. 'What news, Al?' his boss asked.

Denham stopped a few metres in front of him, pushed his hands further into his pockets. 'I heard from Anton an hour ago.'

'Yes.'

'He and Becca managed to successfully remove the laptop from Holt's possession.'

'I know that already. You didn't come all the way here to give me old news did you?'

'No. Something happened at the airport. At check-in they were led down a disused corridor and attacked. Anton says blindfolded and thrown into the back of a van.'

Capricorn was silent for a moment. 'Go on.'

'They were taken to a location; they don't know where. In the countryside somewhere. At some point the laptop was removed from their possession.'

'What do you mean, *removed*?'

'I mean they no longer have it. They don't know who does.'

Another silence. 'Was it Holt? Did he organise this?'

'They don't think so. They don't know.'

'So can you tell me with all confidence that Holt *does not have* that laptop?'

'Becca said to me a while ago that Holt knew some people in Buenos Aires. But she doesn't think he has it. She doesn't see how it would be possible. Those people in Buenos Aires wanted him dead.'

'Have you managed to track down Holt?'

'No. He switched his phone off some time ago, probably got rid of it. I haven't heard from him.'

Capricorn finished his wine. He was silent for quite some time.

'If the laptop contains a copy of Clare Buchanan's statement,' he said, 'which Becca claims that it does... then it's out there. Whether Holt has it or not.'

Denham had no answer.

'Go home to your wife, Al,' Capricorn said at length, his lower jaw sliding forward. 'Give her my regards.'

'I have made arrangements to meet Ray Caulder from his flight tomorrow morning. He was stuck in São Paulo for twenty-four hours. Once I have the contents of the safe I can return them to you.'

'Meet me here. Same time, tomorrow night.'

'I would like to discuss my future.'

'Tomorrow, Al. Tomorrow. We'll talk about where you go from here.'

He arrived back in Streatham Hill on a late train. He sluggishly climbed to the top of the steps of the bridge over the station platform, crossing at the traffic lights with a handful of other commuters, making a cursory glance over his shoulder, as was customary these days. He took his usual route, up the incline of Leigham Court Road, turning right into Culverhouse Gardens, hands pushed as far down into his coat pocket as he could manage in the winter chill. He saw the two males loitering up ahead, scruffy in jeans and trainers, one leaning against the lamp post smoking a suspicious-looking cigarette, the other kicking something on the ground, hoods up. It was only when he walked closer that he realised they weren't wearing hoods at all but balaclavas, with the image of a grinning skull printed on them, covering their faces. The scene irritated Denham. The sight of the fake body hanging from the tree in the private gardens had already set his teeth on edge. Halloween was over for another year, Guy Fawkes too, yet young people still insisted on wearing antisocial masks, the kind that petrified pensioners and small children. He crossed the road.

It took a matter of seconds to feel their stares, to realise they had clocked him, a businessman in a long coat, perhaps somebody worth mugging. He quickened his pace.

Within a flash, they were on the same side of the street. Denham kept moving, didn't break pace.

In his heart, he knew there would be no meeting with Capricorn the following night. A flicker of hope remained, that he might be wrong.

He felt their close presence, picturing Belinda. Wished he could have said his goodbyes. He glanced back, panic exploding in his chest, one of the men taking him out at the knees, sending him splaying forward onto the pavement, thwacking his head on the kerb. His world went horizontal. He felt a searing pain to the kidneys, causing a sharp intake of breath, instinctively curling up in a ball to protect himself. The onslaught kept coming, the kicks and punches harder and harder until he was being pummelled. His nostrils filled with the scent of damp concrete. He clung to the image of Belinda from their wedding day. Only the sounds of the two men grunting were audible. Then Belinda faded away, and there was nothing. The pain at an almost unbearable level, Denham was able to lift his head. A mistake, he acknowledged, a millisecond later. Under the blaze of the street light, he witnessed the bottom of a boot rushing towards his face. There was a sharp pain in his left eye moments before his world turned a brilliant white, then everything went dark.

★★★★★

Monday 14 November, 2016

Ray Caulder woke with a jolt, plane wheels slamming down onto the tarmac, wing flaps going up with a loud whooshing sound that made the hairs on the back of his neck stand on end.

Home soil. In his mind he merrily ticked off all the things he was going to enjoy: a Sunday roast with all the trimmings, a *proper* McDonalds bacon roll, real ale.

His skin felt clammy, eyes hollow. He had been travelling

for two days straight, most of that time spent lying across a set of plastic conjoined seats in the bleak yellow atria of Guarulhos International Airport. Those fuckers at the airline had refused him entry to an overfilled flight and when he'd tried the airport hotel even that had been overbooked.

He felt like he had a case of deep vein thrombosis, knees and legs longing for release, penned in by the economy seat in front. The flight from São Paulo to Heathrow – when he had finally been able to get on one – had lasted a torturous eleven and a half hours.

In Uruguay, the moment he'd left the house in Ciudad de la Costa in the Vitara – not long after putting a bullet in Anil's head – he'd started to hyperventilate, the enormity of what had happened minutes earlier engulfing his psyche. The Indian had always been a cocky shit, it was true, but he had a young daughter back home, a little girl who would never know her father. And what of Holt and Becca? Would they have fled? Would they have buried Anil in the back garden? He knew for a fact that Becca would have been devastated at Anil's demise and that was enough to cause his chest to tighten a fraction.

He had made it to Montevideo airport without crashing into another vehicle. In the car park he found a large empty crisp packet under the passenger seat of the Vitara, made a seal around his mouth and breathed into it, in and out, trying to remember Ray Caulder from the good ol' days, who wouldn't give a flying fuck about that stuff. He had been given a job and he had seen it out to the end. He walked away from the Vitara leaving a gun under the floor mat, a crisp packet on the driver's seat and the steering wheel and gear stick wiped clean. The keys he tossed in a waste bin on the departures level at Carrasco International Airport, moments after he'd purchased his ticket. Both the flight and the onward transfer to London were full: it was cattle class all the way. Ray handed over his credit card to the girl working the kiosk and with a tight smile cursed Denham inwardly.

At Heathrow Terminal 5 arrivals there was already a throng, a sea of handwritten placards, even at 7 a.m. on a Monday. Keeping his eyes down, he made a beeline for the lifts, sticking to his orders from Denham to meet him in person on the top floor in departures. Ray glanced up for a moment, only to find a young twenty-something lad with coffee-coloured skin and wearing an ill-fitting suit looking his way. The lad was clutching a white board with 'RAY CAULDER' written in large letters. Ray shook his head, convinced himself the driver would have been Anton's man – the man Denham hadn't wanted him to meet – and continued towards the lift. Once inside, he pressed the button to go up before the lad had reached out and stuck a palm against the metal door.

'Mr Caulder?' the lad said in an accent not so different from Anil's Hackney twang, 'Mr Denham sent me to collect you.'

Ray rolled his eyes, coming back out of the lift. 'He *fookin'* told me departures.'

'Change of plan. Did you have any bags?'

'None. Lead the way.'

He followed the lad out of the sliding doors, across the paving stones towards the car park. The lad said nothing else. Ray fell in line two steps behind. Bypassing the lifts to the car park they kept to the ground floor parking, weaving amongst stationery vehicles until they were at one corner, within view of the ticket barriers and the exit on the outside. A shiny black Mercedes-Benz GLS Class was parked one space in, Ray taking note of the rear windows completely blacked out. The young driver opened the passenger side door, indicating that Ray should get in. Ray frowned.

'Eyes forward at all times please, sir,' the lad said.

'Where's Denham?' Ray asked.

'No looking behind you please, sir,' the lad repeated. 'Eyes on the windscreen at all times.'

Ray removed his satchel, slid inside the vehicle. Put the satchel in his lap. It was odd being in a right-hand drive again. The lad shut the door behind him, then took up a position at the front of the bonnet, his back to the car.

Inside, the hairs on the back of Ray's neck were bristling again. He sensed a presence in the car; took all his might not to turn and see who was there. A new-car smell filled his nostrils, the odour of fresh leather suggesting he could be in a hire car or that whoever owned the vehicle hadn't driven around in it much.

'Mr Denham?' Ray said out loud.

Whoever it was behind wasn't directly behind him. From the rustling sound Ray concluded that there must have been a second row of seats towards the rear, fold out ones normal for this sized 4x4.

'Good morning, Mr Caulder. I'm afraid Albert Denham won't be joining us. You're speaking to Solomon Capricorn. You know the name?'

Ray tensed. It was unexpected. 'Yes, Mr Capricorn, I do.'

'Good. You have something for me.'

'I do, yes.'

Ray's mind reeled. The voice sounded oddly familiar but he couldn't place it.

'Both items, take them, reach behind you, place them on the back seat, in the middle there, that will do. Keep your eyes to the front, please.'

Ray reached for his satchel, pulling out the certificate and the USB thumb drive held inside the plastic wallet. He did as he was told, placing the wallet on the seat, keeping his eyes fixed on the young lad standing motionless at the front of the bonnet.

'Thank you,' Capricorn said. 'I appreciate you bringing them all the way back to London. I'm sorry for the delay.'

'I was following orders,' Ray replied.

'Indeed. Exemplary work. Tell me, Mr Caulder, where are you from originally?'

'Northallerton. Spent my childhood shuttling between North Yorkshire and Manchester. My mother was Liverpudlian.'

'I need you to do something for me. I need you to disappear. Your time working for Denham is over. Go back up north, or wherever it is you want to go. But not London, not south. If your family is south, move them north. Can you do that for me?'

Ray cleared his throat, still desperate to turn around. He didn't like to be put on the spot. Felt like he was being hurried. Of course he could move, but why should he?

'If you don't mind me saying, Mr Capricorn, Mr Denham always promised me that when I retired I would be well looked after.'

The response was a touch terse. 'Yes I was getting to that. Parked on floor three of this multi-storey car park is a year old silver BMW X Series. The registration document is in your name and address. The car is yours; you may do what you like with it. Inside the glove compartment you will find a percentage of your financial reward in cash. Your safety deposit box in London has also been replenished; you will need to empty it in due course. There will be more than enough money to live out your days very comfortably. When we are finished here my driver will give you the keys to the car and you may go about your business. Do you have questions?'

Ray's heart was slamming against his ribcage. 'Should I contact Mr Denham?'

'Absolutely not. As of this moment, you have never heard of a lawyer named Albert Denham. Do you understand?'

'Yes, sir, of course. Thank you.'

'You may go then, Mr Caulder. We have nothing further to discuss.'

Ray found himself nodding. He opened the door, the lad springing into action and coming round to open it wider for him. He hobbled out of the car, hips still stiff from the flight, keeping hold of his satchel. Before he could even ask, the lad was sliding a key fob into his palm.

'Third floor, other side to this,' the lad said. 'Front row facing the terminal building. You'll hear it unlock with the fob.'

Ray felt like he had a dozen more questions but none came. 'I best get moving then,' he said stoically.

The lad nodded once.

Ray started walking, didn't look back. Thought about Denham for a moment, then kissed the memories of him goodbye. In his mind, he was already calculating a move back up north and how he would be spending his reward from Capricorn.

Chapter 29

London. Tuesday 6 December, 2016

Becca stood on the corner of Glennie Road, allowing her a view of St Peter's Church on Streatham Hill, earphones pressed hard into her ears, the song, 'Lights' by Ellie Goulding dulling her senses for the fourth time in a row. Lilting lyrics filled her world. She had wrapped up, the temperature outside not more than three or four degrees.

She had been back in London for two weeks, the memory of the Buenos Aires's dense humidity still lingering, and all that came with it.

The hearse pulled up to the kerb at five minutes to eleven. A trickle of mourners had arrived in advance, hands in their pockets and murmuring amongst themselves. She flinched when she saw Al Denham's coffin for the first time. Somehow it didn't look big enough to hold the dead man's often imposing frame, as though death had somehow shrivelled him. Becca watched as it was wheeled to the church gate before six men in penguin suits and top hats took up position on both sides. She looked away as Tatiana appeared from behind, wearing a navy-blue suit that didn't quite flatter her slim build.

The Reverend was already addressing the congregation from the pulpit when she made her entrance at the side door.

Her heart sank a little when she witnessed the numbers present for the funeral, a little short of twenty bodies, hardly a sizeable congregation for a professional lawyer still in his fifties. She removed her beanie hat, smoothed down her hair, unzipped her jacket and pushed the wires from her earphones further down into her pocket. She had stopped going to church the day her parents had died. When she glanced down she was standing in the middle of a crucifix on the floor. She shuddered, having lost count of her sins a long time ago.

The interior of the church had been decorated in preparation for Christmas, a nativity scene set up to one side of the altar. Becca took a seat on the fourth row back on the left-hand side of the nave, glancing around at the sombre faces present. Tatiana and her mother were three rows in front, bathed in the light from the rose window. Behind them sat two Eastern European girls with thin lips and hollow cheeks. Further along the row sat three men in overcoats: younger men with slicked back hair like they'd made the journey directly from the City. Young Al Denhams in the making. Perhaps he had been their mentor. On the other side, on the front pew, two women sat holding tightly onto one another. The older of the two Becca guessed to be Orla Drake, a woman Becca had never seen but had been referenced by Denham on several occasions in fond terms, an assistant who had stuck by him 'despite everything'. The younger of the two, an attractive woman in her mid-fifties with sun-kissed skin, expensive highlights and a wide-brimmed black hat clutched a tissue in one hand, tears streaming down her face. She was gazing at Denham's coffin, now parked in the centre of the church in front of the altar, expression still stricken with disbelief, as though more than three weeks after Denham's death following a common street assault she still couldn't quite accept that he had gone. Al had referenced Belinda some years back, an ex-wife for whom he still carried a torch, despite their divorce. Becca watched her closely. A person could tell by the look in her eyes: behind the heart-wrenching devastation, there was love and adoration.

The Reverend announced a hymn. Becca sucked air through her teeth, getting to her feet. She fumbled around for a hymn book, struggling to find the right page as a muted assembly failed to make enough sound to carry above the drone of the organist's mediocre rendition of 'Morning Has Broken'. Had Denham never worked for a man such as Capricorn, he might have had a proper turnout to his funeral: proper friends, more people who cared about him like Belinda so clearly did. Were it not for Capricorn, Denham would never have been coaxed into marrying some faux-wife from Poland, the latter probably rubbing her hands together because now at least she'd get the house. Becca had never heard the full story of how Denham had come to work for Capricorn – not that it mattered now – he was dead, and neither Capricorn nor Anton had had the decency to turn up to his funeral to pay their respects. A little voice resonated in the far recesses of her mind: *the men who you work for, they are men without compassion*, it said. *You let them control you, because you've never known any different.*

He did this, another – louder – voice said. *Don't deny it. Denham is dead because of him.*

Hymn over, Becca reclaimed her seat, removing her

jacket, wiping a stray tear. Under her dress, a necklace was making her skin itch. She teased it out, glancing down at the two rings hanging from a long sterling-silver chain, cradling them in her open palm. The first ring Tom had given her on the ferry ride from Argentina to Uruguay. The second – a proper engagement ring with a cut-price diamond nestled in a thin platinum band – he had presented to her the night before they had gone scoping out the casino in Montevideo in search of some Germans. A smile touched her lips, the memory of his awkward proposal after dinner, how Anil had laughed at them both hysterically. Her smile faded. Those days seemed like a lifetime ago. She squeezed the rings tightly in her closed fist, concealing them both still on the chain back underneath her dress.

At the end of the service, the Reverend announced that Albert Denham would be laid to rest at the West Norwood Cemetery, followed by a drinks reception at a nearby pub. Becca knew she wouldn't be going to either. She kept to her seat as the few assembled mourners filed out behind Al's coffin, the organist now playing a muted tune. No one bothered to look at her, only Belinda, whose gaze gave the impression that they were somehow long-lost friends and Belinda was trying – and failing – to recall Becca's name. Becca looked away, wondering if Denham had ever mentioned her to his first wife.

She took the train from Streatham Hill station back to London Victoria, feet rested on the seat in front of her in the carriage. Capricorn hadn't stuck to his word. Richie was still behind bars. The following day she would visit him again at

Wandsworth Prison, for the fourth time since her return.

A District Line tube train took her as far as Whitechapel before she changed, travelling two stops south to Wapping on the East London Line. The two-bedroom flat she used to share with Richie – before he'd taken up residence in Wandsworth at Her Majesty's pleasure – was situated in Parry House, part of Wapping's Green Bank estate. It was owned by Capricorn. He'd purchased it in the early nineties. Nowadays, flats in the building sold for upwards of four hundred thousand. It needed work: the curtains hadn't been replaced since they'd moved in, there was a spider's web of cracks up the walls and the sofa had been spewing out its fleecy intestines for longer than she could remember. The kitchen cabinets too were falling to pieces. Still, it was home.

Her route took her through Wapping Rose Gardens. On approach to Parry House her pace slowed. Parked at the gate to the Rose Gardens was a black Mercedes Benz 4x4. Expensive cars were the norm for the area, but something about this one looked odd. A young man wearing a white shirt and black trousers was leaning up against the front of the bonnet, legs crossed at the ankles as he smoked a roll-up. He appeared to be waiting for something, or someone. Becca caught his eye as she walked past. He looked her carefully up and down.

Safely inside the flat, she pulled off the beanie hat, kicking the door closed behind her. She paused. The heating was on, the thermostat a couple of notches higher than when she had left that morning. She paused, putting two and two together. Whenever he came to Wapping, he came with a driver, and he always came unannounced.

Shrugging out of her jacket, she pushed the door to the

living room open using one fingertip. He was sat in the moth-eaten recliner chair, the one that Richie liked to sit watching TV in, his legs crossed, stylish overcoat still on, collar pulled up. He glanced up as she entered. She offered him a crooked smile.

'I didn't know you still had a key to the place,' she said.

Capricorn got slowly to his feet. 'I don't,' he said, nodding at a point behind her right shoulder. 'I bought you a gift.'

She turned. Leaning with his back against the wall, hair in disarray, with the beginnings of a beard, wearing jeans and a scuffed pair of trainers, was Richie.

Her heart swelled.

She whispered his name as he approached her, a huge smiling grin on his face, wrapping her up in a bear hug. Felt tears sting her eyes as he crushed her. Underneath her dress, Tom's rings dug into her sternum. 'You're free,' she breathed, the tears flowing now, hardly able to believe they were standing in the same room.

Richie pushed back, eyes gleaming. 'I'm out, I'm done.'

She looked back at Capricorn. 'How?'

Capricorn shook his head, holding up his hands as if he wasn't the man responsible, simply the one who'd had to pay for it. As usual, he wasn't talking. He was a little fatter than she remembered; face tanned yet still decent-looking after all these years. Becca stepped forward, on her tip toes, wrapping her arms around his shoulders. Capricorn smelled of expensive aftershave, laced with a hint of booze. 'Thank you,' she whispered again. 'You don't know what this means to me.'

He pulled away first, taking her fingers in both of his hands. 'Where were you?' he asked.

She tensed involuntarily. 'I went to Al Denham's funeral.'

'I wish you hadn't done that.'

'No one recognised me.'

'You don't know that. I want you to both lay low for a while. You need to help Richie change his appearance. Buy him some new things.'

She nodded in understanding. Capricorn slapped Richie on the back, squeezed his shoulder, for a brief moment placing his palm against her cheek. Then he was heading for the door.

'Wait,' Becca said, to the back of his overcoat. 'You're leaving, that's it?'

He paused at the door, without turning around.

'I delivered Richie to you as promised and now I have a job to get back to,' Capricorn said.

'I have questions,' she replied.

He paused, his hand on the door handle. 'What questions do you have?'

She was silent for a moment, too scared to say what she really wanted to. She didn't know when he would grace them again with a visit.

'The night I took Clare Buchanan's phone from her pocket. In Islington, in 2005. The night she died. Were you there? Was it Anton who killed her?' she asked.

Richie was frowning at her, because he didn't know. He didn't know how many things had changed in her.

She watched Capricorn. He didn't turn around, hand still resting on the handle.

'No,' was his simple answer. 'I wasn't there.'

'But was it Anton? On your instructions?'

She could see the muscle flexing in his jaw. 'What have I always asked of you?'

'Obedience and discretion,' she answered faithfully – honestly – or as it seemed to her now, out of habit.

'And?'

'And in return you will take care of us.'

He opened the door a fraction wider. 'Then let's not forget that, shall we?'

He was about to cross the threshold into the hallway. Becca inhaled, squeezed the rings under her dress for courage. 'What about Sabina Cordero? What's to stop her from talking now?'

Capricorn's arms dropped to his sides. He turned to face her, wearing an expression that told her to be careful, that not even she was exempt from the punishments he could dish out.

'Becca… ?' Richie whispered, out of confusion.

'Why do you think I sent Sancho Belosi to live in Uruguay in the first place?' Capricorn said, pacing back over to where she was standing. 'My darling Sabi has a shadow. I keep my eye on her. I've *always* kept my eye on her. As you know, she has my child.'

'What happened to the laptop?'

He loomed above her. She stood her ground, throat gone dry.

'Anton is working on it. We haven't managed to locate it. Are there any more questions?'

She had a million more. Not about South America, but about her entire life up to this point.

'No,' she whispered.

He was searching her face, laying his palm against her cheek. Perspiration gathered on her upper lip. 'I remember the day you were born,' he said quietly. 'All my sister ever wanted was to be a mother.' He paused, before asking her, 'Can I trust you, Becca?'

'Of course you can, Uncle Charlie,' Richie blurted from behind her when she volunteered nothing. 'Tell him, Bec.'

Capricorn wasn't looking at Richie. His palm had slid down, fingers on his right hand now splayed across her neck. 'Of course, Uncle Charlie,' Becca stated. 'Always.'

'And Tom Holt? Do you care for him?'

He was gripping her now; she felt the pressure of his fingers against her windpipe.

'No,' she whispered.

She held his gaze. He let go, relaxed his shoulders. 'Good. Then we carry on. Go back to normal. Expect word via Anton when I need you next.'

She stood beside the chest in her bedroom, gently unclasping the necklace carrying the two rings, deciding against wearing it for the time being. Richie would have questions and she wasn't sure he wouldn't go running to their uncle with any doubts.

Capricorn had made good on his promise. Richie was out. Outside her bedroom, her brother was lounging on the sofa a free man, laughing at some banal American sitcom on the TV.

It should have felt better than it did.

She looked down at the rings cradled in her palm. It was killing her now. Not knowing if he was alive or dead. If Fede's men had gone after him too. If he'd escaped Buenos Aires. The look on his face lingered, on realising she'd been the one to contact Anton, to have feigned sleep after they had made love in the hotel bed. He had trusted her and she had betrayed him for the men she worked for and to whom she had shown the utmost loyalty. *And for what?* So she and her brother could skulk around an East London flat, waiting for their next job, and the next, and the next after that, following orders as they had been trained to do. Like sheep.

We go back to normal, her uncle had said before leaving.

Becca pressed the two rings to her lips, feeding the necklace into the bottom layer of a pink jewellery box she had been given by her mother when she was nine years old, the same place she was keeping his watch. She planned to return it someday.

The normal she had known would never be the same. Her uncle and Anton were no longer the men she had looked up to all this time.

She closed the jewellery box, turned the key in the lock. The future, *her* future, had already started to look a little different.

Chapter 30

Bariloche, Patagonia.
Thursday 17 November, 2016

The telephone receptionist answered in clipped tones. The line fizzed.

He kept his voice low, asked for Chief Inspector Neil Rawlins and was instantly put on hold.

He was a long way from anywhere. As a student he'd always planned on making the trip south to the alpine town of Bariloche in Patagonia. Falling for Gabi had put a stop to all that. He had finally made it, yet now he couldn't stay. He had to keep moving, get out of Argentina. He sat at a table next to a pine wood wall, coat on, back to the corner, facing the entrance with a view of the TV tuned to Telemundo, and the service counter where a lone waiter plodded about his business. The café, known as El Molinito, was on the corner of a sleepy intersection on the fringes of the centre of town. The owners clearly had a penchant for cheesy motivational slogans, the menu announcing in Spanish that it was 'a good day to have a great day'. He'd ordered a latté and a greasy breakfast plate and hoped there was some semblance of truth in the statement.

He had called the day before from a different café in town. Rawlins had been unavailable. He had been given a short shrift by Rawlins' colleague on refusing to identify himself or speak to anyone else. It was after ten, early afternoon in London.

The line crackled again. 'Rawlins. How can I help?'

The voice was deep, exactly like the one on all the videos available on YouTube. He knew then that this was no imposter, could picture his weathered face.

'Chief Inspector. I can't give you my name. I have some information I need to give you.'

'You sound far away.'

'You were the lead detective on the case of the missing woman Clare Buchanan,' Tom stated.

Rawlins didn't answer immediately. 'I was. That case is with the UK Missing Persons Unit now. There were no more avenues of investigation.'

'I have some information about Clare Buchanan.'

Rawlins went quiet again. 'I'm going to close the door. Don't go away.'

He was back on the line within a matter of seconds. 'What information?'

'It's a video she made before she disappeared. Clare Buchanan was a whistle-blower. She claims Charlie Ebdon, Head of Elate International, was syphoning off money from charitable donations to front companies, the money ending up in the hands of so-called investors, men who may not even exist, who are a cover for Ebdon himself. Her plan was to give her video to police. I'm doing the job for her, eleven years too late.'

Rawlins was silent for quite some time before Tom heard him cough. 'If true this would be a massive breakthrough. How did you come to be in possession of this video?'

Tom glanced towards the windows, down at his frothy latté going cold. He swallowed the lump in his throat. 'That I can't tell you. But I have it. I can assure you, it's genuine.'

The sound of Rawlins' heavy breathing echoed down the line. 'What format is it in?'

Tom glanced at the laptop in his bag at his feet. *Too much information, right there.* A forensic examination by any police force worth its salt would find evidence of planning a robbery, one that had resulted in the death of a British citizen by the name of Anil Choudhury. No, the laptop wasn't going anywhere.

'Right now, I have it on a USB thumb drive. Look, officially, I'm bound by a non-disclosure agreement. I want no record this ever came from me. There can be no emails, no exchanges.'

Rawlins clicked his tongue. 'Then can you send me the hard copy? Can you send me the USB?'

'I can courier it from my location in the next thirty minutes. Priority mail.'

'I'll give you a private address. Things have a habit of going walkabout in this place. Have you got a pen?'

'Yes, go ahead.'

'Send it to 52 Slyfield Gardens, Barking, IG11 8EE.'

'Got it.'

'Mark it for my attention only. How do I reach you?' Rawlins asked.

'You don't. All the information you need is in the video. Apart from one thing. Write down this name: Sabina Cordero. Find out what happened to her. She lives in a secure housing compound in Montevideo in Uruguay. It's called Aves de Las

Colinas. Charlie Ebdon is father to Sabina Cordero's oldest child. I've seen a birth certificate.'

He spelt out the names so Rawlins could write them down. 'You should know that Clare Buchanan talks about an individual in the video,' Tom continued. 'I can't tell you much about him, only that he looks like he's been a few rounds with Tyson judging by the state of his face and nose. He's tall, black hair, doesn't look entirely English. You should know he's a dangerous individual if you ever come across him. His name is Anton.'

'How have you come across him?' Rawlins asked.

'I can't tell you that either,' Tom said, and hung up.

He switched off the phone. Another customer had entered the café.

He had made three copies of the video on three newly-purchased USB thumb drives. The first he planned to courier to Rawlins to the address he'd been given. The second he had made as back-up. Clare's name had flitted in and out of the media over the years. Renewed appeals. A token financial reward for information. He had looked it all up. What her family wouldn't give to know that she had recorded a video prior to her death, accusing her high-profile boss of larceny.

He had spent an hour lying awake and staring at the ceiling back at the hostel overlooking Nahuel Huapi Lake, wondering what had become of her, whether Anton had been given orders by Capricorn to carry out Clare Buchanan's death sentence. How she had died. How her video had ended up in the safe of a woman living in Uruguay, a million miles from London. If Clare had ever known Sabina Cordero personally or if their only connection was a man named Charlie Ebdon, Clare's boss and father to Sabina's daughter. And if Becca had known all this from the get-go.

Becca. He rubbed his brow, tried not to think about her, to push her image from his mind. To think about her being thrown into the back of a van, what her fate had been. Was she back in England now? Sometimes in his dreams she would kiss his mouth and he would wake in a cold sweat.

He gritted his teeth. *Get out of my head*. Becca had given him up to Anton. It had been all lies. She had played him from the start. There had been no genuine feeling and he was a sap for thinking differently.

The third USB he planned on sending to a news outlet. Years earlier he had been dragged to a symposium at University College London on 'Trust and the Media', a love-in for a bunch of millennials that had turned out to be more interesting that it looked on paper. One of the speakers at a round table session had impressed him; Diane Cambridge, the Head of London-based Insight News International. Diane Cambridge would release the hounds, put Clare Buchanan's face back on the front pages, exactly what Charlie Ebdon wouldn't want. Put Ebdon under the spotlight. He would courier Diane Cambridge the third USB and the additional information he had given to Rawlins.

He glanced out of the window again, at the sunlight streaming down onto the pavement. He pictured Charlie Ebdon.

I'm coming for you, he thought.

This wasn't the end of it. The laptop had made sure of that, put a price on his head. Capricorn would want his property back, and would most likely send Anton to come and get it, to put him in the ground. They would likely know now that he'd seen everything. He would need to be shrewd, lay low. Recognise when to run. Do nothing to make him traceable. He needed to get out of Bariloche the moment the packages were sent.

He had kept his eye on the UK press online using an ageing computer at the hostel, searching for any mention of the death of a British Citizen in Uruguay. So far there had been nothing. It had plagued him, what had happened to Anil's body the moment he and Becca had left the house in Canelones. If he was still lying there, putrid flesh decomposing. If Anton had sent in Sancho Belosi to clean up the mess. If Sancho had buried Anil's body in the garden, stopping only to stuff a greasy *chivito* in his face.

Whilst searching for any news on Anil, he had stumbled across a news article relating to a violent attack on a lawyer in Streatham Hill, South London, a few days earlier.

He'd read the article several times to be sure, gut tying in knots.

The lawyer's name was Albert Denham. He had died in the back of an ambulance on route to St George's Hospital in London.

So Capricorn was cleaning up after himself.

In the café, Tom thought about the first time Denham had come to his house. Had the lawyer been a patsy all along? And how had he come to work for Charlie Ebdon? He hadn't seemed like the sort of man to do another's bidding. It was no coincidence his body was now in a South London morgue.

He picked up the phone, yanked off the plastic from the back of the handset, ripped out the SIM card and bent it in two. Wasn't that the position he now found himself in: a trace that required erasing?

He asked for the bill, left the waiter a half-decent tip. Outside he tossed the handset into a public waste bin, heard it hit one side of the metal and land with a thud at the bottom.

He had been played from the start. They had all played their roles: Denham, Becca, Ray, Anil. Even Anton. The road to Capricorn – to the truth – was a treacherous one. Were it not for him standing here, Charles Ebdon would have kept his secret.

He intended to change all of that.

He slung his backpack over his shoulder, walked a block and a half north east to the branch of Correo Argentino, a local courier company. The packages cost him six thousand Argentine pesos to send to London, about eighty US dollars each, to arrive at their destinations three days later. He had to show his passport and would be named as the sender, in his mind not ideal but unavoidable under the circumstances and if he was to guarantee delivery at the London end. He watched the assistant package up the two USB drives for Rawlins and Diane Cambridge in yellow cardboard envelopes. He double checked the names, destination addresses and signed hard copies of the forms, ensuring his signature was an illegible scrawl.

He left the courier's office, considering for a moment the family of Clare Buchanan. The best they could hope for was some kind of closure, to find out where she had gone, or at least where she had been laid to rest. He hoped he would get to see things unravel for Charlie Ebdon, even if it was from afar. And then he might finally be able to go home.

He walked the three-kilometre route from Calle Moreno to the Bus Terminal San Carlos de Bariloche. There was a coach to Osorno in southern Chile, with an onward journey to Temuco, departing at two in the afternoon, journey time ten hours. He purchased a ticket at the kiosk. Thought about Denham again, back to the moment in London that the lawyer had offered him a job, no idea what kind of a world he was opening himself up to.

It was dark outside by the time the coach arrived at the Argentina-Chile border. An Argentinian official came onto the bus and collected up passports. As he waited, Tom listened to a conversation between a lone female backpacker from Spain speaking to a German couple, both sat on the row in front of him. They spoke in English. The German couple urged the backpacker to skip Temuco and head for the adventure town of Pucón, one hundred kilometres south east, back towards the border, a town on the banks of a lake.

As they crossed the border into Chile, he drifted off to sleep.

He stood on a street corner, crick in his neck, weary from the cross-country journey. The town of Pucón was nestled in the shadow of Villarica, an impressive volcano that, along with an imposing lake, had spawned an entire industry based around hiking, jet skiing, biking and white-water rafting. The alpine town was not dissimilar to a ski-town in Colorado, the architecture all log cabins, or *cabañas*, that littered the road back towards Temuco. On arrival he had located a guesthouse, paid up front for a two-night stay with the last of his remaining cash he'd withdrawn using Denham's card two days before the robbery. It was enough to scope out if Pucón was a place he could stay awhile and disappear from view. Capricorn's view. Federico's view. The Metropolitan Police's view. It had a big enough foreign population that he wouldn't stand out. He would require a job in order to survive. It would be a lonely existence, but he wouldn't have a bullet in his head.

It was dark again when he arrived at the self-service launderette, clutching a small plastic bag of his clothes. The owner was a grey-haired woman in her sixties who insisted on being of assistance. A single wash and tumble dry would set him back six dollars. He sat on a bench reading a well-thumbed Spanish-language copy of GQ, letting her get on with it, the scent of petals filling his nostrils.

'Señor?' he heard her say. She was holding out her hand towards him. He got up and walked over. In her hand was a small piece of paper, an Argentinian twenty peso note and a pile of coins taken from his jeans. He pocketed the note and coins, opened up the piece of paper and stopped dead.

The ink had smudged a little, but it was still legible, handwritten. His stomach flipped over, felt like it gave way.

I'm sorry.
I did what I had to do.
B.

He swallowed, ran his thumb over the soft paper. She would have had to have left it in his jeans pocket on the last night they had spent together in Buenos Aires, before Anton had arrived to take the laptop, the same night she'd walked away with his watch, knowing what she was about to do, knowing they would likely be going their separate ways that very night, knowing, he supposed, that he might have ended up dead before ever finding it.

A rush of guilt pulsed through him, followed by the same squall of anger he'd felt towards her before.

You did what you had to, he repeated internally with a mixture of sadness and contempt, screwing up the paper and dropping it into the waste basket, reclaiming his seat.

You stand or you fall.

You did what you had to do, Bec.

Then so did I.

A bell sounded as the door to the *lavanderia* opened. Tom glanced up from his magazine. A man entered, European or American, tanned, in his mid-thirties with bleached-blonde unruly hair and tattoos on his calves, wearing knee-length cargo shorts and a short-sleeved shirt. He exchanged familiar pleasantries with the owner, handing over his bulging bag of laundry, keeping hold of the six-pack of local Kunstmann beer squeezed under his arm, pushing against his ribcage.

He sat two seats away from Tom on the bench, cracked open a can and took a large slug. He leaned back, straightening out his legs across the linoleum floor.

'You want a beer?' he asked and Tom turned his head.

'Sure,' Tom replied. 'Thanks.'

The man slid the can out from its six-pack plastic holder, passing it to Tom, the ring pull letting off a familiar hissing sound when he twisted it back. The beer hit the back of his throat and it tasted like a new day.

'Where are you from?' Tom asked.

'Sweden. You?'

'UK.'

The Swede held out his hand. 'Aksel.'

Tom shook it. 'Tom.'

'How long you been in Pucón?'

'Actually I just got here.'

'Ah,' the Swede grinned. 'Then, my friend, if you don't mind, what I have for you is a job offer. It doesn't pay much, but it comes with free food, a roof over your head and maybe even some beers thrown in. You get to ride a jet ski round a lake all day. Interested?'

There was a twinkle in Aksel's eye. A smile tugged at Tom's lips. He didn't have to think about his answer for very long.

'Sounds perfect,' he said. 'When can I start?'

Acknowledgements

In May 2016, I moved with my husband and our two small children to Uruguay in South America, to work in the small but perfectly-formed British Embassy in Montevideo. I barely spoke a lick of Spanish and had no idea what to expect.

We lived on a secure housing compound known as Lomas de la Tahona, the basis for *Aves de Las Colinas* in this novel. The house overlooked the ninth hole of the surrounding golf course. A few months later, I started writing *Intruders*. Almost all of the places in my story are real: from La Huella in Jose Ignacio, to the vibrant streets of Recoleta and La Boca in Buenos Aires, to the apocalyptic playground on Costa Rica Street in Carrasco, Lagomar Beach and the dusty tracks of the Canelones landscape.

Many good friends have supported me along this journey to publication. I should thank a few by name. Thank you to Heather Cook for reading my manuscript, for your energy, encouragement and belief in the story I wanted to tell. Thank you to Merope Coulson and Nadia Harvey for your long-standing faith in my ability as a writer. Thank you to my mum, Penny Thomas, for telling me not to give up. Thank you to Ben Buley for staying up into the small hours to finish the manuscript and to Emily Cully for your sheer enthusiasm. Thank you to Kronoman for your assistance with the Argentine Spanish.

Grateful thanks to Hilary Johnson and Paul Bennett for your advice and invaluable help in shaping the manuscript. You both taught me so much in a very short space of time. Laura Gerrard, thank you for your incredible attention to detail and whipping my story into shape.

Special thanks to the team at RedDoor Press: Heather Boisseau, Clare Christian, Anna Burtt and Lizzie Lewis. Thank you for choosing to work with me and making my dreams come true. You are the best.

And lastly, to everyone I met in Uruguay, a very special place, a heartfelt thank you. *Besos*.

About the Author

Emma Scullion joined the Foreign & Commonwealth Office in 2003. For the past eleven years she has managed to escape Westminster, working in British Embassies in Beijing, Bangkok, Panama City and Montevideo in Uruguay. She is a graduate of the Faber Academy and *Intruders* is her first published novel. She now lives in Rome with her husband and two children.

Find out more about RedDoor
Press and sign up to our
newsletter to hear about our
latest releases, author events,
exciting **competitions**
and more at

reddoorpress.co.uk

YOU CAN ALSO FOLLOW US:

 @RedDoorBooks

 Facebook.com/RedDoorPress

 @RedDoorBooks